---- ★ ----

"Let him go!" I bellowed as I charged across the lawn. I lifted the paddle to my shoulder as I ran, thinking I could wield it like a club. I let out a few more shrieks interspersed with shouts for help.

The man hammering Don with his fists glanced up. I expected to see features contorted with rage, but the face he turned toward me was expressionless. He appeared as calm, as intent on his task as if he were turning out piecework in a factory. Right, left, right, left. The steady rain of thuds set my stomach churning.

"Stop that! Let him go," I screamed. I gripped the paddle hard, ready to swing.

The man stared back at me with no trace of surprise. "Jesus, some crazy broad's after us. We've done enough here. Come on," he muttered to his companion.

---- ★ ----

Previously published Worldwide Mystery title by
ANNE WHITE

BENEATH THE SURFACE

ANNE WHITE

BEST
LAID PLANS

WORLDWIDE®

TORONTO • NEW YORK • LONDON
AMSTERDAM • PARIS • SYDNEY • HAMBURG
STOCKHOLM • ATHENS • TOKYO • MILAN
MADRID • WARSAW • BUDAPEST • AUCKLAND

BEST LAID PLANS

A Worldwide Mystery/June 2007

First published by Hilliard & Harris.

ISBN-13: 978-0-373-26603-6
ISBN-10:   0-373-26603-0

Printed in U.S.A.

BEST
LAID PLANS

ONE

I̶T̶ W̶A̶S̶N̶'̶T̶ T̶H̶E̶ F̶I̶R̶S̶T̶ trouble I'd found myself in as mayor of Emerald Point, but it could easily have been the last.

More than a year after the election, I was still proceeding—as the sign at our town's entrance advised visitors—with caution. I'd softened the take-no-prisoners style I'd honed during my years in New York, survived a run-in with a secret consortium of area businessmen trying to advance its own plan for the town and adapted myself to the laid-back atmosphere of our sleepy little community. At least I thought I'd adapted.

As Emerald Point struggled to rebuild after a freak tornado the summer before, I immersed myself in filing grant and loan applications and investigating every kind of financial aid available to us. That winter with more funds still needed, I reactivated a plan the town had kicked around for some time—a community center, designed to help us attract a larger share of the lucrative Lake George tourist trade.

One blustery March night, I proposed an updated version of the idea to our local Chamber of Commerce. "John Roberts has agreed to let us use a building on his hotel grounds for a nominal fee," I told the members. "This will give us an excellent location for a center and adequate parking. With a little redecorating, we'll be able to showcase cultural activities, celebrate the area's history and—here's the bottom line—lure tourists away from better-known vacation spots on the lake."

As always, luring tourists proved the magic phrase. The Chamber members responded with enthusiasm. I organized a committee and hit the ground running. No laid-back approach for me this time. Convinced this was our last best hope of competing with other communities on the lake, I raced full speed ahead into micromanaging the effort.

On a warm May afternoon with the summer season hurtling toward us at full throttle, I was perched on a step-ladder, painting a wall in the center's anteroom when I looked down to find Don Morrison staring up at me.

"Do you realize it's almost five o'clock? Quit for the day before you work yourself to death and I'll take you for a pizza," he said.

"Out in public? Like this?" I pointed to my paint-splattered jeans and shirt.

"You'll clean up great. You always do. And if you don't… Well, you look good to me, paint and all." He offered the slow, sexy smile which had the power to melt my firmest resolve.

I caved immediately. Don, in sharply pressed khakis and a green Polo shirt which accented his dark blond hair and beard to perfection, was a guy any woman in her right mind would hang up her paint brush for. "Okay. The rest of the workers have taken off anyway. Let me finish this section and I'll quit, too."

"Tell me something I can do to help, preferably a job which doesn't involve wet paint or dirt."

Don surveyed the entrance area with distaste. The inside

renovations were nearing completion, but the place looked like garbage central. Brown paper wrappings, empty paint cans, discarded drop cloths, even boxes the supplies had been packed in littered the floor.

Clean jobs were in short supply, but I came up with one. "Take a look at the computer on the admissions desk. There appears to be some kind of glitch and we need it ready for the opening."

While Don fussed with the computer, I dabbed paint onto the last remaining section of the bilious green wall I was transforming into a masterpiece of taupe and ivory and pronounced my work done for the day. I closed the paint can, threw a rag over it and tapped the cover down—a trick an experienced painter had taught me after he saw me splashing paint all over myself as I struggled to close a lid. I tucked the can and my drop cloth into a corner and carried the brushes to a nearby bathroom for cleaning. Water-based paint, I'd discovered, proved a godsend to the unskilled.

"Give me ten minutes," I called to Don.

Once I'd washed the brushes, I went to work on myself. The special soap I'd bought quickly dissolved most of the paint from my hands and arms. I shed my work clothes, hung them on a hook and slipped into the fresh shirt and slacks I'd brought with me that morning. My short brown hair, already curling from a day of slaving over a hot brush, fell easily into place. A few swipes of lipstick and I was ready.

"Wow. That's what I call a change." Don, impressed by the transformation, upped his offer to a more elegant dinner at one of the town's classier restaurants.

"Pizza at Mario's is exactly what I've been thinking about," I assured him.

The cheerful little pizzeria provided a home away from home for most of Emerald Point. Food, consistently good. Ambiance, delightful. Patrons, friendly. Even my most disgruntled constituents usually shelved their complaints about my mayoral shortcomings while under Mario's spell.

Don suggested wine with our pizza. I tried to relax, but I couldn't shake a bad case of center-mania.

"Tommy Porter. Can you tell me why I believed that man could paint and get other people to paint? As far as I know he's never managed to do anything right."

"The guy's a screw-up, I'll grant you that," Don said with a smile.

"I thought when Tommy and his Monty Python crew volunteered we wouldn't have to cut into our dwindling reserves to hire professionals. 'How difficult could it be to slap a coat of paint on a wall,' I asked myself."

"And you learned the answer to that the hard way?"

"Starting when they arrived this morning. Understand I took it all in stride for a while. I overlooked spills, goofy jokes, even a damaged section of carpet. But by afternoon, I'd had it."

"Did they quit or did you send them packing?" Don asked.

I seized a sausage-topped slice of pizza from Don's side of the plate and gobbled it down. "They left around three o'clock. I didn't have anything to do with it except to offer up a prayer of thanksgiving as they went out the door."

"Loren, cut yourself some slack. It'll all work out."

"Easy for you to say. You've got a much longer fuse than I have." I reached for another slice of Mario's specialty.

"Not when somebody eats from my half of the pizza, I don't." He grinned and tapped the back of my hand.

"Sorry. I do seem to be in a state."

Don and I had long since established that when we split a pizza, he ordered sausage on his half and I asked for mushrooms on mine. No crossovers.

"You must be upset if you can eat hot sausage without noticing. The work will get finished sooner or later," he said.

"We don't have until later, remember? It's almost the end of May. If we're not ready by Memorial Day…" I didn't have to go on. Everyone on the lake understood the importance of being up and running when the summer tourists arrived. The Lake George season was short. Businesses had only three months—even less time in cold or rainy summers—to take advantage.

"Things will work out, Loren. You'll be having the grand opening before you know it," Don said.

"I wish I had your confidence."

"Speaking of that, my brother and Elaine want to join us at the opening-night party. That okay with you?"

"Sure, although I can't imagine why. This party won't be in the same league as most of their activities," I said.

Don's brother Stephen and his wife lived sixty miles south of us in Albany and, although we got together with them occasionally for dinner, they usually preferred the kind of elegant social life Don and I both tried to avoid.

"I'm not sure why myself, but for some reason they're dying to come. My brother's brought the subject up several times."

"Tell them they're more than welcome." I pushed my plate aside. Too much thinking about the center even affected the taste of Mario's pizza.

"If you're finished, why don't we go to your house? I'll make you a cup of decaf, rub the kinks out of your neck and have you in bed and totally relaxed in no time. How does that sound?" Don leered expectantly.

"It sounds great." And it did. So I was almost as surprised as he was when I begged off. "But I'm really beat tonight. Can I get a rain check?"

Don acted appropriately disappointed, I appeared properly contrite, and we left Mario's on good terms. At least, I thought so at the time.

Since we both had our cars, we exchanged a casual good-bye outside the restaurant and I headed home. More accurately, I intended to head home. On impulse, I swung north toward the center, thinking I'd sleep better if I made sure Tommy and his gang hadn't returned for more painting.

By then it was almost dark. I did a double take when I saw a light in one of the windows, a light I hadn't meant to leave on. As I parked next to the building, I noticed the front door was ajar. I must have failed to shut it tight.

In the shadows of the anteroom, I could see the ladder and paint cans tucked in the corner where I'd left them. I skirted the contour map and a display of artifacts and switched on the light at the entrance to the main room. On the wall opposite me a large glass case contained life-sized figures of our local hero, Major Robert Rogers, and three of his Rangers. The Rangers, wearing the gray-green homespun our research confirmed was their traditional garb, stood with muskets raised, prepared to fire into the simulated forest at the edge of the display. A placard explained they were waging a new kind of warfare against the combined forces of French and Indians as they struggled to secure the lake and its environs for the British.

In the dim light the four figures looked no different than

usual, but something had been added to the diorama. A body, dressed not in a Ranger uniform but in shabby denim, sprawled motionless on the floor of the case a few feet from the other figures. The face was turned away from me and was partially obscured by a tangle of thick, dark hair.

"What the hell?" I hurried over for a closer look. Reggie Collins and the other re-enactors who'd planned the exhibit had spent hours debating the merits of including figures of wounded or dead from either side.

Reggie, who portrayed Rogers himself in the re-enactments, had opposed the idea. "Not what we want. Too scary for the kids," he'd insisted.

"So why shouldn't they know folks got killed around here, since so many of 'em did?" George Tyler, always the dissenter, had argued.

But Reggie had the clout to win the field. No bodies. At least, no bodies until now.

I moved closer and cupped my hands on the glass, struggling for a better look. The body hadn't been part of the diorama when I left the building that afternoon, I could swear to that. Had Tommy or one of his buddies with a warped sense of humor come back and played a practical joke?

But this wasn't a joke. The man lying in the display case looked dead, or close to it. I planted my hands on the glass and shoved hard, trying to slide open one of the panels. The glass wouldn't budge. When I leaned in close, I could see the dowel in the lower track which kept the panel from moving. I hustled around to the door which led to the hallway behind the case. No luck there, either. The door was locked tight. Reggie and his crew prided themselves on leaving everything shipshape when they quit for the day. The body must have been put in there somehow after they'd left.

I ran back into the entry and grabbed the telephone off the admissions desk. No dial tone. Lee Daniels, one of the committee members, had assured us two days ago he'd completed arrangements to have the phones hooked up. Apparently, something had gone wrong. If only my cell phone wasn't sitting home on my kitchen table.

I yanked open the door and rushed outside. Darkness crept out from under the trees and obscured the narrow road. No sign of cars or walkers. A hundred yards up the hill toward the Inn faint lamplight shone from a small roadside bungalow. Faster not to take the car, I thought, and took off for the house.

The man who answered my frantic knocking on his front door was short and middle-aged, one of the Patterson brothers, I thought, but I couldn't come up with a first name. He listened to my breathless explanation of a body in a display case, registered surprise, disbelief, then eventually, willingness to help. He called 911 and handed the receiver to me. I took a deep breath and calmed down enough to describe what I'd seen.

"Don't go back inside the building," the 911 operator advised. "I'm notifying the sheriff's department. Wait for them near the entrance."

"Thanks for your help." I thrust the phone back into my Good Samaritan's hand, wheeled around and took off down the hill toward the center. It was after nine now, pitch black, with no glimmer of light anywhere. I raced along the road, anxious to be at the center when the sheriff's car arrived. I knew I was moving too fast, taking chances I shouldn't take, but I kept going. I felt the tip of my shoe catch on a root or branch that reared up at the edge of the pavement. I tripped, pitched forward, tried to slow down, but my momentum proved too strong. Powerless to stop, I staggered a few steps ahead, then sprawled flat on the rough macadam. My head hit against something, cracking against it hard enough to send flashes of light exploding behind my eyes. I wanted to get up, but I couldn't seem to move.

TWO

As THE LIGHTS flashed and faded behind my eyes, I lay on the side of the road and took stock of my injuries. The pain in my head lessened, but my ankle stung like fury. My left cheek rested against a hard, cold surface which I recognized as the edge of the pavement. When I tried to lift my head, waves of nausea washed over me.

A man's voice floated in from above me. Someone on a cell phone was calling for help. "Rescue squad, too. Get 'em here fast. The mayor's been hurt."

A flashlight beam played along the ground next to me. A figure moved closer, the face a blur behind the light.

"Wait. Tell me who you are." I intended to take command, but my words came out in weak little chirps.

"Mayor Graham? What happened?" The man holding the phone leaned over me.

"Who are you?" I lifted my head. The nausea came roaring back.

"Bob Patterson. You came to my house and asked me to call 911. Then you tore off ahead of me. Rescue squad will be here in a minute."

Maybe if I sat up in stages. "Bob, can you give me a hand here? Pull me up a little?"

"Oh, I don't think so, Mayor. Not a good idea. Appears like you hit your head hard when you fell. Squad will be comin' in a few minutes. You best lie still, let 'em take a look at you."

"The body? The display case?"

Bob put his finger to his lips. "You better shush, Ms. Graham. You shouldn't be talkin' so much. Help will be right along."

I gave up and let my eyelids droop. There was more I needed to tell him, but it could wait. A few minutes later I heard Rick Cronin's voice—he must have been the sheriff's deputy responding to the call—and then, after a while, the voices of the rescue squad.

"What were you doing here so late, Mayor Graham? Don't you know you're not supposed to paint in the dark?" someone asked with a chuckle.

"She was in Mario's a couple hours ago. I saw her there myself. She must have come back here after that," another voice said.

An EMT knelt next to me and attached a blood pressure cuff to my arm. He ran his hands gently over my skull. "Your blood pressure's okay, Mayor. And it doesn't look like you're bleeding anywhere, but you got quite a bump on your head and I don't like the look of that ankle. We'd best run you down to Glens Falls Hospital for some x-rays."

I wanted to argue, but my head hurt too much. Out of the corner of my eye I saw a stretcher being set down next to me. All this fuss and they kept ignoring the most important thing. I didn't dare raise my head, but I forced the words out. "Never mind that. Check the body inside, in the display case. Maybe the guy's still alive."

"What body do you mean, Mayor?" Rick Cronin, dressed in the dark gray uniform of our county's sheriff's department, dropped to one knee next to me, his boyish face lined with concern.

"In the diorama. Lying there with the Rangers," I said.

"The diorama? You mean that display case Reggie Collins and the re-enactors set up?".

"That's where the body is, Rick. I think the guy's dead. I couldn't get the case open."

"You stay quiet now, Mayor. Don't be trying to get up. Paul's gonna take over here, make sure you're okay." Rick spoke in the slow, even tones I'd heard him use with accident victims. He stood up and changed places with the EMT.

"Let me talk to her a minute before you move her." Jim Thompson's voice drifted in from somewhere nearby. Jim, an investigator with the sheriff's department, handled many of Emerald Point's thornier law enforcement problems. The man in the display case must be somebody important for Jim to drive up here at night even before the deputies had finished their work.

I could hear Rick explaining in low tones how I'd asked Bob Patterson to telephone 911. Since Emerald Point didn't have its own police force, calls like this went directly to the county sheriff's department.

Jim leaned over me. "Loren, they want to take you to the emergency room for x-rays."

I must be hurt worse than I thought. Not only had Jim been sent for, he was calling me by my first name, not his usual practice.

"That's not necessary. I'm all right. My head hurts like crazy, but I think the guy in the diorama is dead. Has anybody checked him?"

"What were you doing painting so late, Loren?"

"I wasn't. I finished painting hours ago. I'd gone to

Mario's for pizza. When I drove back by, I saw the light on and the door open and went in to check."

"But the ladder, the paint. They're tipped over near the entrance. Wasn't that where you were painting?"

I gritted my teeth. At least I started to, but tensing my jaw muscles sent the pain in my head spiraling off the charts. I settled for enunciating in a slow, deliberate way. "Listen to me, Jim. I was not painting. I saw the body in the case. I couldn't get to it so I went for help. When I came back down the hill in the dark, I tripped."

I could see Jim glance toward Rick. "Try to remember more about what happened. Maybe you were on the ladder and you fell."

I don't know what made me angrier—Jim's refusal to believe me or my own whiny efforts to explain. I wanted to shout at him, but I knew my head couldn't handle anything more than a whisper. "Damn it. Why are you talking to me as if I don't know what happened? I saw a man in the display case. Tell me who it is."

"Loren, we're going to get you to the hospital now."

I sputtered out a protest, but he paid no attention.

"I'll be down to check on you," he continued. "I'll be in touch with the doctors. If they think it best, I'll let you get some rest and stop by in the morning." He stepped back.

As the EMT eased me onto the stretcher, my thoughts spun off in a new direction. "Oh no…the body. Jim, is it somebody I know?"

One of the squad members opened the back doors of the ambulance. Two men secured the blanket and straps around me and raised the stretcher. No one answered my question.

"Wait. It's somebody I know, isn't it, Jim? That's why you won't tell me." The words caught in my throat. The man's face had been turned away from me and I'd only seen one side of it. Had it been someone I knew lying there injured, maybe dead?

Jim moved closer and touched the stretcher. "Loren, don't work yourself up. I don't know what you thought you saw. The ladder and the paint you were using are tipped over near the entrance, but there's no body in the display case or anywhere else in the building."

THREE

An EMT sat next to me in the ambulance as we raced down 9N and onto the Northway. He silenced me every time I mentioned the body in the Rangers' exhibit and bombarded me with questions about my health history, allergies and previous hospitalizations until I didn't have the energy for any more talk. They'd find the man sooner or later, I told myself. Maybe he wasn't dead; maybe he'd managed to crawl out the back door into the woods behind the center. Granted, I'd only seen him for a few seconds, but he didn't look like a guy going on any long trips.

Even though the emergency room was busy, I rated my own cubicle, an IV line and a harried but efficient doctor who examined me and ordered x-rays.

The nurses on the eleven-to-seven shift were starting their rounds when Josie Donohue, my friend Kate's sixteen-year-old daughter, burst into my cubicle. "Somebody called my mother and told her you were here. She's parking the car, Lor. What the hell happened to you this time?"

I probably should have expected Josie, never long on tact, to remind me of my poor record of injuries and trips to the ER. I tried to get the upper hand.

"Isn't this late for you to be out? Don't you have school tomorrow?" I asked her.

"Won't get much out of school, Lor, if you die on me."

Before I could assure Josie I didn't plan to die, Kate rushed in. "Loren, what happened? Are you in pain?"

"I was running too fast and I fell," I admitted, then described what had happened at the center.

As Kate, her blue eyes wide with alarm, heard me out, Josie leaned over me, bombarding me with a steady stream of questions. "Are you saying you saw a body, Lor, and the deputies claimed they didn't find one?"

"I saw one in the display case, I swear it. But all Jim found was the ladder lying on the floor with the paint spilled next to it. So it looked like I was painting and fell."

Kate pushed my hair back, her hand cool and gentle on my forehead. "Of course, a blow on the head…"

"I know. I know that's what everybody's thinking. But I wasn't painting, I saw the door open. I went in to check. There was a body in the diorama. I'm not crazy, you know."

"Of course, you're not." Kate's tone reminded me of Jim's, much too reassuring for my taste. Even Josie slacked off on the wisecracks—not a good sign.

The time in the Emergency Room dragged mercilessly. When it looked as if I would be kept overnight, I told Kate, "You should get out of here. You have to open the coffee shop in the morning and Josie has school. I'll be okay."

A half hour after Kate and Josie left, the doctor who'd wanted to admit me was replaced by one willing to discharge me as soon as he saw the results of one more test. As the last of my patience evaporated, I slid off the end of the stretcher. To my relief, I found I could put weight on my feet and stand without dizziness. I experimented with a few cautious steps, then limped into the hall pulling the

IV pole behind me. I spotted a phone on an empty desk, called Rick Cronin and talked him into coming after me.

"Give us a few more minutes to finish up your paperwork and we'll disconnect your IV," the nurse at the desk said.

"Better hurry. My ride will be here any minute."

Fifteen minutes later the sheriff's deputy came striding through the ambulance entrance. At twenty-five, Rick might be the youngest man on the force and cursed with the chubby pink cheeks of a preschooler but, in his neatly pressed uniform and wide-brimmed hat, he commanded respect. I was out of there in record time.

AT NINE-THIRTY the next morning, I was sitting behind my desk at the Village Building, nursing the grandmother of all headaches with black coffee and pain pills, when Jim Thompson tapped lightly on my door. Without waiting for an invitation, he marched in and folded his lanky, six foot three frame into my visitor's chair. "So you conned poor Cronin into springing you from the ER, I hear."

If he wanted an apology, he'd have a long wait. "You know how those emergency room doctors are. Once they get you in there, they never want to let you go. Tell 'em you're leaving and they immediately find the test results they insisted they had to wait for."

Jim nodded. "I've heard that complaint before. And then you felt duty bound to pick up your car and come to work, even though you look like death warmed over."

"Why, thank you, Jim. Remind me to comment on your appearance the next time you have a bad day," I said with mock sweetness.

We both knew it was an idle threat. I'd never seen Jim looking less than neat and ready to face the world. As an investigator in the sheriff's department, he didn't wear a uniform, but his height, along with his well-tailored suits and crisp white shirts, made him an imposing figure. No crumpled Columbo look for this guy.

Jim refused coffee, but I poured myself another cup in my ongoing effort to quiet my head. Then I got down to business. "You still haven't found a body or a wounded guy crawling around outside the building, I take it. Otherwise, I'm sure you'd tell me and apologize for doubting my word," I said.

"Wasn't that I was doubting your word, Mayor. You were pretty banged up, and with the ladder and the paint tipped over, it sure looked as if you'd taken a fall."

I couldn't really blame him for that, so I kept my cool. "I spent most of last night going over what happened. My first reaction when I went by the center and saw the front door open was that I'd been careless about locking it. Then I went through the rooms and noticed the back door open, too."

"And you didn't think to beat it right out of there?"

"Of course not. I thought maybe some of the guys who'd been painting there earlier had come back."

"Okay. Better give me their names and the approximate times they left. We might get something from them."

As I jotted down the names, I heard footsteps in the anteroom.

"Loren, you're here? I thought you'd still be in the hospital." Pauline Collins, village secretary and jack-of-all-trades, poked her head into the room. Pauline—plump, white-haired, early sixties—had served the former mayor for more years than she liked to tell and now performed the same duties for me. Her encyclopedic knowledge of the town's past and present made her an invaluable resource.

"I'm here," I said.

"I came in early, thinking I'd cover the office this morning. You sure you're all right?" she asked.

Jim winked in her direction. "Now that you mention it, Pauline, maybe it would be a good idea for her to take the rest of the day off. Who knows? She might listen if you suggested it."

Pauline was too loyal to side with Jim right then, but I knew she'd jump on the idea the minute he got out the door. But first, she had something else on her mind. "Jim, somebody called Reggie early this morning, asked him to come to the center and look at the diorama. Did something happen to it last night?"

"We're checking the place out. The mayor can fill you on the details. I'm heading over there right now."

Before Jim had reached the door, Don Morrison barged past him into the office. He ignored Jim and Pauline and zeroed in on me. "Loren, for God's sake, what happened to you? Weren't you headed home? They tell me you went back to the center to paint."

By that time, I knew better than to grit my teeth, but I managed an ugly snarl. "I wasn't painting. I can't convince anybody of that. I found the door unlocked and I saw a body in the display case."

"A body? You mean somebody was dead?" Pauline said.

"I couldn't tell. The case was locked and I couldn't open it. So I ran to a house up the road to telephone for help. On my way back I fell."

Don unleashed another barrage of questions. "You went back to the center? What in the devil did you do that for? Didn't you say you were going home?"

I saw the problem. Hell might have no fury like a woman scorned, but men weren't far behind in that department. This wouldn't be easy to explain, but I tried the truth. "You know what? I drove by just to make sure Tommy and the other painters hadn't gone back there. When I saw the door open, I thought either I hadn't shut it tight or they were in there painting."

Don shook his head, as if amazed at my stupidity. "Right. You saw the door open and you breezed right in. Their cars weren't parked out in front, were they?"

"No," I admitted.

"You didn't see any of them around, did you?"

"No," I said again.

Before Don could warm up for a full-scale lecture, Jim interrupted. "I'll leave you two to work this out. You might want to take it a little easy on her, Morrison, until she's feeling better. Then I'll be happy to join any campaign aimed at getting her to use better judgment."

Pauline didn't usually interfere in my business, but the two-pronged attack on me swung her solidly to my defense. "Hindsight's a wonderful thing," she snapped. "Loren probably wishes she'd gone straight home herself, but she can't change things now. And she obviously has some work she wants to get done this morning."

Our visitors took the hint and disappeared fast. As soon as the door swung shut behind them, Pauline turned her attention to me. "So what is it about a body in the display case? Did somebody vandalize the diorama or something?"

"Worse than that," I said, and described the body lying in middle of the Ranger exhibit.

Pauline's cheerful face clouded with concern. She knew

most of the re-enactors personally. "You're telling me one of those guys might be dead and we don't know who it is?"

"I'm not sure the man was a re-enactor. He didn't have a uniform on. He looked dead, but he could have just been knocked out. The case was locked and I couldn't get it open to check him. They probably think Reggie will know who it was—if they decide to believe I saw somebody."

Pauline mulled over what I'd said. "Well, if the fellow's dead or hurt bad, we'll find out eventually, and there's nothing you can do in the meantime. You probably should go home and rest up. You'll accomplish lots more at that meeting tomorrow if you're not all played out."

She was right. Much as I hated to admit it, she was right. The center committee had planned an important meeting for the next day. I'd need to be at the top of my game if I was going to get us back on track for the opening.

"And I mean home," Pauline said as I picked up a few papers and started for the door. "Never mind checking out the center on your way. Let the sheriff's department do what they gotta do."

I nodded as if to agree but of course I didn't listen. I drove directly to the center. Jim's car was already parked out front along with Reggie's truck and two other sheriffs' vehicles. Looked like they were still checking the place.

The front door of the center stood open but the screen door was locked. I knocked and called Jim's name—and called again.

Several minutes passed before he appeared in the entrance hall. He stopped several feet away from the door. "We're checking on what you told us, Mayor."

"But I can come in, can't I? I want to see if anything jogs my memory."

Jim rubbed a hand over his head. He was perspiring, his wiry, salt and pepper hair curling along his forehead. "Another day maybe we could do that. Right now, it'd be best not to contaminate these rooms."

"Wait, you mean you invited Reggie Collins in and not me? I don't believe this."

"Mayor, trust me on this. Let us do our job and tomorrow you can look around all you want to. I guarantee it."

"At least tell me if you found anything more this morning, anything you didn't see last night."

"Not yet. I swear I'll tell you the minute we do. Now, use good sense and go home and get some rest. Let us do what we have to do here."

Everyone's advice sounded annoyingly alike. Much as I hated to do it, I gave in and went home.

FOUR

I WANTED NOTHING MORE than to take Jim's advice and sleep the day away, but I couldn't stop my mind from racing. Eventually, I gave up trying and paced restlessly around the house, unable to distract myself with reading or television. At seven o'clock I answered a knock on the back door and found Don Morrison peering through the screen.

"I've been hoping you'd stop by." I shoved open the door and threw my arms around him.

To my surprise, his brother Stephen and his wife appeared on the walk behind him.

"Loren, we wanted to make sure for ourselves that you're really all right," Stephen said.

As always, when I saw Don and Stephen together, I was struck by their resemblance to one another and also the differences between them. They were both in their mid-thirties, slightly over six feet in height, trim and muscular, with light brown hair and light coloring, but there the similarity ended. Don, an easy-going extrovert, refused to give up the thick beard he'd grown to celebrate his move to Lake George Village a few years before, avoided dress-up clothes whenever possible and reveled in every aspect of his new, relaxed lifestyle. Stephen, far more intense, drove himself hard as chief operating officer of an Albany engineering firm, as well as finding time for a wide range of civic and social activities. In the two years I'd known him, I didn't think I'd ever seen him completely at ease.

As the men stepped into the kitchen, Elaine Morrison, dressed for an evening out in a beige silk suit and elegant silver earrings, pushed past them and embraced me with a careful hug. "I doubt you feel like company, Loren. We won't stay, but we've been worried about you."

"Banged up a little, that's all," I said, conscious of the wrinkled slacks and top I'd been lying around in all day.

Stephen reached out and patted my shoulder awkwardly. "Loren, how awful. You saw a body at the center, Don said. We would have driven up earlier, but this was Elaine's night at the shelter."

"Elaine, is that how you dress to serve up meals at the shelter?" Don asked.

"Silly. Of course not," she said with a smile. "As soon as we finished, I rushed home to change. This is the earliest we could get here. Loren, we want to hear about the body you saw."

"I saw a man lying in the display case. I thought he was dead, but he disappeared, so I guess he wasn't. I tried to get the glass open to check, but I couldn't move it."

"In the display case? What was he doing in there? Was it someone you know?" Stephen rattled off questions one after another.

I offered the same answer I'd made that day to everyone who'd asked. "I didn't get a very good look, but I don't think he was anyone I've seen before."

"Won't the sheriff's department be able to identify him?" Elaine said.

"I'm the only one who saw him. By the time the deputy

got there, he was gone." I sensed more questions coming, most of them questions I couldn't answer. I glanced toward Don, sending a message I hoped he'd pick up.

He did. "We probably shouldn't keep Loren talking. I thought I'd fix her a light supper and make her stay quiet."

His brother took the hint at once. "We'll go right along. We just had to make sure you weren't hurt worse than they said, Loren."

Elaine gave me another hug. "Let me know if I can do anything for you, anything at all."

I thanked them for coming and Don walked them out to their car.

"I hope we didn't offend them, but I really wasn't up to company," I said when he returned.

"They didn't plan to stay. Just wanted to check on you. And you really should eat something. Eggs okay?" He swung open the refrigerator door.

"Eggs will be perfect." I didn't offer to help, just sat back and watched him whip up one of his special omelets.

While we ate our impromptu meal, I made another attempt at fence mending. "I hope I've convinced you I didn't go back to the center to paint."

"So you said this morning."

"And you still don't sound convinced."

"I haven't quite got the picture yet. You say you drove by on your way home and saw the front door open?"

"That's part of what puzzles me. And I still haven't figured out how that body got into the display case or how it disappeared."

We kicked around a few possible scenarios, then faced the fact we'd hit a dead end and moved to less disturbing topics. At nine o'clock, Don picked up our dishes and slid them into the dishwasher. "You look tired, Loren. You should go to bed."

"Maybe you could join me." I got up from my chair and walked over to him. I took hold of both his wrists and pulled him toward me. He hesitated for a few seconds before he let me lead him up the stairs.

When we crossed the threshold into my bedroom, he stopped and turned me around to face him. "I'm not sure this is a good idea."

"But I am. I'm okay now," I said.

He kissed me gently, then studied my face, his concern for me apparent.

An almost-full·moon had risen over the lake and a soft evanescence flooded in the windows on the east side of the house. Silver light filled the bedroom, forcing the thick, violet shadows back into the corners. This was my favorite time of day in my favorite room. After I'd decided to stay on here in the house my grandfather had left me, I'd furnished it with my most cherished possessions, made it my special place. It was my retreat, my sanctuary, a haven to share with someone I cared for.

I put my arms around Don and kissed him with a long, lingering kiss. Our lovemaking progressed slowly, familiar now, yet never predictable. His face as he leaned above me radiated concern, affection, maybe even love, although we were both reluctant to leap that hurdle too quickly. We slipped out of our clothes and lay down across the bed.

As we stepped up the tempo of our movements, I felt myself respond to him eagerly, my thoughts focused only in the moment, until we fell apart, gasping for breath.

We lay quietly for a time. Finally I said, "To think I

passed this up last night in favor of a bump on the head and a twisted ankle. I must really be losing it."

"Remember that next time."

"Remind me if I forget." I smoothed the thick brown hair back from his forehead, touched the soft skin above his beard gently with my fingertips.

"I'll do that."

"You're the best," I said. I couldn't use the word love. I'd been hurt by someone who used it too freely and I suspected Don had been, too. We treated each other carefully, leery of reopening old wounds. At least most of the time. If one of us were careless—well, I was usually the one who took what we had together for granted. That I might pay a price for that carelessness didn't occur to me, at least not on that tranquil summer evening as I lay quietly while Don dressed.

"Sure you're okay? Really sure?" he said as he pulled the sheet back and helped me straighten myself in the bed.

"I feel as if I could stay here for a week."

"Do it then. Stay right there just like that. I'll turn out the lights and lock up as I go out." He bent down to caress my cheek.

"Perfect," I said. And right then as I drifted off into the sleep which had eluded me all day, I felt as if everything was.

THE NEXT MORNING, after nine hours of uninterrupted sleep, I limped downstairs to find the coffee maker ready to start and an affectionate message next to it. Apparently, I'd been forgiven.

As my favorite brand of Starbuck's coffee dripped into the carafe and filled the kitchen with its welcomed aroma, I opened the door to pick up the *Post Standard,* our area newspaper, from the porch. To my astonishment, Madeline Hathaway jumped out of a white convertible parked in my driveway and hurried toward me.

Madeline, an attractive blonde in her thirties, was a relative newcomer to the Point. Two years before, she and her husband Ted had bought a deteriorating mansion on the lakeshore north of town and poured a fortune into restoring it. Once the work on her home was completed, Madeline began volunteering in local organizations and quickly established a reputation as a hardworking, congenial presence in the community. Ted, fifteen years her senior and rumored to be the richest man on the lake, devoted himself to amassing more and more wealth and left his wife to manage all the other aspects of their lives.

"I've been watching for signs of life." Madeline bounded up the steps and into the kitchen. "I didn't want to wake you in case you weren't feeling well. I have a group of people meeting at the center at nine o'clock. They've agreed to pitch in and help, but I want to clear everything with you before we start. Make sure we do things the way you want them done."

"A group?" I had trouble picturing any volunteer arriving for work at nine o'clock, much less a group.

"Eight or ten definite right now, promises from others. If everyone pulls together, we should be able to get the place whipped into shape in no time."

I stared in disbelief. "Come in. Have a cup of coffee with me. Tell me what you plan to do."

"Anything you want us to. Finish the painting first, I'd say. You've got most of it done, anyway, so that shouldn't be any problem. Clear out the trash. Maybe do something about the floors."

"This sounds too good to be true," I said as I set out a plate of Kate's croissants and poured coffee for us both.

"Tell me your priorities, Loren. You probably want to put in some time at your office this morning, if you're feeling up to it. Then maybe you could stop at the center when you're through. We've got a committee meeting there this afternoon anyway, haven't we?"

Madeline ran through more things she intended to do while I listened in amazement. As soon as I approved her plan, she finished her coffee and took off, anxious to get started.

When I arrived at the center that afternoon, I shook my head in disbelief at what Madeline and her group of volunteers had accomplished. She'd convinced a professional painter to stop by and offer constructive criticism and, with his guidance, Tommy Porter's crew had finished painting the walls and woodwork. Since redecorating the inside of the building was a major component in the face-lift, the center was well on its way to acquiring the update we wanted.

Other volunteers had completed the unpacking and setting up of the remaining displays, and a clean-up crew was already piling a truck with the first load of trash for the dump.

"Things are really coming together," Madeline said, as she swept up after her workers, "but now that the walls look fresh and clean, you see how much the floors need work. I bet I could talk Ted into paying to have them sanded."

"Exactly the finishing touch the rooms need," I said and filed the idea under too-good-to-be-true. Ted had already earned the nickname Ebenezer Scrooge from several local fundraisers. I didn't hold out much hope for the floors.

The next day, to my amazement, Ted sent in professional sanders to remove the years of stain and grime from the hardwood floors and varnish them to basketball-court sheen.

"The sanders you hired did a fantastic job," I told Ted when I called to thank him. Before I could elaborate on how much I appreciated his gift, he growled that I could thank Madeline instead of him and banged down the phone.

Madeline mentioned the conversation when she stopped by that afternoon to inspect the job. "That was sweet of you to call Ted," she said. "He really appreciated it. I hope he didn't sound too abrupt on the phone. When he's at work, he comes across as grumpy sometimes when he doesn't mean to."

"I probably should have waited until evening and called your house," I said.

"Not at all. Don't give it another thought. He was glad to be able to do it."

I wasn't convinced, but Ted's sour response didn't make a dent in my euphoric mood. After months of foot-dragging, the committee and the new workers Madeline had recruited had thrown themselves whole-heartedly into the renovations and whipped the center into shape in record time.

I hadn't understood the reason for the turnaround until Pauline spelled it out for me. "They're ashamed of themselves and well they might be. Here you almost got yourself killed, painting late at night, trying to do so much alone. Made 'em realize they were slackers."

"Why won't anyone believe I wasn't painting that night?" I asked her. Those words had been my mantra, and people still weren't convinced.

"Let 'em think what they please if they pitch in and get the job done," Pauline insisted.

At that point I didn't have much choice. Unless the body I'd seen in the display case turned up—and there'd been no sign of that so far—no one was going to give more than lip service to believing me.

I knew Pauline's advice made sense. I tried to remove the body from my list of things to worry about, but I couldn't get it out of my mind. Finally, I came up with an idea. It was a long shot, but maybe I could find a clue to where that disappearing corpse had gone.

At that point I hadn't quite made sense of those
rocks I'd seen in the display case turned up—and they'd
been no type of rock—many... noise was something with nature
that hadn't... bottle opening...

I knew I'd find a diet... my senses. The only reason
I'd woken from my bed of flowers... going to was that I
couldn't get out of my mind. Finally... calling on with an
idea. It was a pity that... the clouds I could find a clue, a

FIVE

I POLISHED UP my plan. With both my head and ankle now
almost pain free, I pronounced myself fit for limited
exercise again and plotted a new course for my morning
run. I'd start at the center, I decided, and check out the
hiking trails which wound through the woods behind the
building. The back door of the center had been open the
night I'd seen the body in the display case and, even though
several days had passed, maybe—just maybe—I could spot
a clue as to how the man had managed to get out of there.

"Cool," Josie Donohue said when she overheard me
telling her mother what I intended to do. "I've been
thinking of doing some running myself this summer. I'll
go with you."

"You can't be serious. Sacrifice your shot at being
named Couch Potato of the Year?" I said.

Josie rolled her eyes toward Kate who was whipping up
an assortment of hors d'oeuvres for the freezer. "Why not?
I might be going out for soccer this fall. I need to get in
shape."

Disagreement was useless; I'd learned that the hard way.
Fortunately, I'd developed other strategies for dealing with
Josie. "Fine. I'll pick you up in my car tomorrow at six forty-
five. We'll drive over to the center to start our run. That's
morning, you realize. Be outside if you want to go with me."

I saw Kate nod almost imperceptibly, as convinced as I was that Josie's involvement would come to a screeching halt.

Wrong, both of us. The next morning I found my young friend, dressed in jeans even more disreputable than her everyday denims, doing squats and stretches outside her front door.

"I know you have an idea. What is it?" she asked, as we drove to the center to begin our run.

"Whether anyone believes me or not," I said, "that man I saw in the display case was either dead or close to it. If he managed to drag himself out the back door, he may have left blood or some other kind of trail. Maybe it's not too late to find it."

"You want to search the woods? Didn't they already do that?"

"I doubt the deputies made much of a search, since nobody was quick to believe me."

"Shows you what us teenagers go through all the time, Lor. A little circumstantial evidence—like spilled paint and a tipped ladder—and you might as well plead guilty and be done with it."

"I suppose," I said, but her remark made me stop and think. Most of the time, I assumed people believed what I said or at least accepted my statements in the context of well-intended political spin. For the first time, I'd been forced to deal with open disbelief and the covert glances that accompanied it.

We left the car and set out on one of the trails behind the center. My ankle gave me more trouble than I'd expected and slowed the pace, but before we'd gone half a mile, I heard Josie's breathing grow labored.

"Might be a good idea for you not to go too far your first

day," I said as the path we were following wound steadily uphill.

"I'm all right. You're the one hit your head. I don't want you dropping dead out in the woods someplace all alone."

"You want me to drop dead while you're with me?" I asked her. But I was touched enough by her concern to promise a five-minute break at the top of the hill.

We were both puffing when he reached the crest. The lake stretched below us, a long sweep of its thirty-two-mile length visible from our resting place and picture perfect in the morning sunlight. Even at this hour, sailboats bobbed on its smooth, slate blue surface and one of the big lake steamers, gleaming like a huge white wedding cake, churned along on its first trip of the day.

"I never get over how beautiful the lake is. Let's sit a minute and enjoy it," I said.

Josie stifled a sigh of relief as she sank down on a rock.

From our vantage point, we could look back at the woods behind the center. Still relatively untouched, this land was located far enough from town that no one had turned it into building lots, at least not yet. Evergreens and hardwoods dotted the rough terrain; jagged rocks, bushes and undergrowth filled in the open spaces.

This may be how these woods looked two-hundred-fifty years ago, I thought, when Rogers and his Rangers harassed the French with a new kind of warfare they'd learned from the Indians—traveling light, moving with stealth through the wilderness, pulling back when necessary to Fort William Henry at the southern end of the lake or even farther to their home base at Fort Edward.

The path we'd followed that morning was one used today by picnickers and hunters. We'd seen no sign of a body, no trail of blood, no scraps of clothing, no clues of any kind. Plan A gone sadly awry. I'd have to come up with another idea.

SIX

LATER THAT DAY, with the center nearing completion, I turned my attention to preparations for our grand opening. As I'd done with other Emerald Point projects, I called on friends for help. I asked Diane Anderson, who taught English in nearby Lake George, to manage the center during her summer vacation, and she agreed to do it. With a little skillful persuasion on my part, Don volunteered to catalog our exhibits on the computer. I contracted with Kate Donohue to provide refreshments for an opening-night party. Pauline and I mailed out special invitations to members of our common council and local civic organizations, even to our state assemblywoman, Cynthia Smith.

What had seemed an impossible undertaking a short time before was becoming a reality. I heaved a sigh of relief and accepted accolades for the center like a proud parent. Nothing small town or amateurish about our effort—the place would have held its own in the heart of Manhattan.

On the night of our grand opening, I arrived to find Kate, her cheeks flushed with excitement, laying out a buffet which far exceeded the agreed-on offerings. Instead of the modest hors d'oeuvres we'd contracted for, she'd set out chafing dishes piled with chicken wings, shrimp, mushrooms, meatballs, even her special Clams Rockefeller. I surveyed the buffet table in amazement.

"Are you out of your mind? You'll bankrupt yourself."

"I haven't been able to work on the building, so this is my contribution. And it's too late to argue about it," she said as early arrivals, scarcely able to believe their good fortune, began storming the table.

Kate, cool and calm in her long black skirt, white shirt and red bow tie, handled the rush with her usual aplomb. She'd even prevailed upon Josie to help out and—more shocking still—to adhere to Kate's dress code for her servers.

"I never thought I'd be seen in public in this get-up," Josie muttered. She tugged at her own bow tie, suspended on an elastic cord under her white shirt collar. Fortunately, Kate let her young staff wear black slacks instead of long skirts or Josie would surely have rebelled. "I'm lucky my friends don't usually show up at these kinds of things, but I'm afraid word may still get out."

"And you'll be disgraced for life? Helping your mother in public and dressing like a dork at the same time—I don't blame you for being upset."

"I'm doing it for you, Lor. Don't forget it. You owe me big time." She whirled around and snatched up a tray of hors d'oeuvres. I held my breath as she flounced off, the tray tilted at a precarious angle.

An hour later most of the residents of Emerald Point, along with dozens of visitors from neighboring towns, had crowded into the center. When I saw Madeline and Ted Hathaway escorting a group of their new neighbors through the exhibit area, I caught Madeline's eye and we exchanged smiles of satisfaction. The hard work had paid off.

Cynthia Smith, our assemblywoman, arrived with an entourage. As I showed Cynthia and her staff through the rooms, she was lavish with her praise for our efforts. "Your people have done an amazing job with this, Loren. I love the displays, and that history of boats on the lake is beautifully done. You've included everything from French and Indian War bateaux to present-day lake steamers."

"Did you notice this diorama of the lake bottom Jay Brown made for us?" I asked, as sixteen-year-old Jay jumped up from his seat to point out the special features of his exhibit. "And we want to be sure you see our environmental display. The Lake Protection Group and Bateaux Below members did it as a joint project."

Cynthia took her time examining everything. When we reached the Rogers' Rangers display, she pulled me aside and whispered, "Isn't this where you saw the body, Loren? This must be hard for you to have this constant reminder."

I appreciated her concern. Every time I peered through that glass, I flashed on the man I'd seen lying on the floor of the case.

"And they still don't know who he was or what happened to him?" she went on.

"No idea," I said and moved the group quickly to another exhibit.

By the time Cynthia and the others had said their good nights, the party in the main room had swung into high. Don had arrived with Stephen and Elaine and staked out a table.

When he saw I was free, Don signaled for me to join them. "I've saved a chair and a glass of wine for you, but if you don't sit down right now, I can't promise there'll be any hors d'oeuvres left," he said.

"He's implying I'm gobbling more than my share," Stephen told me as he reached across the table for a giant shrimp wrapped in bacon. "This food is top of the line,

Loren. Elaine's already wondering if she can get the caterer to come to Albany to do a party for one of her civic groups."

Elaine nodded as she popped the remains of a crab puff into her mouth. Although the men wore sport shirts and summer slacks, Elaine, elegant as always, was dressed in a trim, black sheath, obviously expensive, and eye-catching gold jewelry. Her perfectly styled black hair and the rich, burnished leather of her shoes and bag completed the look. I might not be wearing New York's best these days, but I still knew it when I saw it.

"He's right," she said. "I have to get your caterer's name. Don says she's a friend of yours. Maybe you could talk her into catering for us. The people I used last year for our fall festival were nothing compared to this."

"I'll give you her number and e-mail. I'm sure she'd like to discuss catering the festival with you." I knew Kate would be pleased by the compliment. She wanted to keep expanding her business, if she could, but Albany was probably too far away for her to travel for an event.

And there was no telling what that event might be. Besides her volunteer work at the soup kitchen, Elaine organized fund raisers for several charitable organizations, oversaw everything from an annual black and white New Year's ball for the historical society to a cleaning and painting party at a homeless shelter. Her own entertaining was equally eclectic. She hosted large, elegant soirées for clients of Stephen's engineering firm and small, intimate dinner parties, all of which Don, who hated formality of any kind, did everything in his power to avoid.

"How about your brother? Does he like being involved in these things?" I'd asked him once.

Don had hesitated over his answer. "He goes along with

it, anyway. For a while I got the feeling he was just going through the motions, but lately he seems happier, more like his old self."

One evening shortly after I met Stephen and Elaine for the first time, Don had filled me in on his brother's long history of problems with alcohol. "He racked up some bad years, quite a few of them to be honest about it, came close to losing his company a couple of times," he said.

"And Elaine stuck by him?" I asked.

"She threatened to leave more than once. Then, five or six years ago, he turned his life around. As far as I know, once he stopped drinking he never went back to it. Elaine moved them to a more upscale neighborhood, cultivated wealthier friends and launched them on that round robin of social activity they're always involved in. They both see it as good for his business, I guess."

Still, to me, Stephen never seemed totally comfortable in any group. Tonight he kept glancing around the room, checking out the crowd, although I doubted he knew anyone else there.

As we stuffed ourselves on Kate's delicious hors d'oeuvres, Don proposed a toast to the success of the evening. "And especially to you, Loren, for pulling this off. There were times when I didn't think you could swing it."

"So now you tell me." I raised my plastic wine glass and bumped it against his and Elaine's. Stephen waved his soda bottle in our direction.

When our guitar player, Eddie Nerone, took a break, I borrowed his microphone to welcome the guests and acknowledge the contributions made by our committee. I offered a brief but sincere thank-you and sat down.

When I returned to the table, Don leaned close and

whispered to me, "Perfect. Short and to the point. This crowd wants to party." He nodded across the room to where Eddie had already picked up his guitar and the guests were besieging Kate's buffet for seconds.

At nine o'clock, the evening showed no signs of winding down. By then, most of the guests had checked out the exhibits, gorged on Kate's hors d'oeuvres and exchanged greetings with friends and neighbors. As the crowd gathered around Eddie, he let loose with a Fleetwood Mac medley that had the gang clapping and begging for more. The decibel level was already shattering eardrums when a tremendous crash ripped through the building.

Eddie stopped in mid-chord. The crowd fell silent for a few seconds. Then pandemonium set in as people tried to figure out where the noise had come from and shouted for friends and relatives.

Don jumped up, looking wildly around the room. "What the hell was that? Do you have any idea what happened?"

Before I could hazard a guess, Melba Williams—plump, dignified Melba Williams—staggered through the door of the main exhibit room. Her eyes glittered with fright, tears streamed down her face. "Oh God, I was almost killed! A bomb went off in the ladies' room right next to me. We're being attacked!"

SEVEN

IN SECONDS OUR festive evening degenerated into chaos. While I comforted Melba, Sheriff's Deputy Rick Cronin, who'd been assigned to keep an eye on the entrance and parking lot, rushed inside and made a careful check of the building. The explosion, he quickly announced, had been caused by a cherry bomb set off in the ladies' room. But even after Rick had searched the rest of the center without finding anything suspicious, the guests weren't willing to hang around. September eleventh had altered people's thinking. A prank, once seen as harmless, no longer amused anyone when it mimicked something serious. The building emptied quickly.

Don and I saw Stephen and Elaine to their car and returned to help Kate pack up the remains of the buffet.

"This stuff used to happen in school all the time," Josie told me as she swept empty paper plates and cups off the tables and into a black plastic garbage bag. "Not so much anymore, though. I can't imagine who'd do a dumb thing like that here. There weren't any kids around except for Jay Brown showing that diorama he made and he's too wimpy to do something like that."

While Josie helped Kate load her van, Don and I stacked the folding chairs he'd borrowed for the party. As we took a short break, I said, "You're coming home with me when we're finished here, aren't you? I've been looking forward to some time alone with you."

He shook his head. "Afraid I can't tonight. Madeline made me promise to get these chairs back to the Legion Post in Lake George before they close at midnight. They've scheduled some big event for tomorrow, told her they wouldn't loan them otherwise."

I'd forgotten about the chairs. Pick-up truck owners like Don often did that kind of favor. "Own a truck, you're fair game," he'd say cheerfully. But tonight…tonight I wished he hadn't been so agreeable.

The next morning the center opening made the papers, but not quite the way I'd hoped. Although my friend Stephanie Colvin, a *Post Standard* columnist always quick to promote Emerald Point activities, wrote a glowing review of the event, one of the editors, famous for his slash and burn approach, used his column to speculate about the cherry bomb and the body which may or may not have been left in the display case. Not exactly the kind of PR we'd hoped for.

"We didn't need this," Pauline and I agreed as we bad-mouthed the editor and his column.

The man's attitude may have been mean-spirited, but I had to admit I shared his concerns. Why would someone leave a body in our display case, spirit it away before it could be identified, and set off a cherry bomb on our opening night? Was the cherry bomb connected to the body somehow? If only I could identify the man in the display case, other pieces of the puzzle might fall into place.

Fortunately, the Plan B I'd been searching for presented itself later the same day when Ramona Dolley called my office. Despite the forty-year difference in our ages,

Ramona and I had been friends since my childhood visits to the lake.

"If you say you saw a body in that display case, Loren, that's good enough for me," she'd told me the day after the incident. "I'm no stranger to people talking about me behind my back, you know. The trick is not to let them get you down."

The year before, Ramona had been the subject of more than her fair share of gossip when her husband Deke committed suicide after running their motel business into the ground. Even with help from her daughter, Lake George realtor Jeannie Spenser, Ramona had been struggling financially ever since.

That afternoon when I picked up the phone, she jumped right to the point. "I don't know why I didn't think of this sooner, Loren. There's a guy staying here won't leave his cabin. I don't mean he won't leave it at all. I've been offering a breakfast buffet—thought it might help me get some business. Nothing special—juice, a couple kinds of Danish I pick up at Kate's, and coffee. Well, every morning this guy scurries onto the back porch where I lay it out, slurps up most of the food and coffee and takes whatever's left back to his cabin. Then he stays in there all day 'til the next morning."

I wasn't sure where our conversation was going, but I went along. "You mean he eats everything you put out? Where does that leave your other guests?"

"Truth be told, I haven't any others. This guy's the only one."

"And you don't think he leaves the cabin except to get his breakfast?"

"He has a car, but I never see him go anyplace. I've been

keeping an eye on him. I swear he stays right in there from one day to the next."

I took a wild guess. "Do you want me to help you evict him?'

"No. He paid in advance. He's all right with me financially. The reason I'm telling you—he checked in the same night you saw that body. I'm wondering if it could have been him in that display case. Suppose he was hurt, but managed to get out of there some way or other, then holed up here to hide out?"

"I don't know, Ramona. That's quite a stretch. You say he has a car?"

"An old, beat-up Chevy. Been parked out by the cabin since the night he came."

I hesitated. Local motel owners grumbled about noisy tenants, extra guests sneaked in, tourists who skipped without paying. A complaint like this was a first for me.

"Here's what I'm thinking," Ramona went on. "Come over and have coffee with me tomorrow morning before you go to the office. I lay the buffet out on my back porch. You can watch him through the kitchen window, see if you recognize him."

Definitely a long shot. I'd only seen part of the man's face, a shock of black hair standing up from his head like a rooster's comb and a worn denim jacket. I wasn't sure I'd recognize him. Still, I'd enjoy having coffee with Ramona. At least she believed I'd seen somebody. I was grateful for that.

EIGHT

I'D INTENDED TO STOP by Ramona's motel the first thing the next morning, but a seven o'clock phone call altered my plans. I'd managed an early run—without Josie this time—and was just finishing my shower when the phone rang.

Don didn't waste time on preliminaries. "Loren, I've got some bad news. Madeline Hathaway had an accident last night. You know those steep stairs from their house to the beach? She fell all the way down them."

"Oh no. Is she hurt bad?"

"She's dead, Loren. Apparently, she hit her head. Other injuries too, I guess. There's a short account in the paper, so it must have happened before midnight."

I hung up quickly and ran to the porch for my newspaper.

Emerald Point Woman Dies in Fall, the headline in the *Post Standard* read. The account was sketchy, with only the information available at press time and no other details besides the ones Don had given me.

My hands shook as I read the article. I'd liked Madeline Hathaway. She'd been a real help on the center committee—good natured, efficient, willing to tackle any job. I'd been looking forward to getting to know her better.

I thought back to the first time I'd met her. Shortly after she and Ted had moved to the Point, they'd attended a meeting for owners of lakefront property. Ted had seized the opportunity to accost me about the condition of the road which ran behind the big houses on the shore. "You'd think with the damn high taxes you sock us for up there we'd be entitled to decent upkeep on that stretch of road. Bad enough most of us have to maintain the drives into our houses ourselves."

"I'll see what I can find out and get back to you," I'd promised.

Ted, still dissatisfied, had gone on snarling about one thing or another while Madeline ignored his tirades and chatted easily with the other people there.

The next day I'd asked Pauline the question I assumed would clarify the relationship for me. "I assume he has money. Is that why she puts up with him?"

Pauline could usually be counted on for the inside scoop, but this time she wasn't quite sure. "Everyone thinks so, anyway. He wheels and deals, apparently hits a jackpot once in a while. No solid info on how much he's got, though."

But on the morning I learned of Madeline's death, I knew where to go for details. Kate opened her coffee shop and catering business early. By seven-thirty, the second or third wave of regulars would be ensconced at the counter and tables, gobbling the breakfast specialties and catching up on the news. No Emerald Point happenings escaped discussion at Kate's.

A short time after Don's phone call, I took a seat at the counter where Herb the Baker, Kate's roly-poly helper, was pouring coffee and serving his special breakfast combos. "Herb, isn't it terrible about Madeline Hathaway? What have you heard?"

"We're just talking about it here, Mayor. Our town is

sure having a run of bad luck. She and Ted was outside on
their patio last night, they say. She maybe started down to
the beach and slipped."

One of the men at a nearby table interrupted him. "You
might as well hear the truth, Mayor. Everybody's gonna find
out sooner or later, anyway. The Hathaways were arguing
something fierce. Madeline was yelling her head off."

"Madeline? I've never heard her raise her voice," I said
in surprise.

"She raised it last night, that's for sure. Teena Wilkinson just left here, claims she heard quite the fight, and it was
mostly Madeline's voice, not Ted's," the man continued.

Herb swung around from the grill and echoed agreement.

"How did Teena manage that one?" I asked.

Teena Wilkinson, a notorious gossip, lived miles away in
Lake George Village. She was reputed to know everything
that happened on the lake, but an argument at the Hathaways'
place would have been a challenge even for her sharp ears.

Bill Donor at the next table jumped in to explain. "Teena
was babysitting next door for the Cliffords. Says there was
a big argument goin' on at the Hathaways. Real knock-
down, drag-out, Teena says."

I'd wanted news, but this was more than I'd bargained
for. I picked up my coffee. "Kate out back?" I asked Herb.

"Go right along out," he said, as he flipped a stack of
pancakes onto a plate.

Kate, her black hair tied back and her jeans and shirt
covered by a big white apron, was mixing a bowl of
seafood salad at her favorite workstation. "Too much for
you out there?" she asked.

"I came for news on Madeline. Then when they started
giving it to me, I wanted to bolt out the door."

"I know what you mean. Unfortunately, they've got the basic facts right, I guess. There was an argument. She fell. Fill in the blanks as you see fit."

"Wait a minute. Do people think Ted pushed her? Is that what this is about?"

"I don't know if anybody's spelled that out yet, but I suspect it's just a matter of time until they do." Kate refilled my coffee cup from a pot on the counter and slid a croissant onto a plate.

"Thanks, but I plan to buy some from Herb. I promised Ramona I'd stop by her place this morning and croissants are her favorite."

Not that I'd have to bribe Ramona to find out what she'd heard about Madeline's accident. I was confident she'd have every detail down pat by the time I got there.

TEN MINUTES LATER I gave Ramona a hug and handed her the box of croissants. "Sorry I'm late," I said.

"These'll make up for it, if they're what I think they are. Coffee's ready. You've got time, I hope." She led me into the big country kitchen she'd repainted during the winter in a cheerful shade of yellow.

I pulled out one of the old-fashioned wooden chairs at the table and sat down. "Have you heard about Madeline?"

She nodded as she poured our coffee. "Two or three phone calls already. I figured that was what delayed you. And it wouldn't have made a speck of difference what time you got here, anyway. He's gone."

"The man staying here? He finally went out somewhere?"

"Took off for good would be my guess. His car was gone when I got up this morning. I walked out to the cabin and peeked in the side window. No sign of him."

"Are his clothes gone, too?"

"Don't know that he had much. He always wore a beat-up shirt and old, shabby jeans. He looked pretty much the same to me every time I saw him."

"How about his hair, Ramona? Did he have a big shock of dark hair? That's what I remember seeing in that display case."

"Can't rightly say. He wore a cap when he came to get his breakfast."

"So he's gone. Did he owe you for the room? Is that why he skipped?"

"No. He paid me in advance when he moved in. His rent was due again today. But he didn't even wait around for his breakfast. That sure wasn't like him."

"Do you think he could have overheard you talking to me on the phone?"

Ramona shook her head. "Anything's possible, Loren. I just wish I'd called you sooner so you could have got a look at him. But there is something you can do for me as long as you're here."

"Sure. Anything you say."

"Go in the cabin with me. I don't really want to face it alone. It's the same one Deke was in when—you know—when he..."

I understood. I'd spent time with Ramona after Deke shot himself. I hadn't seen him lying fatally wounded in that blood-splattered cabin, but I still got shivers when I thought about that morning. "Sure. I'll go in by myself if you want me to."

"I'll be all right. I've worked in the cabin a lot, fixing it up. I just don't want to find the guy's still there, even with his car gone. If you're with me, I can say I thought he'd left and you might want to rent it."

I followed Ramona across the yard and up the two steps onto the cabin's rickety little porch. Ramona might have worked on the place, but to say she'd fixed it up was a stretch. The door's paint was pockmarked with ugly blotches; the finish on the once shiny log walls, cracked and peeling.

Ramona rattled the knob a couple of times, then pushed open the unlocked door. She threw me a look over her shoulder and stepped inside. I followed close behind her. The room contained an unmade bed, a Depression-era dresser, a chest of drawers and an old TV on a small stand—that was all. The closet-size bathroom I checked out was as bereft of personal belongings as the rest of the cabin.

"It sure looks like he's bailed on you," I said.

"I can't pretend I'm sorry. I had a bad feeling about that guy." Ramona gathered up towels from the bathroom and began stripping the sheets from the bed.

I wasn't sorry he was gone, either. Ramona had probably been overly suspicious, I told myself as I drove to the office. She'd connected her tenant with the body in the display case for only one reason—the date of his arrival. Chalk that up to coincidence. Case solved.

An hour off my usual schedule, I unlocked the door of our little white frame Village Building and embarked on my morning routine—open the blinds, switch on my computer, set the coffee maker to supply my favorite Hazelnut blend. I sorted through my IN box, but I knew I didn't have much time. Jim Thompson, the always dependable sheriff's investigator, would arrive any minute to update me on Madeline Hathaway's death.

A little before ten Jim, eyes dull with fatigue, plodded in and collapsed into my visitor's chair. His pallor and the heavy lines around his mouth testified to a long night.

I didn't ask if he wanted coffee, just got up and poured him a cup and set it on the desk in front of him.

"Thanks. I can use this. You've heard about Madeline Hathaway, of course. She always seemed so full of life. Hard to believe she's dead."

"For me, too. They say she fell? I suppose the stairs down to the lake from those big houses can be treacherous."

Jim didn't reply. He sipped his coffee and stared at me as if waiting for me to ask the question.

So I asked it. "Is it true they were quarreling? Over at Kate's this morning they said the neighbors heard them, but you know how people are around here. Doesn't take much to start a rumor like that."

"It's no rumor we've got another suspicious death here. I may have to look into finding us one of those crime scene consultants you hear about on TV."

I picked him up fast on his remark. "Suspicious? Crime scene? Are you saying it was a crime, not an accident?"

"Hang on, Mayor. They don't pay me to jump to conclusions, or you either. Anyway, as I understand the role of those consultants, they also help establish when something isn't a crime. Though the way Teena Wilkinson was talking this morning, nobody's apt to believe that."

"Teena was next door, someone said."

"Babysitting for the Cliffords. Insists she heard Ted and Madeline arguing."

I nodded. "That's the story I got, too. Bad enough for Ted to lose his wife. People start hinting he's a murderer."

Jim drained his coffee cup and set it on the desk. "You

know, Mayor, that's the trouble with making enemies in this town. Ted Hathaway's made a lot of 'em, and they're anxious to think the worst of him."

"I know he's an abrasive guy," I said. "From the day he moved here, I've heard negative comments about his business dealings. Still, he seemed devoted to Madeline. You don't really think he killed her, do you?"

"Those steps," Jim said as if visualizing the scene in his mind, "you're right about those steps being treacherous. She could have started down and fallen, I suppose. There's a railing on one side, but she might not have taken hold of it. We'll have to see what the coroner says."

I recognized a successful change of subject when I heard one.

"Does it look as if she died instantly?"

"Coroner will tell us that, too. It's not like your grandfather's place, you know, with that gentle slope down to the water. The houses up there are maybe twenty, twenty-five feet above the beach, and it's a steep drop. Plus, there are a lot of rocks at the foot of the stairs she could have hit."

I didn't answer. My grandfather's place. Not mine. I'd lived in Emerald Point for five years. Just when I started thinking I belonged here, I got clobbered with a remark that made it clear I was still an outsider.

NINE

SHORTLY AFTER THE door swung shut behind Jim that morning, the telephone rang. When Diane Anderson had something on her mind, she didn't waste words. "Loren, I want to pay a sympathy call on Ted Hathaway. How about going with me? These things are always easier with two people."

She was right. I'd have to see him sooner or later myself.

Better not to delay. I arranged to pick Diane up at two o'clock.

The Hathaway place—Ted sometimes referred to it as the Hathaway estate—was situated north of the Point in an area of stately homes, a top-of-the-line location. That part of the shoreline had been colonized in the late nineteenth century by wealthy entrepreneurs who'd amassed their fortunes in the days before income tax and similar annoyances. The property had been passed down through several generations of the Tucker family until the death of the last descendent a few years before. Ted, who'd been scouting the area for lakefront property, bought it fast and spared no expense in restoring it to its original grandeur. Now, the elegant stone mansion with its landscaped grounds and circular drive surpassed most of the other multi-million-dollar homes along this section of the lake. Diane and I both stole admiring glances at the house and plantings as we walked up to the side entrance and rang the bell.

Ted answered the door himself. He appeared to have showered and shaved and his dark brown slacks and beige dress shirt looked fresh, but his haggard appearance suggested a sleepless night. Ted Hathaway had probably been a good-looking guy in his youth, but now, somewhere in his fifties, he was balding and losing the battle with weight.

"Come in." He ushered us into a big, showy living room overlooking the lake twenty feet below. A wall of floor-to-ceiling windows offered a breathtaking view of sun-kissed water dotted with white sailboats, speeding motor craft and a chugging lake steamer. The view of the tree-lined east shore and the mountains rising behind it reminded me of landscapes Georgia O'Keeffe had painted during the summers she spent a few miles south of here.

As Diane and I seated ourselves in a pair of wing chairs, I found myself picturing Madeline in this room, wondering how many times she'd sat here enjoying this view, never dreaming she'd pay such a high price for it.

Diane offered her condolences. "I'm so sorry about Madeline. She was a wonderful person. I knew her through her committee work."

"Yes." Ted appeared too shaken to say more.

I added my words of sympathy. "And she was such a help at the center this spring. I really appreciate all she did."

"Yes," Ted said again.

"And she was involved in other projects, too. She was always quick to pitch in," I went on.

Ted finally found his voice. "Too much so, if you ask me."

I didn't want him to start on that subject, so I cast around for a new approach. "Have you made plans for the funeral, Ted? Is there anything we can do to help?"

He shook his head slowly. "They're doing an autopsy. I don't know how long it will take."

Diane added a few remarks, but she got even less response than I had. Finally, we each muttered a few additional words of sympathy and said our good-byes. Ted remained in the doorway, staring after us. I wished I'd thought to ask if he had friends or relatives to stay with him. He seemed very much alone.

THE BUDGET COMMITTEE meeting that night ran late and my head was spinning with proposals and counter-proposals when I pulled into my driveway a few minutes after ten o'clock. I noticed a large black car parked on the street near the house, then did a double-take when Ted Hathaway swung open the door and strode over to me.

He didn't bother with a hello. "Can I come in? I wanted to talk to you today but not in front of somebody else."

I unlocked the back door and pointed him into the kitchen. Despite a refreshing breeze which had sprung up at sunset, the inside temperature of the house was uncomfortably warm. "It hasn't cooled off much in here. Why don't we sit on the front porch?" I said.

He dropped into a chair at the kitchen table and looked around the room. "This will do. Is anybody else here?"

The question surprised me. Anybody else in the house would have been sitting in the dark. "No. We're alone. You wanted to talk to me?"

"People think I killed Madeline. Don't bother to deny it. I know they do."

I couldn't deny it. A groundswell of rumor to that effect had been building all day.

"Nobody's come right out and said it, but people won't look me in the eye. I finally asked one of the guys who works for me. He admitted there's a lot of talk."

Did that surprise him? Ted Hathaway had acquired more than his share of enemies. Still, that didn't make him a murderer. I searched for an appropriate response. "I'm sure it's painful for you, Ted, but you can't worry about gossip. People here love spreading rumors. Has Jim Thompson given you any reason to think he suspects you?"

"Not yet, but he plans to meet with me again tomorrow. 'To clear up some loose ends,' he called it."

I felt as if I were walking on quicksand. "Do you know why there'd be talk?"

"Some woman at the neighbors' place claims she heard us arguing. But damn it, it wasn't me Madeline was arguing with. I don't know who it was."

"You were there, weren't you?"

"I was home earlier that night. We had a disagreement, I admit it, but nowhere near a fight. And we didn't talk loud enough for anyone else to have heard us. But I did take off in my car, went for a ride, thinking it would cool me down. Somebody else must have come in. I don't know who it was."

"Wait. Are you saying you argued with Madeline and left, and then someone else came to the house and argued with her, too?" Did he really expect people to buy this about a woman who I'd never heard disagree with anyone?

"I know. I know. It sounds like I'm making this up. No one's gonna believe me."

He was right. This story wouldn't be an easy sell. If he

couldn't convince me… "Tell me where you went. Maybe somebody saw you."

"I doubt it. I just drove around for a while. When I got back, I looked for Madeline. I figured she'd gone off with somebody. Her car was still parked in the driveway. Then I went over to the stairs and glanced down. She was lying across the rocks. Just lying there, not moving."

"You didn't see her fall?"

"Hell no. I'm not even sure she did fall. Maybe she went down to the beach for some reason and somebody killed her there. You got anything to drink? I could use a drink, a beer even."

Actually, I felt I could use one myself. I got up from the table and pulled two cans of beer out of the refrigerator. Before I could take glasses from the cupboard, Ted had popped the tab on his can and gulped down a long swallow.

"Did you tell this to Jim Thompson the first time he talked to you?" I asked him.

"Sure. But I don't think he believed me. I admit it sounds like a fish story. I need you to help me."

I was trying so hard to sort through what he'd been telling me, I didn't react at first. Then I realized what he was asking. "You want me to help you? How? What can I do?"

"I think you know who came to see Madeline, who was there when she fell. She's spent so much time with you lately you must know who she was involved with." He drained his can and glanced pointedly at the refrigerator.

I pretended not to notice. "Hold on, Ted. What do you mean she spent so much time with me?"

"She said she was working with you a lot. She took off most every night and all day on weekends to help get that damn center finished on time."

I did a fast recap. Every night? All day on weekends? That was a stretch. I made a fast calculation of how often Madeline had worked at the center before the week of the opening. She'd been there frequently, sure, but not always every day or for very long.

"She was generous about helping out," I said, choosing my words with care, "but we weren't necessarily there at the same time or even in the same room."

"'Generous' isn't the right word for it." Ted's voice coarsened. "I was really disgusted the night of the opening when you didn't say more about all she did. That half-baked thank-you of yours wasn't enough considering the hours she spent there. I wanted to tell you that right then and there, but she wouldn't let me."

Fortunately, Madeline had better sense than to let Ted spoil the opening. My mind raced back over my conversations with her. I'd told her several times how much I appreciated her efforts. Had she expected more herself? "Ted, I'm sorry to hear this. I thought Madeline knew how grateful I was for all she did."

"Oh, she would never ask for special thanks. But you know what I think? You want to know what I think?" He jabbed a finger in my direction. His voice dropped even lower; his tone had an ugly edge.

I pulled myself up straight in my chair. Right then, I didn't give a damn what he thought. "Ted, you're way out of line. If you want to calm down and discuss this in a rational way, I'll listen to you. Otherwise, this conversation is over."

He started to argue the point, then backed down. "Sorry. I get upset talking about this. I think she was interested in somebody on that damn committee of yours, somebody she worked with at the center." He glared at me, searching my face for a reaction.

I raced through a mental list of the volunteers—Tommy Porter and the other painters? Hardly. They weren't in Madeline Hathaway's league. Billy Weston? Even an irascible husband would be better company than Boring Billy. The Dobson brothers? No way. I shook my head. "Ted, I never saw any signs of it."

He wasn't convinced. "I know she was interested in somebody. She practically told me so."

"Did she tell you that on the night she fell? Is that what you two were arguing about?" I was pushing my luck, but I wanted to know.

He started to flare up again, then got hold of himself. "I told you we weren't arguing. I asked her what the hell was going on. That time at your house. That's when it started with him, I'd bet money on it. She came home late that night. Thought I was staying over in New York. She looked dreamy-eyed, flushed even, like she did sometimes when we first started seeing each other. Give me another beer, will you?"

Not good. Runaway train here. Time to throw a switch or two. I shifted in my chair and ignored his request. "I know you're upset, Ted, but it's late and I'm exhausted. Besides, I don't have any idea what you're talking about. What night at my house?"

Afterward, I congratulated myself for not blurting out that Madeline had never been at my house, not the night he was apparently talking about or any other. I'd learned a few things since I'd been elected mayor. Keep your own counsel, my grandmother used to say, and I'd finally caught on. I didn't have to tell everything I knew. When Ted didn't answer the question, I asked again. "What night at my house?"

"The night you moved the committee meeting there. The first Thursday of May. I remember because I was supposed to have a meeting in the city and it was cancelled. Things had been a little cool between us, so I went to the center, thought I'd pick her up and we'd go for a drink or something. The place was all dark, no cars, no lights, nothing. When she came home, she said you'd moved the meeting to your house. You'd turned it into a goddamn party for the committee. She'd been drinking, I could see that plain enough."

"And you argued about that?"

"Not really. I said something about her not being where she said she'd be, but…well, she could always get around me." He looked away sheepishly, actually flushed as he remembered.

Too much information. I flashed on a scene I didn't want to picture, a scene of Madeline defusing Ted's anger. Was this some kind of sick game they played?

"Ted, I'll have to think about this. I'm so tired right now everything's a blur. Let me try to piece some of this together in my own mind. We can talk again if you want to. But I assure you, I saw no sign of Madeline being interested in someone on the committee, not at any time. I don't know what more I can tell you."

"If you really don't know who she was seeing, you could ask around. I can't do it. Nobody's going to tell me. Jim Thompson would suspect me of making this up if I told him what I've just told you, but you could find out."

I stood up and walked to the back door. "Ted, I really can't talk any more right now. Let me think about this." Ted hesitated, then got to his feet reluctantly. Before he could say anything more, I swung the door open and leaned against it, waiting for him to leave. As I pushed it shut behind him, my mind raced back over the things he'd told me.

Madeline Hathaway had apparently taken the simplest approach to deception: start with the truth and improvise as necessary. Except that now she couldn't do any more improvising. The facts were going to come out. In a few days, Ted Hathaway would be looking for answers to a whole new set of questions.

TEN

I'D SPOKEN THE TRUTH when I told Ted I was exhausted, but my conversation with him that night left me too wired to sleep. I tossed restlessly for an hour, then sat up and turned on my bedside lamp. Ted's accusations had forced me to see Madeline in a whole new light. Could she really have been interested in someone else, so interested she would have considered leaving Ted? And how would that have affected his life?

The way most people in Emerald Point saw the Hathaways was that Ted made the money and Madeline handled everything else. Madeline served on the committees, supported the causes, entertained at the lavish parties and cultivated the lake's old guard until, slowly but surely, she and Ted had maneuvered their way into the area's upper-crust society.

Even after they'd gained a toehold, they must have realized that initial acceptance didn't come with any guarantees. The people in this tight-knit circle were old money, linked by marriages or business partnerships, often for several generations back. Emerald Point's Millionaire's Row might lack the elegance of the Newport cottages, the Saratoga Springs mansions or the country estates along the lower Hudson, but its residents cherished their lakeside domain as an enclave of grace and beauty. No matter how much wealth Ted amassed, I doubted his new neighbors would tolerate his surly behavior without Madeline to act as a buffer.

The morning after my conversation with Ted, I shortened my run and paid another visit to Kate's coffee shop. That day the little restaurant could have served as a model for a Norman Rockwell painting. Uniformed working men from the power and telephone companies crowded the counter. Elderly retirees—also mostly men—exchanged news and views at the tables. As always, Herb the Baker presided over the room with his usual hang-dog expression.

"Okay if I say hi to Kate?" I asked him and left Norman Rockwell's small town America for Martha Stewart's kitchen.

At the butcher block work table Kate, wrapped in her signature white apron, was chopping celery, peppers and onions. Next to her, a picture-perfect roast turkey, obviously just out of the oven, filled the room with a succulent aroma.

"Don't tell me you cooked that turkey this morning? It's only seven-thirty now. What time did you start work?" I asked her.

"I came in around three to bake the sweet rolls for Brown's Hotel. As long as I was here, I figured I might as well roast the turkey, too."

"And I complain about the long hours in my job. The next time I whine to you, remind me of this."

Kate poured a mug of coffee and slid it over to me. "Not to worry. There's an up side. I get to take off right after lunch and catch a couple hours sleep before Josie comes home from school."

I sat down on a stool near her and sipped the coffee. "Delicious as always. Those croissants look great, too."

Kate took the hint at once. She arranged one of the fluffy, buttery creations on a plate and passed it over. "You're out early yourself. Are they still talking about Madeline out there?"

"I didn't wait to find out. I can't get her off my mind. I understand people are already whispering about Ted, wondering if he killed her." I watched for Kate's reaction.

"I can't imagine why he'd do that. He always seemed crazy about her and she was such an asset to him." She turned away quickly and opened the refrigerator door, but not before I'd noticed a faint flush of color in her cheeks.

"One reason comes to mind," I said. "I know you hate post-party talk, but you've probably catered most of the events she attended this spring. Could she have been interested in someone else? Or was someone showing interest in her?"

Kate brushed away my questions, looking even more uncomfortable. She hated gossip about the parties she catered. I'd heard the speech she made to her staff. "These people are paying a big price for our services," she'd tell them, "and they expect us to be discreet. If they hear we've spread stories afterward, they'll think twice about using us again."

"Sorry. I know you hate to be asked questions like that," I said.

She hesitated, as if considering how to respond. "You could ask Diane. She might know something," she said finally.

Subject closed. We chatted about other things until I'd finished my croissant and checked the time. "Thanks for breakfast. I'll pay Herb when I go by. And don't tell me not to." I took off fast before Kate could object.

A LITTLE AFTER NOON, I was finishing one of the reports we had to file with the state when Pauline arrived for the afternoon shift. No sense neglecting one of the best sources of information in town. If I pressed the right buttons, she might answer a few key questions. I pushed one.

Her response surprised me. "Oh, you know how this town is about talk. Madeline Hathaway is—I guess I should say was now—an attractive woman, not above a little casual flirtation. Linked to men off and on, but nothing definite."

"Linked to…"

"Oh, different ones. Don't know how serious. Husband traveled a lot, you know, and she was no hand to sit home."

"Like what men?" I pressed her, hoping for at least one name.

"Ralph Forrester, for one, I've heard."

"But that's old news, Pauline. Wasn't it a year or more ago people buzzed about the two of them?"

Pauline glanced down at the papers on her desk. She sorted through the pile twice before she spoke. "Yes, I suppose it must have been. I hear Ralph's thinking of moving south next winter. Retired now, you know."

I got the message. If she knew something, she wasn't about to tell it. My fact-finding expedition was going to require a lot more work.

THE NEXT NAME on my list was my friend Diane Anderson.

"Yes, there's been gossip," Diane admitted as we shared a pizza at Mario's that night. "Madeline definitely preferred the company of men, but there was never any scandal as far as I know. With Ted away on business so much, she went places alone. She obviously didn't want to sit home every night. You couldn't blame her for that."

"Are you saying she was never linked to anyone romantically?"

Diane shrugged. "There was talk a while ago about Ralph Forrester, but I suspect it was nothing more than a casual flirtation. She wasn't much for women friends, but you know who she got together with once in a while? Ellen Davies, that writer who's staying in the Village. Maybe she could tell you something."

I mulled over Diane's suggestion. I did want to know more, not because Ted had raised questions about Madeline, but because I found her death troubling, too. I'd planned to contact Ellen about another matter anyway. Maybe that conversation would provide the opening I needed to ask about Madeline Hathaway.

ELEVEN

TWO DAYS LATER, on a perfect June afternoon, Ellen Davies and I sat on the deck of the Shoreline Restaurant in the heart of Lake George Village. Once again, the lake had come roaring back to life for the summer, at least here in the Village where a million and one activities were taking place. Tourists sauntered in and out of the shops. Families, eager for a trip up the lake, boarded the boats moored at the Shoreline's docks. The parasail business was literally in full swing and the brightly colored sails floating over the sun-kissed waters offered thrill-seekers the dips and chills they longed for.

"One of those perfect early summer days, isn't it?" Ellen said, as she and I gazed out at the glistening lake and the lush green hills cradling it. "It's easy to see why neither of us could tear ourselves away to go back to New York."

I'd been pleased when Ellen accepted my invitation to lunch. She and I had made similar changes in our lives a few years before. Like me, she'd visited the lake and decided to stay on. At that time she'd been researching Lake George's most famous summer resident, Georgia O'Keeffe, for an article she'd planned to write. Then, after stumbling across a collection of what appeared to be long-lost O'Keeffe paintings and almost getting killed in the process, she'd turned the experience into a mystery novel.

"Another summer and we're both still here. You must have been bitten by the same bug I was," I said.

Ellen nodded in agreement. "I'm staying for a while longer anyway. Most of the time, it's so peaceful here. Yet in summer the place bustles with life. I love the changes. What's to go back to New York for?"

"My thinking, too," I said. "Emerald Point may not be as lively as Lake George Village, but we're working on it. Our goal right now is to acquire a little more business, but not enough to destroy our tranquility."

We sipped glasses of wine while we chatted easily about her research on Georgia O'Keeffe and my projects as mayor. If she wondered why I'd invited her to lunch, she didn't let on. As we started on our club sandwiches, I took the plunge. "What we need now is an experienced writer to handle some publicity for us, especially about our new community center. Help us get that little more business we're looking for, make people aware of what the Point has to offer."

"But hasn't the *Post Standard* been publicizing your projects?" Ellen asked.

"Stephanie Colvin has done a good job for us, but that's not going to be enough. I'd love to see articles in *Adirondack Life* and the Capital District newspapers and magazines."

"You mean articles about your new center?"

"That and anything else that would give us a little buzz. What I'd like to do is talk you into doing a piece or two for us."

Ellen hesitated, staring past me at the lake. *The Horicon,* one of the largest of the lake steamers, sounded three ear-splitting blasts of its horn as it pulled away from the dock. The delighted passengers leaned over the rail, waving at friends and strangers alike.

I continued my pitch. "I want to be up front about this. The pay wouldn't be much at first, but if the periodicals paid you, you'd have those fees. And I'd do everything I could to make things easy for you."

Ellen turned back to me with a smile. "No wild promises. I like that. But I'll need to think about it. I'm not sure I have the energy right now for something new."

"You mean because of Madeline Hathaway's death? I understand you and she were friends." I hadn't planned to bring up the subject of Madeline so quickly, but she'd given me an opening I couldn't ignore.

Ellen nodded. "Good friends. We'd only known each other a short time, but we had so much in common. We both used to say how pleased we were to have found each other."

I understood exactly what she meant. I'd felt the same way about Kate and Diane. "Finding friends can be difficult in a new place. I've learned that, too. You make acquaintances, but it takes a while before you count them as friends," I said.

"That's the way it's been for me. There are only a few people here I consider friends. Now with Madeline gone…" Her voice trailed off.

"I'm sorry. It's hard to lose any friend, but especially one as full of life as Madeline. The news must have come as a terrible shock."

"It did. And I don't like what I'm hearing about her death. Apparently, they're not convinced her fall was an accident. Have you heard that, too?"

"Yes. There's a lot of talk." I hesitated, then took the plunge. "You know more about Madeline's private life than most of us. Do you think she could have been involved with another man?"

Ellen looked away again, watching a second group of tourists as they disembarked at the Shoreline dock. "Are people saying there was someone else?"

"I've heard speculation to that effect."

Ellen slid her drink back and forth, leaving wet splotches on the table. "I suspect there'll be a lot more talk before this is over. Do people at the Point think Ted killed her? He seems to be the prime suspect around here."

I considered how to answer her question. "I guess. The Point's a bad place for gossip. A few have's and a lot more have not's. Some folks love the idea that the upper crust—and that's how many of the locals see the Hathaways—can take a hit."

"I know what you're saying," Ellen agreed. "Something worse than having your unemployment insurance run out or the bank threaten foreclosure. Isn't that why people love the scandal sheets and those unsolved mystery programs on TV? Whatever takes your mind off your own troubles."

I waited, not sure where the conversation was going.

Ellen moved her chair closer to mine. "I feel as if I should tell someone this, but I don't want to go to Jim Thompson. Maybe I can get your reaction."

I leaned forward slightly, feeling a knot form in the pit of my stomach. I'd thought I wanted to know more about Madeline's secret life. Now I wasn't so sure.

Our clumsy young waiter, obviously a new hire for the summer, brought the coffee we'd ordered.

Ellen waited until he had settled the cups on the table and moved off. She spoke slowly as if she were choosing her words with care. "Madeline played some weird games with Ted. I don't know if people were aware of that. Maybe the games were more dangerous than she realized. She knew he was crazy about her, thought he couldn't stay mad at her no matter what she did."

"I'm not sure what you mean by 'games,'" I said, although I remembered Ted using almost those same words.

"She could usually get Ted to do anything she wanted. So she needled him, teased him, just enough to keep him on edge. She claimed he loved it, that it kept things hot between them. She didn't like to sit home by herself, so she went out alone when he was away. She was always smiling, remember? Always bubbly…full of life?" Ellen blinked away tears as she remembered her friend.

"And maybe she didn't always go out alone?" I realized I was asking Ellen the same question Ted had put to me. Was she about to confirm Ted's worst fears?

"I really can't say. Maybe Ted played his own games with her. She told me not long before she died she thought somebody was following her."

"Really? You mean somebody checking on her for Ted?"

Ellen hesitated. "I don't know. It might not have had anything to do with Ted. She was flirtatious, I know. She spent time with men on committees, working on the center. But anything more?" Her voice trailed off.

"Seems funny she wouldn't have told you," I said. But perhaps Madeline had confided in Ellen about an affair, and Ellen was too good a friend to betray her confidence.

"I can tell you there was a pattern with her and Ted," she continued. "She'd stay out late, rile up his suspicions. Then she'd convince him he was imagining things. She knew he was crazy about her. Maybe she thought the game-playing kept him that way."

"You think this was a game they played?"

"I guess. When she knew she had upset him, she'd walk

a narrow line for a while, make a point of coming home early, not giving him cause for concern. Once everything quieted down, she'd start up again. After a while, he wasn't so easy to convince. He began checking on her, found out she wasn't always where she said she'd be."

I remembered the party I'd supposedly thrown at my house. Were lies like that part of the web Madeline wove? "Yet even then, he stayed crazy about her?" I asked.

Ellen nodded. "He adored her. He wouldn't have wanted to lose her, I know that. If he thought she was going to leave him, I don't know what he would have done."

Now I was the one who looked away. What had she just told me? How much should I read into what she'd said? I'd just opened a Pandora's Box without any idea what winged creatures might come flying out.

TWELVE

ELLEN AND I MOVED to other topics as we finished our coffee and, when we left the Shoreline a short time later, I'd learned nothing more about Madeline's possible involvement with other men. On the plus side, however, Ellen had agreed to query *Adirondack Life* about an article on our new center. Coverage like that by a professional writer, I thought, should counteract the negative editorial about the opening.

Since I was only a few miles from the Warren County Municipal Center, I decided to pay a visit to Sheriff's Investigator Jim Thompson. I found him in his office and agreeable to conversation.

I skipped the preliminaries. "Anything more on Madeline Hathaway's death?" I asked as I settled into his visitor's chair.

"You've probably heard rumors already. I'm sorry to say at least some of them are true. She didn't fall down those stairs on her own. Doc says she was struck by a heavy object, probably at the top, then fell or was pushed. She was hit several times, maybe with some kind of club or board. No sign of the weapon yet. It may have been taken away from the scene."

"So it's definitely murder?"

"I'm afraid so."

"Does that make Ted a suspect?"

"We'll question him again, of course. Right now, we're planning to talk to Lee Cameron. The rumor mill says he and Madeline had been spending time together lately. He may have been the mysterious visitor Ted claims he passed on the road that night."

"You think he might have been going to see Madeline, that he's the one who killed her?"

"Slow down, Mayor. Let's not to jump to any conclusions. Step by step. Slow and easy. That's our approach to this."

I slid forward in my chair, started to get to my feet. Then I hesitated, considering how much I should say. "Jim, are you thinking Madeline was romantically involved with Lee? Or with someone else? Is that what's behind all this?"

Jim spoke slowly, deliberately. He'd obviously considered the possibility already. "Madeline Hathaway was an attractive, vivacious woman. She put herself out there, if you know what I mean, made herself seem available. Someone may have thought she was more available than she actually was, maybe read the signals wrong. It happens, you know. A lot of ways this thing could play out."

I thought about Lee Cameron as I drove back to the Point. He was at least fifteen years older than Madeline, but he was a good-looking, easy-going guy who made an attractive party date for middle-aged widows and divorcées here at the lake. He and his wife had split years before and Lee hadn't been in any hurry to marry again. "I never make the same mistake twice," he'd told me one night at a party after he'd downed a drink or three too many.

Maybe in your love life, not necessarily in your party conduct, I'd been tempted to say. But I let his remark pass. I found Lee a likeable drunk—if there was such a thing.

He overindulged sometimes, but he usually tapered off before he embarrassed himself or anyone else.

What if he had been the visitor Ted passed on the road that night? Could Lee have quarreled with Madeline at a time when he was drunk enough to lose control? Or could the visitor have been someone else, someone no one knew about yet? Jim was right. There had to be other possibilities.

As soon as the autopsy was completed, Madeline Hathaway's body was disposed of quickly and with little fanfare. A brief obituary in the *Post Standard* announced that there would be no viewing hours and the funeral service and burial would be private. Then, the day after the funeral, in a complete about-face, Ted began telephoning people to invite them to a reception at his home.

"He's asked me to do the food," Kate Donohue told me when I stopped at the coffee shop. "I'm not at all sure what he wants me to serve. He's set the time at two in the afternoon, agrees that it's too late for a luncheon and too early for a cocktail party. We decided on something like a tea, but I'm still not sure what he wants."

"How many does he plan on inviting?" I asked as I watched Kate whip up a batch of her double chocolate chip brownies, my personal blue ribbon winner.

"He can't tell me that either. No alcohol, he said, so I'm concentrating on flavored teas and coffees. I'll bring a selection of sweets and hope they suit him. I've done parties for Madeline. She always knew exactly what she wanted to serve and planned everything down to the nth degree."

"Could you repeat one of those menus?" I asked.

"Not really. Madeline entertained at A-list cocktail parties. Splurged on drinks and elegant hors d'oeuvres. She was a class act and she got Ted to foot the bills, which I don't think could have been easy. He's questioned me about how much everything costs numerous times."

"What do you think that means? Is money tight for him?"

"One thing I've learned in this business—there's no connection. Sometimes the people with the most money are determined not to spend a cent more than they have to. On the other hand, the ones who can't afford much will often get carried away and run up their bills like there's no tomorrow. In fact, I've started asking for a hefty down payment from a couple of my regulars after they've dragged their feet on paying one time too often."

"Are you including Ted and Madeline in that category?" I asked, astonished that Kate would disclose so much about her business.

"Not at all. Madeline took care of their bills. She paid right away and she always added a generous tip for my servers. I loved doing business with her. But I can see Ted might be tough."

"Don't go overboard. You know how easy it is for you to throw in the extras."

"I'm sure Madeline wouldn't have wanted anything tacky."

"Kate…" I warned, but I didn't expect her to listen.

As I drove home, I thought about the turns Ted Hathaway's life had taken in recent weeks. He'd been forced to juggle the roles of suspicious husband, grief-stricken widower and murder suspect. Why would he want to add party giver to that mix? Ted had something more on his agenda. I was sure of that.

THIRTEEN

THE DAY OF TED'S reception, I arrived at the Hathaway house at two o'clock to find several dozen people congregated in small groups in the living room. In addition to friends and neighbors, Ted had apparently invited members of committees Madeline had served on, including—to my surprise—two of the men people were gossiping about, Lee Cameron and Ralph Forrester.

I spotted Ellen Davies, huddled in a chair in the living room, staring out at the lake. Diane Anderson stood chatting with a group of her fellow teachers near the door. She waved and signaled to me to join them.

"Where's our host?" I asked her.

"Haven't seen him. Kate let us in. She has a couple of her staff pouring tea and coffee. You help yourself to the desserts. A really strange event."

"Is there a reason for it? I don't quite understand why he invited us here."

"Kate says he's going to make an announcement. We're supposed to stick around until then."

"Did he invite any of Madeline's family? I don't remember ever hearing about her relatives, but she must have had somebody."

"An uncle. Over there on the couch. A little out of it, I think. I spoke to him, but not much came of it."

"I'll give him a try," I said and walked across the room to where an elderly man sat alone, almost swallowed by the thick royal-blue couch cushions.

"I'm Loren Graham, a friend of Madeline's." I extended my hand.

The man, who looked to be eighty or more, was thin, balding, and very frail. He'd acquired all the hallmarks of aging we hope to be spared—rheumy eyes, a blank stare, dark liver spots splattered across a face which looked as if it were carved from ivory. He stared up at me without responding.

I dropped my hand, considered walking away, but my better nature asserted itself. I perched on the edge of the couch next to him. "I liked Madeline very much. She was always working on projects here in town, very giving, very quick to help out," I said.

He nodded his head. He appeared to be trying hard to focus. After a minute he gathered up the energy to answer me. "Yes, she was a good girl. Tell me again what happened. How did she die?"

Nothing like starting with the tough ones. How much did this poor guy know, I wondered, and how much did he need to know? I made a quick decision. I'd start with the first report and see how things progressed from there. "I understand they found her body at the foot of some stairs, down on the beach. They're investigating to determine what happened."

"Was she dead when they found her?" His voice sounded stronger. He seemed more alert somehow.

"Yes. I believe she was. They thought she'd fallen, but now they're not sure."

"They think somebody killed her." It wasn't a question. The man was more with-it than I'd thought.

"Yes, they do," I conceded.

"Do they think Jordan did it? He could, you know. He's mean enough."

I hesitated, then managed an answer. "I don't believe I know Jordan. Who is he?"

"Why, he's Connie's boyfriend. I've never liked him. Like I say, he's mean, mean enough to kill somebody, if you ask me. I think he hits Connie. I've seen the marks on her. She claims I'm imagining things."

This was going to be a wild ride. "I don't believe I know Connie, either. Is she here today?"

"They brought me, but they're not here. I don't know where they went." He glanced nervously around the room.

"Are you relatives of Madeline's?" I asked.

"I am. I'm her uncle. I take care of Connie. But I don't know where she went. Do you see her? Pretty girl, fifteen, dark hair. I'll need to get a ride home with her." He squinted at one group after another, pushing himself forward on the couch, struggling to get up.

"You sit back and relax. I'm sure she's not going to leave without you, but you'd better stay right here where she can see you."

I patted him on the shoulder as I stood up.

My words calmed him. He sank back into the cushions. "All right. I'll wait here."

Kate was standing in front of the window wall, keeping an eye on the buffet table.

"How's it going?" I asked her.

"Madeline would be appalled, and you know what? I have no idea how it's supposed to go. Ted's outside showing someone where her body was found. I'm surprised the whole crowd hasn't rushed out there. Like that's the big attraction, I guess."

"Who's he showing around?"

"Some relatives of Madeline's. A young couple I didn't meet."

"I bet they're the people that man over there is looking for. He's starting to worry because he came with them and he's afraid they've left without him."

"That's Madeline's uncle. Lives over near Lake Luzerne somewhere. I have no idea why the young couple's here or why Ted isn't back. He's got some kind of announcement he wants to make."

The crowd began losing patience. Several people got to their feet and scouted around for a place to put their cups and plates. I saw a couple of Madeline's friends from Bolton Landing slip out through the kitchen door. As others prepared to follow them, the sliders to the patio were shoved open and Ted burst into the room.

"Hey, don't be leaving for a minute," he bellowed at the escapees. When everyone had turned toward him, he went on. "I said I've got an announcement to make and I'll make it right now. I'm going to give a sizeable donation to the new center. Madeline loved that place, thought it was a great idea to put something like that here in town. She worked on it day and night. I'm not sure how much people appreciated all she did." He glanced pointedly at me. "But I'm willing to go along with what she wanted. I guess you could say I'm willing to put my money where she put her time. I'm making a big donation—my accountant's going to come up with some figures—and I'd like to see the place named after Madeline. I think it should be called the Madeline Hathaway Community Center."

Silence greeted the announcement. I knew Ted had been complaining to everyone that Madeline's work on the center hadn't received proper recognition. As if there wasn't enough talk already about her death, his ranting had given the town another juicy topic for gossip. Here was Ted making a fuss because he thought Madeline was working at the center so many times when she was…where? Nobody really knew, unless maybe Ellen Davies did. I glanced across the room toward where she was sitting.

Ellen stood up and—although she was staring at Ted in astonishment—began to applaud. Others followed suit.

"Nice idea," someone said.

"Madeline would be pleased," another voice added.

"Thanks, Ted. Very generous of you," someone else called out.

I had no idea what to say. For the first time since I moved to Emerald Point, probably—if the truth were known—for the first time in my life, I was speechless.

FOURTEEN

As SOON AS TED made his announcement, many of the guests surged toward him to congratulate him on his largesse. Others seized the opportunity to escape out the back door. I stood motionless near the windows as Kate packed up the silver tea and coffee services and her helpers scurried around gathering cups and plates.

Ted accepted the congratulations with a stolid dignity which I read as smugness. No matter how much time Madeline had or had not put in at the center, I could hardly come out publicly against naming it for her. And it wouldn't matter if the amount of Ted's gift turned out to be no more than the donation he and Madeline would have made anyway. This wasn't the time to call his bluff, but the idea of thanking him publicly for what I saw as a questionable gesture made my flesh crawl.

"I suppose that was a sample of the decisive business style people talk about," I whispered to Kate, as I checked out possible escape routes. From where I stood, I spotted a small anteroom, opening onto the lakeside terrace. "I see a way out," I told her, "and I'm taking it."

Once outside, I scooted down the stone steps from the terrace to the immaculate green lawn and took off around the house toward where my car was parked. A few yards ahead of me on the grass, I noticed an old-fashioned lawn swing, a two-seater covered by a green striped canvas awning. I remembered lawn furniture like this from my childhood visits to the Point. I walked toward it, wondering if this was a sparkling new reproduction or a meticulously restored antique. I'd almost reached the swing when I saw a girl curled up on the seat facing away from me. Josie Donohue.

Poor Kate. Josie, often at odds with her mother, had apparently come to help serve, then found a reason to lose her temper and stalk off.

"Josie, what are you doing out here?" I said.

As the girl turned around, I took a step back in surprise. I'd heard that everyone has a twin somewhere in the world and now here was Josie's, huddled in a swing only a few miles from her double's home turf. The same dark hair, tangled and in desperate need of a wash; the same wrinkled, unbecoming clothing, mostly denim, the same pale face devoid of makeup. Except...

I moved closer. As I approached her, I realized this girl didn't so much resemble the Josie of today as the one I'd met for the first time several years ago. Until this moment, I hadn't realized how much my young friend had improved. For Josie, change had come slowly, but it had come, and it was change for the better.

"I'm sorry. I thought you were someone I knew," I said.

Her answer was worthy of the old Josie—a scowl and a grunt. "So?"

"You look just like her. I'm sorry to stare at you, but I can't quite believe it. You two could be twins."

Not quite, I thought even as I said the words. This girl was taller and slimmer than Josie with a hint of a shapely figure beneath the baggy clothes. Her matted hair might be the same color, but her features were more finely drawn. Even the disreputable get-up, the unpleasant set to the mouth, the hostility in the dark eyes as she glared at me didn't mask a delicate beauty.

"So?" she said again.

Word choice, tone of voice, manner. In those ways, this girl could easily have been twin to the earlier Josie. "Are you a relative of Madeline's?"

"Don't you mean, was I a relative? She's dead, you know. Uncle Ted just took us down to the beach to show us where they found her."

I couldn't disguise my surprise. "Is Ted your uncle?"

"That's what I call him, anyway."

What did that mean? "I met an elderly gentleman inside. Are you the Connie he mentioned? Did he come with you?"

Her expression softened. "Yeah. My great uncle. He sounds like he's not quite with it, but he's okay."

"So you're here for the reception. Do you think you'll be coming back to visit sometime? I know somebody you might like to meet."

"Nah. We don't visit. Uncle Dwight said we had to come today for Maddy's sake. Ted didn't want us to."

"Really? Did he want this to be private?"

"Yeah. Him and a few hundred of his closest friends. But he shouldn't have counted us out. My uncle told Ted we were gonna be here whether he liked it or not and that was it."

"How did you get here? Do you have your license?"

"I wish. I'm gettin' one soon, the minute I hit sixteen. Jordan drove us over from Luzerne."

"Jordan?"

"He's a guy I hang with. There he is. Comin' up the

stairs from the beach." She pointed toward a figure silhouetted against the sky.

Jordan probably had a few years on Connie. Other than
that, they were a matched pair. Both wore scruffy jeans,
black tee shirts and denim jackets pockmarked with stains.
Jordan hadn't found time to shave and the dark stubble on
his jaw, along with his greasy blond hair, gave him a slight
edge in the grunge look.

As annoyed as I was at Ted, I could understand his reluctance to include these relatives. With many of the area's
prominent business people invited to his reception, this couple
would definitely start tongues wagging. Perhaps Madeline
herself hadn't been quick to acknowledge this branch of her
family. I'd heard her more than once answer questions about
where she came from with a casual "not anywhere around
here." As far as I knew, family members twenty miles away
in Lake Luzerne had never been mentioned.

Jordan marched across the lawn toward us with what my
grandmother would have described as a puss on. He
ignored me and glared at Connie. "We gotta put this show
on the road. Where the hell's your uncle?"

Connie wasn't intimidated. "So go get him. Tell him we
need to make tracks."

"He better not give me any argument. I've got to work
tonight. I'll be lucky to get there on time as it is." He spun
around and took off toward the house.

For some reason, maybe to offset Jordan's rudeness,
Connie thawed a little toward me. "I would have introduced
you, but he's in a bad mood and I don't know your name."

"Sorry. Loren Graham." I considered mentioning I was
the mayor, but decided against it.

"He tends bar in a joint up there, a real dive, but it's all he can get. There aren't a lot of jobs for kids over where we live. Jordan dropped out of school, so that makes it even harder to find something."

"Do you live in Lake Luzerne?"

"Near it. I'd like to get out of there, but there's no way I can see to do that. I thought maybe Ted would help now with Maddy gone, but he's bein' a real pain. Of course, that's not anything new and different."

Did that mean Maddy had been helping them? Before I could ask anything more, the girl jumped up from the swing and glanced off toward the parking area.

"I'd better be there when they come out," she called back over her shoulder as she trotted off. "My uncle can get real mixed up sometimes. If he doesn't see me, he'll give Jordan an argument and this isn't a good time for that to happen."

I watched her as she moved quickly away from me, a frail little figure off to deal with two difficult males. "Connie," I said as I hurried to catch up with her, "are you going to be all right?"

"Oh sure. Nothing I haven't dealt with before. But hey, thanks for askin'. That's a helluva lot more than Ted did."

FIFTEEN

TWENTY MINUTES LATER I was seated in the back booth at Mario's Pizzeria sipping a glass of wine I hoped would smooth out the bad effects of the afternoon's roller coaster ride.

A few minutes later Diane, who'd waved and mouthed the word Mario's as I pulled out of the Hathaways' parking area, slid into the booth opposite me. "You got here fast. You must be even closer to the edge than I thought."

"Mad enough to kill that stupid Ted. The more I think about what he pulled, the more furious I get."

"Better ease off the mad enough to kill talk until they decide who did Madeline in. No sense making people think you're inclined that way."

"Okay. I retract the statement. My remark was poorly timed, although that doesn't necessarily make it inaccurate."

"Loren, calm down. You know Ted's a jerk. And I'm sure you'll find a way around naming the center for Madeline if you want to. Give yourself a little time to decide if this is something you can live with or not."

Something I could live with. That remark was as much hyperbole as mad enough to kill, but no warning bells went off for that either.

Kate joined us a few minutes later. "Loren, I didn't like the way things went today. You looked like a thundercloud when Ted came out with his announcement. I wanted to be sure you were all right."

I swallowed hard. I'd known Diane and Kate since I moved to the Point five years earlier, and I couldn't have asked for more loyal friends. "Annoyed by his presumption, but otherwise fine," I assured her.

She reached over and touched my hand. "I sent my helpers back to the restaurant by themselves. All they have to do is put the leftover food away and fill the dishwasher. They ought to be able to manage that much."

"They'll be okay," Diane said. "You deserve a little time off. Have a drink with us. We're badmouthing Ted if you want to join in."

Before we could return to that subject, Don Morrison sauntered in the front door and over to our booth. He glanced from one of us to another. "I see I've missed something important. Somebody better fill me in."

"Why weren't you at Ted's gathering? You would have found out for yourself," Diane said.

"Wasn't invited. Apparently, I'm not on Ted Hathaway's A-list."

"Well, you're on ours. Join us," Diane told him.

Don glanced over at me, and I smiled to second the motion. For some reason I hadn't seen him or talked to him much since the opening-night party. Despite my resolve to be less independent, I'd been preoccupied with the center and with planning its day-to-day operations.

After our waitress brought the rest of the drinks, Diane repeated Ted's speech almost verbatim, even replicated the dirty look he'd thrown in my direction.

Don leaned toward me. "So, Loren, you resented the steam roller approach? Is that the crux of the problem?"

"You've got it. At least that's part of it," I said.

"You mean there's more?" he asked.

I hesitated, then searched for the right words to express what I'd been thinking. "I'm really not convinced the center should be named for Madeline. Not just because Ted announced his bright idea in public without running it by anybody first, but because it's unfair to some of the others on the committee. Madeline really pitched in at the end, but some people had been working hard since February. They deserve a share of the credit."

Don stared straight at me with a look I couldn't read. "Are you thinking it should be named the Loren Graham Center?"

For the second time that day, I found myself speechless. I saw Diane's startled look, heard Kate's gasp of surprise.

Diane recovered first. "Don, what the hell kind of crack was that?"

Don made a quick attempt to smooth things over. "Hang on. I guess that didn't come out the right way. I've heard people say the center should be named for Loren. She's the one who deserves the recognition. That's all I meant."

"No one's worked harder on it," Kate said.

"There's fat chance of that happening now," Diane added.

"I know. I know. I didn't mean the remark the way it sounded. Sorry, Loren," Don said.

I made a quick, brushing motion with my hand. "Let's drop it and talk about something else. I've had enough of the Hathaways for today."

We did talk of other things; at least three of the four people in the booth managed to do so. I inserted a few appropriate comments from time to time, but what I wanted more than anything was to go home. As soon as the pizza came, I ate a slice, pasted a smile on my face and said my goodbyes. Then, I bailed out of there as fast as I could.

SIXTEEN

When I left Mario's that day, I was still bristling at Don's remark. I'd learned a trick or two in the last few years about keeping my mouth shut when I felt like exploding, but hiding my reactions still didn't come easily.

As I drove to my house, I saw that the storm which had threatened for most of the day had been swept away by a light summer breeze. The dreary afternoon had turned into a perfect June evening. I did a quick check of my watch. Even after wine and pizza, I could manage a walk before dark. Maybe that would improve my mental state.

I unlocked my kitchen door and rushed straight for the closet where I'd stashed some sportswear—an institutional gray shirt and shorts perfect for my bleak mood. I did a couple of dozen stretches and took off from my own backyard, headed for a quiet section of the Point where I wouldn't encounter much traffic.

I concentrated on the beauty of the scenery around me, the recurring glimpses of the lake shimmering like a series of elongated photographs between the houses I passed. I tamped down my feelings of annoyance at Ted for his announcement, but adjectives kept boiling up in my brain—premature, ill-timed, out-of-line, arrogant. And I was barely scratching the surface. Ted, I suspected, would probably get his comeuppance sooner or later. If Madeline had been hiding a secret life by claiming to be working at the center, he was bound to find out. Still, I took no pleasure in the thought. Why couldn't he put the past behind him and let her rest in peace? There was no reason now for anyone to dredge up her indiscretions.

As for Don, I was too frazzled to tackle that topic at all. His remark about naming the center for me had dropped like a stone into the conversation. Maybe my commitment to the project had rankled more than I suspected. Or, maybe—as he'd put it—he hadn't meant his comment the way it sounded. Best to leave that one until another day.

By the time I turned back toward the house, the sun had dipped behind the mountains to the west and a soft, golden twilight was settling over the lake. Against the outline of the opposite shore, I saw one of the lake steamers starting its swing, ready to turn south for its return to the Village. The happy sounds of music and voices floated across the water.

Despite the annoyances of the last few hours, a feeling of peace washed over me. I was living in one of the most beautiful places in the world. I'd be crazy to let anyone spoil it for me.

My feelings of contentment evaporated fast. As I approached my house, I saw two shadowy figures slumped in the Adirondack chairs under the trees in my back yard. I'd almost reached them before I recognized Connie and her uncle.

"Hi," Connie called, giving me a jaunty wave. "Sorry to barge in on you, but we've got a problem and I couldn't think of anyone else to go to."

I stifled a groan. This wasn't the best time for me to tackle somebody else's problem. Still, my heart went out to them. They were a pathetic-looking pair. The uncle's face had gone even paler, and his eyelids drooped as if he could barely hold them open. Connie, despite her show of bravado, appeared exhausted and close to tears.

"What happened to your ride?" I asked.

"Dumped us. Ted picked a fight with Jordan and he took off. We walked down to the highway in case he was trying to find us, but that didn't do any good. Even if he came back, he wouldn't have known which one of the turnoffs to take. I had the directions in my pocket and Jordan's got no sense at all when it comes to remembering where he's supposed to go."

"How did you get here?"

"Bummed. Some guy in a pickup gave us a lift. I told him your name and he said you were the mayor of the town here. I didn't know that. Guy said anybody would know where you lived. Started to drop us off a few miles back, then ended up bringing us all the way himself."

A complete stranger moved to sympathy for them. I was embarrassed at my own reaction.

"Thought maybe you'd give us a ride to Lake Luzerne," Connie went on. "Ted's not home. He took off right after the guests left, passed us on the road without so much as a wave. And you and him are the only two people I know around here."

I did a fast assessment. I was tired, sweaty and in desperate need of a shower. Connie and her uncle could easily have said the same about themselves. Even worse, they were miles from home, probably hungry as well and dependent on the mercy of strangers. I took a deep breath and resigned myself to the inevitable.

SEVENTEEN

"I can give you a ride," I said, struggling to inject an upbeat note into my voice.

Connie shoved herself up out of the chair. "Thanks. I figured I could count on you. Come on, Unc. She's going to give us a ride home."

"Let's go in the house for a few minutes. You probably want to use the bathroom and maybe have a quick bite to eat before we leave." I did a fast recall of the contents of my refrigerator. Nothing fancy, but at least I could offer sandwiches.

"'Preciate your kindness, ma'm." The uncle forced the words out with difficulty. He strained forward in the chair but, with the seat slanted backward, he was working against impossible odds. Connie seized both his hands and pulled him toward her slowly until he was able to stand. With her arm around him, she guided him into the house.

"I'm afraid I don't have many choices in food," I told them, as Connie eased her uncle into a chair at the kitchen table.

"Cereal would be good for my uncle, if you have it. That's probably what he'd like best, wouldn't you, Uncle Dwight?"

That was the first I'd heard the man's name. "Dwight…? I don't believe I know your last name," I said.

"Sorry about that, ma'm. Dwight Tanner. 'Preciate your kindness."

My hope of giving my guests a fast meal and getting them home quickly died a prolonged death during the next hour. Uncle Dwight spent some time in the bathroom, then returned with an expectant look to the kitchen table. I fixed him a bowl of Corn Flakes and a glass of milk, and ran upstairs for a quick shower and change. Connie refused to accept anything I offered, although I felt sure she was hungry.

After Dwight asked for a second bowl of cereal and began eating it even more slowly than the first, she agreed to a glass of milk and an orange. Then there was another trip to the bathroom for Dwight and the long, slow trek to my car.

With her uncle finally strapped into the back seat, Connie hopped into the front and I began to relax. A trip to Lake Luzerne, a pretty little village nestled in a region of lakes in the Adirondack foothills southwest of us, shouldn't present any problems, I told myself. I'd take them there and head right back. Their visit had taken my mind off Ted's announcement and Don's unfortunate remark. Once home, I might even rack up a decent night's sleep.

Darkness came on fast as we drove along. Traffic was light. We reached the Northway at Lake George Village in record time. South of the town, I took the exit for 9N. Good highway, few cars. The lights of Roaring Brook Dude Ranch twinkled through the trees on our left. Several bars and restaurants along the highway boasted full parking lots, even on a Wednesday.

Connie checked out the places we passed, but didn't comment. The sound of Uncle Dwight's slow, even breathing signaled that he'd fallen asleep almost immediately. As the road climbed steadily, I ran a few questions by Connie, but she limited herself to short, almost meaningless replies.

"How did you say you were related to Madeline?" I asked at one point.

"Shirt tail, I guess you'd say. She's really not my aunt, more like a cousin."

"And is Dwight her uncle, too?"

"Not exactly. It's more like we're all cousins."

"You and your uncle live together, just the two of you?"

Connie bristled at what she thought I was implying. "He wasn't always like this, you know. He took real good care of me. Now, I figure it's my turn to take care of him."

"A lot of responsibility for a young person, though," I said. I found myself full of sympathy for this child forced to grow up so quickly. I wondered what role Madeline had played in their lives and how they'd manage now with her gone.

We passed through the Lake Luzerne business district, the main street quiet, the stores closed for the night. A few miles outside town, Connie directed me to a blacktopped road which zigzagged up the side of a mountain. I watched for landmarks, aware that I'd have to find my way back to Lake George.

A few minutes later Connie pointed out a log cabin restaurant, its windows blazing with neon beer signs, its parking lot overflowing with cars and pickups "This is the place Jordan tends bar. His car's parked over there, so he must have made work all right," she said.

"You must be ready to kill him, aren't you?" I blurted out before I could stop myself. Another poor choice of words. Diane was right. My vocabulary needed a serious makeover.

"Yeah, he did leave us in the lurch. Good thing you were willing to bring us," Connie said mildly.

"Does he pull stuff like that on you very often?" I asked.

"Nah. Jordan's all right. Ted can drive anybody up a wall. Even Maddy used to get royally pissed at him."

Maddy? How could Connie know that, I wondered. Did Madeline discuss Ted with her relatives?

A few miles beyond the roadhouse, we turned onto a narrow road, little more than hard-packed dirt. Four or five houses huddled together surrounded by fields, some planted, some lying fallow.

"Here. Turn in here." Connie gestured toward a driveway next to a small bungalow. In the beams of the headlights I caught a glimpse of scaling paint, un-curtained windows, and a sagging front porch.

We bumped along the rutted drive until she signaled me to stop next to a side door. Uncle Dwight was crumpled against the back seat in what appeared to be an exhausted slumber. With my help, Connie pulled him up and out of the car and we half carried him into the house. She hit a wall switch and we supported him along a narrow hallway and into a downstairs bedroom.

"He won't wake up now for hours," she assured me. "I'll just get his shoes off. He's okay in his clothes. It's better not to disturb him."

As I stood quietly in the doorway watching her settle her uncle for the night, I wondered how many times she'd performed this same task. Something in her manner hinted at what she planned to do. "Are you going down to that bar to see Jordan?"

She waited a minute before she answered me. "I might."

"How? How will you get there?"

"I'll walk. Maybe somebody will pick me up. I'll definitely be able to get a ride home."

Again, I bowed to the inevitable. "Look. I'd like something to eat myself. Why don't I treat you to a burger or something?"

She hesitated again, probably considering how she could accept the ride and send me on my way. Then she agreed to my suggestion.

The bar—roadhouse, joint, whatever you wanted to call it—proved to be even tackier than I expected. Loud, dirty, full of testosterone. The outfits of choice for both sexes were worn, faded jeans and grubby tee shirts. Most of the male patrons needed a shave. The few women sprinkled through the crowd showed a lot of skin.

No one paid much attention to Connie even though she was obviously much too young to be in there. I rated stares, once-overs and, even before we sat down in a booth, an invitation to polka.

"Thank you, no," I told the scruffy-looking guy who'd sidled over to us.

"Bug off, Kenny. We're here for a burger and that's all," Connie said.

Kenny beat a hasty retreat.

"How was the funeral, hon?" the middle-aged waitress asked Connie as she whipped out her pad to take our order.

"Wasn't one. Just a reception," Connie said.

"Jordan says your stepfather was ugly as ever."

Connie shrugged, then glanced quickly toward me, as if hoping I hadn't picked up on the woman's designation of Ted.

As soon as we'd ordered our burgers, she answered my question before I could ask it. "I tell people that's what Ted is sometimes. Easier than trying to explain. But I've told Jordan not to call him that."

"Is he? Your stepfather, I mean," I asked.

"Nah. 'Course not."

"But people know him. Does he come over here sometimes?"

"He's been here a couple times, I guess. Not that much. Hey, do you mind if I get a side of onion rings with my burger? They make really good ones here."

When I agreed, she popped out of the booth to track down our waitress. Then it was only a step to the bar where she stood talking to Jordan until one of his customers signaled him for a drink.

By the time she came back to the booth and sat down, we'd shifted gears from questions about Ted (mine) to comments on the bar's burgers and onion rings (Connie's). I hated to acknowledge that Connie had outsmarted me, but she'd managed it smoothly.

My burger and the onion rings Connie insisted I share turned out to be delicious. We gobbled our meals in silence, finding it difficult to talk over the steady bleat of the juke box. By the time we finished eating, I'd had enough of the bar scene. I was debating the pros and cons of taking off and leaving Connie there by herself when she surprised me.

"I'm really pooped tonight," she said after a couple of major yawns. "Would you mind giving me a ride home?"

As she got out of my car at the side door of her house, I experienced a strong sense of relief. I'd delivered her to her own house, out of harm's way, at least for the night. It wasn't until I backed out of the driveway and noticed she'd left the outside light on that the truth dawned on me. Jordan would be joining her when he finished work.

EIGHTEEN

I WANTED NOTHING MORE than to fall into bed the minute I got home, but I knew I was too wired for sleep. I grabbed a cold beer out of the fridge and made myself comfortable on the hammock in the screened section of the porch.

I stared out at the lake, opening myself to its magic.

As always, the lake did its best to placate me, sounding its slow, rhythmic beat in counterpoint to the gentle lapping of waves against the dock. The sky above the black water blazed with stars. Night noises I loved—the occasional burst of laughter and the muted sputt-putt of a boat going past the camp—floated toward me. Things didn't get much more perfect than this.

But I couldn't relax. I kept seeing Connie disappear through the door of that shabby little house with nothing more to look forward to than a visit from the irascible Jordan. Of course, I told myself, maybe he turned into a prince when they were alone together. But I didn't believe that for a minute. And also, didn't Connie have to go to school tomorrow? Shouldn't this be exam time? I'd never thought to ask.

I slept eventually, but not before I'd made a plan. I was involved now, dragged in by Madeline's lies about working with me at the center and by Ted's demand for information. Today, I'd found myself pulled in even deeper by my reaction to Connie. Underneath the unkempt look and the inappropriate clothes, she was a beautiful girl—intelligent and kind—and she needed help. If I didn't offer it, who would?

THE NEXT MORNING at the office I whipped through the day's agenda at top speed. The minute Pauline arrived I left to pay another call on Ted Hathaway. He sometimes worked at home, I knew, and I decided to take a chance on finding him there.

Ted answered the door himself. He didn't speak, just bristled at me with an unpleasant grimace—a look he'd probably developed for business enemies.

I summoned my best official tone. "Ted, you asked me to do something for you. I'd like to come in and talk to you about it."

Ted paused a half-beat longer than necessary before he pushed back the door. I considered the gesture an invitation to enter and stepped into the hallway before he could object. He was dressed for business—dark suit, crisp blue cotton shirt, maroon tie. He didn't look like a man who planned to hang around the house much longer. He glanced pointedly at his watch—a Rolex, of course.

"This way," he said and led me into an office—beautifully appointed, a decorator would have called it—and waved me toward a chair. He sat down behind an impressive mahogany desk and ignored the papers strewn across it.

"Go ahead."

"You asked me what I knew about Madeline. Apparently, there were a great many things I didn't know," I said.

Ted's answer was terse, borderline rude. "Isn't that to be expected?"

"To some extent, of course, but I was surprised to meet

Connie and her uncle. Connie's boyfriend took off after his exchange with you and left them stranded."

Ted snorted, not at all sympathetic. "I could have arranged a ride for them. All they had to do was ask me."

"Unfortunately, you left before they could do that. They walked down the road, hoping the boyfriend would come back for them, but he didn't. When they saw you take off, they realized they were stuck."

Ted managed a small moue of surprise. "Unfortunate, yes. But hardly my fault. I didn't particularly want them to come to the reception anyway."

I waited, expecting Ted to ask if I knew how they got home. I was considering volunteering the information when something changed in his face. He stared past me at the door.

I turned. A woman stood framed in the doorway, a tall, stunning woman who'd appeared without making a sound. Platinum blonde hair, exquisitely styled; a charcoal business suit, perfectly cut—an icy presence which commanded attention. She didn't enter the room but stood motionless, her gaze focused on Ted.

Again, Ted delayed a few seconds too long, then made the introductions. "Finn Lattimore. This is Emerald Point's mayor, Loren Graham."

When the woman failed to respond or move toward me, I didn't get up. "Good afternoon," I said over my shoulder. I would have liked to ask Ted to repeat her name. I'd thought he said Finn. I ran through a quick checklist of names Finn might be short for—Finola, Finney, Phineas. I couldn't come up with many possibilities.

"The plane. We really need to leave in the next five," she said. Her voice was soft, but loaded with authority. Before Ted could reply, she vanished from the doorway.

Ted turned back to me. "Loren, why don't we plan to get together the first of next week? I have meetings in the city and it's important I leave right now. You're a busy lady yourself. I know you understand."

If only he hadn't let the note of condescension creep into his voice. I stood up at once, letting my annoyance show. "Then call me and we'll set up a definite time. You asked me to do something for you, remember?"

"Yes. Yes. I remember." He came around the desk and shook my hand, moving us both toward the door.

I refused to quit. "Also we need to discuss your idea about naming the center for Madeline. I wish you'd spoken to me about that before you made your announcement."

Ted started to answer, but his desire to get me out of there choked off his reply. "All right. All right. I'll call you. You can show yourself out, can't you?"

I took my time leaving, but Ted didn't notice. He turned his back to me and began stuffing papers from the desk into a briefcase.

On my way out, I looked around for Finn, but there was no sign of her. The rooms off the hall yawned dark and empty. Outside, under the portico, Ted's black Lexus was parked with its motor running. I moved close enough to check out the driver, but there was no one in it.

As I left Ted Hathaway's house that morning, a jumble of partially formed questions ricocheted around in my brain. Not only had my conversation with him failed to provide me with answers, I found myself even more puzzled than before. Fortunately, I came up with another idea. I telephoned Ellen Davies and asked if I could stop by her house.

Ellen may have been surprised by my call, but she was

gracious enough to tell me to come ahead. She gave me directions to the cottage she rented from her uncle at the southern end of the lake. I pulled into her driveway thirty minutes later.

From the outside, the camp—as people here called the lakeside cottages—came across as rustic and a little rundown. The interior caught me by surprise. Ellen had given it a simple, almost Spartan look which she'd told me reflected the style of Georgia O'Keeffe, the painter she'd come to the lake to research and write about. She'd painted the interior walls white, covered the overstuffed furniture in white duck and hung simple wooden shutters on the windows, all choices inspired by photographs she'd seen of O'Keeffe's New Mexico home in Abiquiu.

I glanced around the living room with appreciation. An enormous rendition of the Black Iris hanging over the white fireplace formed an eye-catching focal point for the room. Since I'd moved to the lake, I'd learned more about O'Keeffe's work, especially the giant flower paintings she'd done during her fifteen summers here. I knew she'd painted several versions of the Black Iris. This one with its luxurious shades of black, gray and white and accents of rich reds and pinks struck me as magnificent. It was sensual, breathtakingly beautiful.

"What's it like to be greeted by something like this every morning when you come downstairs?" I asked.

"The Black Iris III, you mean? Overwhelming, awe-inspiring, inspirational. Take your pick. As you can imagine, being in the presence of genius either makes a person try harder or give up and throw in the towel."

"It does inspire awe, doesn't it?" I said.

As I looked more closely, I realized to my surprise that

the painting wasn't a poster or a print, that it appeared to be genuine. But it couldn't be the real thing, could it? I wanted to ask, but something held me back. From time to time, rumors circulated that O'Keeffe had left paintings behind during her summers at the lake. A few years ago, Ellen herself had investigated one of those stories and narrowly escaped being killed by a ring of art forgers. If this painting were real, it would be worth a fortune. I glanced around for wires or some other sign of a security system, but I didn't see anything.

"I think of all her works, this is the one I like best," Ellen said. "Stieglitz—he was her husband, you know—saw O'Keeffe herself as the Black Iris. Open, yielding, incredibly sensual. He fell in love with her soon after they met. Wouldn't you like a man in your life who saw you that way?"

I thought about her question. "You know, I'm not really sure. I suspect being adored may be better in theory than in practice. Not that I'm speaking from experience, you understand."

I really wasn't. I'd thought Richard adored me in the early days of our marriage but...there were indications that Stieglitz hadn't stayed faithful, either. Being adored didn't come with any guarantees.

"Do you think Ted Hathaway adored Madeline?" I asked Ellen a short time later as we sat at her kitchen table drinking coffee.

"I'm not sure 'adored' is the right word. He wanted to keep her, didn't want her to leave him for another man, that's for sure."

I waited, anxious not to interrupt her train of thought. I thought she was ready to tell me the very thing I wanted to know, but she didn't go on.

I prompted her gently. "People think she was involved with someone else, but nobody is willing to give me a name."

"And you don't know why? Seems funny, doesn't it, when people are so quick to gossip about everything else that happens around here." She picked up the coffee carafe and refilled my cup.

Our conversation drifted to other topics. Ellen mentioned the article she'd promised to write about the center, then spoke of her research on famous art forgers of the past for her mystery. "Art forgery is a fascinating subject. You can't believe the scams some of those forgers got away with. They'd paint something in what they liked to call the style of a famous artist, then breeze right into a gallery and make a pitch to sell it. You'd be surprised how often they got a dealer to buy it without checking the provenance, or at least without checking it very carefully."

When I looked puzzled, she added, "The provenance is what they call the history of the work, its lineage, I guess you could say."

"You mean even reputable art dealers might buy a painting without knowing for sure it's genuine?" I asked.

"And maybe get a famous artist's work for peanuts? Sure. Greed is a great motivator, you know. Why not take a chance?"

Was Ellen referring to her own Black Iris III, I wondered as I left her cottage that afternoon. She'd piqued my interest in art forgery, made me wish I knew more about the topic. But she'd done something else that day, even though I'd been too dense to realize it.

She'd told me who Madeline Hathaway had been involved with, told me and expected me to be smart enough to figure out what she'd said.

NINETEEN

TWO DAYS LATER I drove back to Lake Luzerne. Shortly after two o'clock I counted the cars and pickups in front of Dave's Diner and was pleased to find that Dave accommodated a late lunch clientele. I took the first empty stool I came to and ordered coffee while I studied the menu.

"Try the egg salad. It's one of our specialties," the woman working the counter told me. A silver-haired grandmother prototype, she was short, plump and dressed all in pink, right down to her tennis shoes. Even the word Jane on her name tag trailed pink flowers and ribbons.

Jane knew her sandwiches. The egg salad, accented with chopped olives and a lively dressing, was served on fabulous bread which I recognized as one of Panera's from nearby Glens Falls. "You're right. I do love it," I told her when she came back my way. She flashed me a pleased smile.

"I knew you would. Everyone does. A little variation on the usual way of making it. That's all it takes. Dave invented it himself. Hasn't been off the menu in twenty years."

She'd given me an opening and I took it. "Really? Dave's been here for twenty years? How about you?"

"Almost as long."

"So you know just about everybody in town then?"

"I'd say so. Sooner or later they all find their way to Dave's."

"I'm here to see a girl named Connie Leland. Lives outside of town, part way up a mountain. Know her?"

"Sure. Connie stops by once in a while. Dave told Jordan Barstow, the guy she runs with, not to come back, but Connie's a nice kid."

So I wasn't the only one who didn't warm up to Jordan. "Did Connie ever come in with an older woman? Attractive, friendly. Madeline Hathaway's her name."

"Sure. Maddy. The poor thing that got herself killed. Seemed like a good soul. Spent time with Connie. The kid needed that."

"She came here? To Lake Luzerne?"

"Checking on an old uncle of hers lives here. Poor guy's gettin' along in years now."

"Did she come alone?" I couldn't quite fit Ted into this picture.

"Brought a guy with her sometimes. Said they were fixing up the uncle's house. Good thing, I'd say. I hear it's in pretty bad shape, but poor Dwight can't do much work around there anymore."

The waitress moved away to drop checks in front of customers at the end of the counter. Damn, I thought. Just when I might be learning something. As soon as she was free, I pushed my cup forward and signaled for more coffee.

"Think the man with Madeline Hathaway might have been her husband?" I asked Jane as she refilled my cup.

"Doubt it. Most of 'em don't act like he did. At least, not the ones I know. She called him a handyman. Classy guy for that line of work. He could fix up my place anytime, if you know what I mean." She gave me an exaggerated wink.

I nodded. "A handyman, you say?"

"The kind everyone wants to find. Good-looking, great manners. Hung up Maddy's jacket for her on the rack over there before they sat down. Pulled out her chair, stuff like that. Treated her real nice. Even paid for both of 'em. Not like most of the yoyo's we get in here."

"Really?" I lingered over the word, hoping for more.

No such luck. Jane had told me enough. Now it was my turn to answer questions.

She leaned across the counter and lowered her voice. "So tell me how Maddy managed to get herself killed. We heard she fell going down some stone steps in the dark. But you know what? I don't believe that. She was afraid of heights. What's that disease where you can't climb mountains or go up in tall buildings? Well, she had it."

"Something-phobia. Give me a minute and I'll think of it," I said.

"Maddy wouldn't go down steps like that in the dark, not without hanging on tight to something or somebody. I'd bet on that."

I considered how much I should say. Tomorrow's papers would probably have the whole story. "Acrophobia's the word. And you're right. They're not sure she did fall. Sheriff's department suspects somebody killed her."

"You don't mean it. Dave, you hear this? We was right. This lady says maybe somebody did kill Maddy."

Dave lumbered toward us. A high-speed lumberer, he was on us in seconds. "So what's this? Somebody killed Maddy, you say?"

I hesitated. "They're looking into that possibility, I guess."

"Ain't that the damnedest? Sow the wind and reap the

whirlwind." He was shaking his head as he pushed through the swinging door to the kitchen.

"Dave reads the Bible a lot. Don't approve of folks running around."

"Did folks think that was what Maddy was doing?" My question sounded casual. At least I hoped it did.

"There's been talk off and on about her and Connie's dad. He died last year. Maddy was mighty good to him. Folks wondered. Then lately, she started coming up with this new guy."

"To work on the uncle's house, you said."

"With maybe a little fun stuff afterward. Stayed up at Boone's Motel sometimes. Miz Boone owns those cabins on the river. Nothing much, but Maddy was no snob. Billy Pringle—he's one of the sheriff's deputies patrols up here—he'd spot the guy's pickup tucked around back under the trees."

"Really?"

"Maddy'd leave her Caddy big as life out front, but the handyman would park around back where nobody could see him. Thought they were pulling off a neat little shack job. Out-of-towners don't think folks here are smart enough to figure what's going on."

I couldn't tell if she'd meant to include me in that remark or not, but I was ready to take off anyway. Connie would be home from school by now and I wanted to pay her a visit.

I TOOK THE SAME ROAD I'd taken that night with Connie, found the turnoff easily and ten minutes later was bouncing down Dwight Tanner's driveway. The little house looked even shabbier in the daytime. Either Maddy's handyman hadn't been very handy or he'd directed his energies elsewhere.

I saw Connie sprawled in an unpainted rocker on the porch. "Hi," I called as I got out of the car.

She watched me approach with the same coolness she'd displayed when I came on her sitting in Ted's swing. Her greeting was almost inaudible. "Hey."

My explanation was simple, maybe too simple. "I wanted to make sure you were all right."

"Sure. Why wouldn't I be?"

"And your uncle, too. He seemed pretty wiped out the other night. Was he okay the next day?"

Connie gave me a look Josie would describe as the hairy eyeball. "Like I told you. He gets tired easy, but then he's okay after he's had some sleep."

I'd overstepped. I hesitated, ready to admit defeat. "I didn't mean to intrude. Sorry."

Connie thawed a little. "You know, as long as you're here, maybe you can tell me something. Do you know about jobs for kids my age around Lake George anyplace? Summer jobs, I mean."

I stalled for time. "When do you get out of school?"

"Today was my last day. There's not much work around here and I'm going to need something."

"Have you worked other summers?"

"No. But Maddy was helping us out. I don't think Ted's gonna be that generous."

I would have loved details on that topic, but I didn't dare push my luck. "You couldn't take a job at Lake George, could you? How would you get back and forth?"

"Wouldn't have to if I worked at one of those hotels where they give the help room and board."

"What about your uncle? Could he manage here by himself?"

"Reckon he'd have to. We got a couple neighbors would look in on him. I could probably come home on my day off and get him set up for the next week."

"Connie, are you on your own here? Isn't there somebody else responsible for your uncle?"

"Nah, he's the one responsible for me. And don't you go tellin' anybody he isn't up to it. We could both end up in homes somewhere." She stood up and crossed the porch toward me, her hands clenched into fists at her sides.

"Your parents?"

"Both dead. My dad was sick a long time. He died last year. Unc and I do all right long as folks leave us alone." She glared at me again to make sure I got her meaning.

Definitely time to leave. My visit to Connie had netted me zero information. Fortunately, I had another card to play.

TWENTY

ON MY WAY HOME I took a side trip.

A few miles from town I found the sign I'd been watching for—Boone's Motel. Just beyond the sign, a long, white-frame building consisting of maybe a dozen rooms huddled in a grove of trees. Not fancy, but definitely in better shape than my friend Ramona's log cabins.

I parked and tapped lightly on the door marked Office.

"Come in," someone called.

The room I'd entered wasn't much larger than a walk-in closet, but it contained motel office essentials—computer, desk and chair, compartments on the wall for mail and keys. A hot plate was tucked into a corner and a metal shelf unit held videos under a sign offering to loan them to guests.

A clean-cut young man seated at the desk glanced up from a physics textbook propped open in front of him.

"I thought exams were over," I said.

"For most people. I doubled up on my science and math this year, so I still have one more to go."

"Sorry to interrupt. Is there any chance of seeing a room?"

"You want it for tonight?"

"Actually, no. I'm coming back this way next week. I thought I'd see what you have available."

He nodded. "Sure. I guess. My mother usually likes to show the rooms herself, but she's not here. I can take you."

The boy pulled a key from the wall rack behind him and we stepped outside. He led me past three doors, then stopped and unlocked the next room we came to. He reached in to flip up the light switch, then stood back to let me precede him inside.

Jane the waitress had been right. If Maddy, as she was apparently known in this part of the world, had stayed here for romantic getaways, she was no snob. The room appeared clean enough, but definitely not a candidate for a five-star rating. Everything in it had been scarred by age and use—the king-size bed with its shabby navy coverlet, the old-fashioned TV, the chipped wooden dresser and the beige vinyl chair in a style I dimly remembered from my childhood. Nothing a weary traveler couldn't make do with for a night or two but, when I pictured the Hathaway place at the lake I found it hard to imagine Madeline staying here.

"A friend of mine told me about this motel. Maybe you remember her—Madeline Hathaway," I said.

"The woman who got killed over at Lake George?"

Why did I keep assuming people over here didn't get the news? "That's the one. She stayed at your motel sometimes, I understand."

His manner shifted from friendly to suspicious. "You with the sheriff's department?"

"No. No. I was a friend of hers."

"So?"

"I might be coming over here once in a while to visit someone."

"Connie? To see Connie?"

I had to stop underestimating this guy. "You know her?"

"Sure. We go to school together. She doesn't have that

great a life. And now with her cousin dead, she could use somebody in her corner."

Her cousin. That day at Ted's house Connie had said Madeline was her cousin, then referred to Ted as her uncle. Strange, I thought, as I headed home. Still, the young man at the motel was right: Connie did need somebody in her corner. Maybe I should try to be that somebody. It wouldn't be a problem to drive over to see her once in a while. I hadn't liked her idea of finding work at Lake George. At Lake Luzerne, people knew her and wanted the best for her. That counted for a lot.

I kept thinking about Connie as I traveled back along 9N. I reached the entrance to the Northway a little after four and, on impulse, turned south instead of north and drove to the Warren County Municipal Center. I found Jim in his office.

"Anything new on Madeline's death?" I asked, as I sat down across from him.

"The autopsy's confirmed homicide. Everybody's been saying that, anyway. I doubt that it comes as a surprise to you, so we might as well talk about it now. You spent time with her. What did you know about her social life?"

I chose my words carefully, as if they were hot chestnuts ready to explode. "I did spend time with her working on the center, but probably not as much as some people think."

My response merited an annoyed glance. "What's that supposed to mean?"

"From something Ted said, I think she let him believe she was working with me sometimes when she wasn't."

"Well, she apparently had some extracurricular activities going on. We're looking into that. It might save time if you told us what you know."

"I've heard those rumors, too, but I can't put a name with them. Are you thinking Ted found out about what she was up to and killed her?"

"Slow down, Mayor, let's agree not to jump to conclusions. Right now, we have no evidence pointing us in that direction."

"Or do you think the man she was involved with might have done it?"

Jim made a low, rumbling noise in his throat. He glanced down at the papers on his desk. "We'll consider all possibilities."

"So, do you know who the man was?" I asked.

"Why? Do you?" The sharpness in his tone surprised me.

"Jim, I just told you I didn't. If I knew, I'd certainly tell you, wouldn't I?"

"Would you? I seem to remember times in the past when you didn't tell me everything you knew."

I waited for him to smile to soften the crack. He didn't. Instead, he bent forward over his desk and shuffled the papers—the universal signal for visitors to get lost.

"You maybe have things to do," I said.

No response.

"I probably should go along," I said.

Still no reply.

I sat a few minutes longer, hoping he'd offer one additional tidbit of information.

He growled. That was all.

I'd driven halfway home before the pieces of the puzzle fell into place. Finally, I got the message—or more accurately the lack of message. Kate, Pauline, Ellen Davies, and now Jim—all of them had pulled up short when our conversations touched on the mysterious stranger in Madeline

Hathaway's life. With Kate, I understood her reticence. She didn't gossip, especially about her clients. Ellen had practically told me she knew who her friend was seeing, then stopped before giving me the answer. Pauline, who sometimes dished more dirt than I wanted to hear, had clammed up and changed the subject when we spoke about Madeline. And Jim—I now realized the growls and furtive glances at his papers meant not that he didn't know, but that he didn't want to say. All these people knew who Madeline was seeing, and nobody wanted to tell me.

Why not? I'd find out sooner or later.

The answer smashed into me like a January gale off the lake. How could I have been so stupid? The general rule for gossip in Emerald Point was that sooner or later somebody told it. If somewhere, at some time, people were keeping their mouths shut, it had to follow that somewhere else others were letting the genie out of the bottle.

In this case, no one had been talking, at least not to me. Five years ago, I might have attributed this wall of silence to my newcomer status, to the fact that I hadn't yet qualified for the town's inner gossip circle. But that situation no longer applied. Pauline rattled on freely now. Diane chattered about local events and people, both past and present. Ellen Davies had come close to telling me, but I'd attributed her reluctance to give me a name to loyalty to a friend.

Ergo, as an old professor of mine used to say, look for what's right under your nose. It wasn't that people didn't want to tell, they didn't want to tell me. And as soon as I realized that, I had the answer. I knew the name of the man Madeline Hathaway had been seeing—Don Morrison.

TWENTY-ONE

EVERYTHING FELL INTO place, made perfect sense. I hadn't spent as much time with Don in the last few weeks as I usually did. Even when we both helped at the center, we'd been busy with different projects. Sometimes he worked on fine-tuning the computer program in the morning while I was at my office and left before I arrived later in the day.

I knew I'd been preoccupied with the center, but I hadn't exactly been fighting him off either. There'd been no more shared pizzas, no calls to suggest we get together. Then, that crack about naming the place for me instead of Madeline. I hadn't thought much about any of this, suspected he might have still been ticked because I'd gone back to the center the night I saw the body. But that was my interpretation. That was me again, putting my own spin on things.

I'd been slow to see the truth, but now I saw how it all pieced together. Don Morrison was the man Madeline Hathaway had been involved with, maybe the man Ted had seen driving up to their house the night she was murdered, maybe even—my mind recoiled at the thought—maybe even the man who'd killed her. That couldn't be true. Not Don, the gentle, good-natured academic. Had something dark and sinister, violent even, been lurking beneath that easy-going, college professor surface? Had Madeline, the consummate tease, tapped into a hidden well of rage the rest of us never saw?

I couldn't go home. I couldn't spend a night alone wallowing in these suspicions. I drove past the entrance to my street and straight to Kate Donohue's house.

Kate responded quickly to my urgent knocking on her front door. "Come in. Josie's gone for the evening. We can talk."

That was the great thing about a friend like Kate. I didn't have to tell her I finally knew the truth. She read it in my face the minute she opened the door. "Come out to the kitchen. Have you had dinner? Try a little of this linguine. I hate to see it go to waste, but I can't eat another bite and Josie doesn't like it."

I sat down on a kitchen chair. "Stop. Don't ply me with food. Information is what I want."

"Loren, take it easy. Coffee, then." She walked over to her coffeemaker, filled a mug and set it in front of me.

"You knew. Everybody knew."

"No, everybody didn't know, not until a day or two ago. How did you find out?" She pulled out a chair and sat down across from me.

"I finally figured out what everyone wasn't saying. It took me long enough. I feel like such a fool."

"Stop. Don't start berating yourself. You're not a fool, and you're not in the wrong here. And everyone didn't know. Diane and I discussed this for the first time last night. We wondered if we should tell you."

"Yes. Of course you should have. Don't you know me well enough to realize I'd want to know? Don. Don of all people—the mystery man in Madeline's life. I should have picked up on the clues, should have suspected something sooner. How long do you think this has been going on?"

Kate got up from the table and refilled my coffee cup. "Loren, slow down. Take this one step at a time. I really have no idea what's been going on, as you put it, or for how long. I heard a little buzz a few weeks ago, just a hint or two at first. Someone made a crack about Madeline having a new guy in her life. No name mentioned. Then when Don wasn't invited to Ted's house after the memorial service, the gossip mill really started grinding."

"Damn it, I was the beard. Although doesn't there have to be another name for the role when it's a woman? He trotted me out in public to throw people off." I slammed down my coffee cup and jumped up to pace around the kitchen.

"Loren, take it easy. You've had a lot of experience dealing with problems. This isn't the right approach, and you know it. Get all the facts before you work yourself into a frenzy."

Kate was right, of course. But I'd verified the central fact and I couldn't handle anything else right then. Her confirmation of Don Morrison as the man Madeline was seeing had sent my thoughts galloping in a dozen directions at once.

"You know what? Ted suspected she was involved with someone. I didn't mention this to you before, but right after Madeline was killed he came to my house and questioned me. He thought I could tell him who it was."

"Really? Ted asked you who it was?"

"This makes more sense now. I thought he asked me because Madeline claimed to be working with me at the center when he suspected she wasn't. But I bet he'd heard rumors about Don then, thought I'd be hurt enough to rat on him."

"Do you think Ted is that devious?"

"Sure he is. Don't people question his business ethics, speculate about some of those deals he pulls off? Doesn't everyone claim he wheels and deals to make his money? He probably thought he could trick me into telling him."

Kate shook her head. "I don't know, Loren."

I continued my tirade. "Damn it. All this time, it was Don."

"Not all this time. I don't think this has been going on very long."

"Why not? Don must have been damn good at keeping the secret." I thought back to the night I'd gone back to the center and seen the body, dredged up the way Don had feigned disappointment when I hadn't invited him to come home with me. For all I knew he'd run straight to Madeline the minute I drove away.

And then the next night at my house when I thought I'd smoothed everything over. Maybe the last thing he'd wanted was for me to drag him upstairs to make love. Maybe he'd been dying to get out of there and go to her. For all I knew, that was exactly what he had done as soon as he could disentangle himself from me.

As if she could read my thoughts, Kate reached across the table and laid both her hands gently on top of mine. "I'm so sorry about this, Loren. I know you're hurt, but don't you think your first move should be to talk things over with Don, hear what he has to say?"

"Kate, you must be a helluva lot bigger person than I am to suggest that. If I got within a hundred feet of Don Morrison tonight, people would be gossiping about another murder tomorrow."

She squeezed my hands. Her eyes beamed sympathy,

but the little half smile on her lips made her look exactly like Josie. "Well, you've been trying to think of ways to put Emerald Point on the map. That would be one way to do it."

TWENTY-TWO

BY THE NEXT AFTERNOON at four o'clock, I'd accepted the fact that planning Don's murder probably wasn't the best course of action. On the other hand, asking him for an explanation smacked too much of playing the passive victim role. The answer, I decided, lay somewhere in between. I telephoned him to say I wanted to drop by his house.

He hesitated a fraction longer than necessary, probably considering how fast he could get out of town. He knew something was up. Then he folded. "I'm making spaghetti sauce. Why don't you plan on dinner here?"

"All right." I didn't dare say more. I didn't want anything in my voice to trigger a question from him. I hadn't figured out exactly what I intended to say, but one thing for sure—I didn't want to say it in a phone call.

The night before, as I stared wide-eyed into the darkness, I'd asked myself a million questions and I hadn't been satisfied with the answers. I'd been down this road with Richard, but now the circumstances were different. I wasn't married to Don. He and I viewed each other as friends, good friends, but neither of us had pushed for commitment. We'd never talked about a future together, never even discussed being exclusive.

Madeline Hathaway had been a beautiful, seductive woman. I could understand how any man would have been attracted to her. I didn't like the idea that she was married and playing around, but that was her business—hers and Ted's, and whoever she chose to play around with.

What I hated most was the fact that Don hadn't been honest with me. But then I hadn't spent much time alone with him in the last few weeks. Maybe he'd put off telling me until after the center opening and then couldn't get up the nerve to do it. Much as I hated to let a perfectly good snit dissipate, I could feel it happening. I decided to listen to his side of the story.

A little after six that night, still not convinced I hadn't taken leave of my senses, I drove to Lake George Village. Don had bought a small cottage on the water when he moved from Albany a few years before. He loved the place, viewed it as the realization of a longtime dream. The white clapboard bungalow featured a wide veranda and an un-obstructed view up the lake. A few too many downtown lights twinkled through the trees for my taste, a little too much boat traffic disturbed the quiet, but I had to admit the setting was spectacular. I parked in the driveway and knocked on the screen door to the kitchen.

I spotted a couple of pans simmering on the stove and smelled the irresistible aroma of the spaghetti sauce Don loaded with herbs and garlic. A tray on the counter held wine glasses, a fresh-baked loaf of Italian bread and a bottle of Merlot. The Merlot made a statement. Don pre-ferred Chianti with Italian food. He'd apparently gone to the store and bought my favorite red wine. An obvious sign of guilt. Or was it an attempt at conciliation?

When my second knock went unanswered, I pulled open the door and stepped inside. I called his name as I poked my head into the living room. He obviously was expecting me, but I saw no sign of him anywhere. I walked out onto the porch.

Don's front yard sloped down to a small beach area, flanked by two docks where he tied his canoe and motor boat. Figures huddled together near one of the docks—Don and two heavy-set men I didn't recognize. The three leaned in close to each other. I needed a few seconds to understand what was happening. One of the men, well over six feet tall, stood behind Don, pinning his arms to his sides. The second guy, muscular as a Sumo wrestler, pummeled Don's motionless body with one sickening blow after another.

"Hey, what the hell's going on?" I scanned the porch for a weapon, spotted a canoe paddle leaning against the wall near the door. Without stopping to think, I grabbed it by the narrow end and went crashing out the door and down the steps.

"Let him go!" I bellowed as I charged across the lawn. I lifted the paddle to my shoulder as I ran, thinking I could wield it like a club. I let out a few more shrieks interspersed with shouts for help. Don had neighbors nearby. If I made enough noise, maybe one of them would come running.

The man hammering Don with his fists glanced up. I expected to see features contorted with rage, but the face he turned toward me was expressionless. He appeared as calm, as intent on his task as if he were turning out piece-work in a factory. Right, left, right, left. The steady rain of thuds set my stomach churning

"Stop that! Let him go," I screamed. I gripped the paddle hard, ready to swing.

The man stared back at me with no trace of surprise.

"Jesus, some crazy broad's after us. We've done enough here. Come on," he muttered to his companion.

The other man loosened his grip on Don's arms. As he stepped back, Don crumpled, limp as a broken doll, into a heap on the ground. The men, surprisingly fast for their size, galloped off toward the driveway. I stood over Don, not daring to drop the paddle, afraid to take my eyes off his assailants. A wave of nausea hit me as I watched their retreating backs. Huge, they were huge. Once my adrenaline rush slowed down, I realized the chance I'd taken. Either of them could have smashed me like an annoying insect without missing a beat.

Don moaned but didn't move. I kept my hand on the paddle as I knelt down next to him. His body had twisted when he fell, but I didn't dare try to straighten him out.

"Don, Don. Can you hear me? Open your eyes."

He didn't respond.

My heart jumped as someone ran into the yard. I turned and saw a middle-aged man in sports clothes, definitely not one of the attackers. A woman followed him.

"What happened? Do you need help?" the man asked.

"Call 911. Tell them to send an ambulance and notify the sheriff's department. This is Don Morrison. He's been attacked. I think he's badly hurt."

"I'll do it," the woman called and hurried back the way she'd come.

The man rushed over to me. "I'm Don's next door neighbor. Tell me what I can do."

"I don't think we should try to move him. I don't see any blood, but he may have broken bones or internal injuries. We'd better wait for help," I said.

The neighbor and I hovered over Don for what seemed

an eternity, fearful of doing anything to injure him further. His breathing was shallow; he didn't groan or try to move. When the emergency squad arrived, the man and I stepped back to let an EMT kneel down next to him. He slipped a cervical collar around Don's neck and unbuttoned his shirt to examine his injuries.

I was still rooted to the same spot when I saw the flashing red lights of a sheriff's car. Deputy Rick Cronin strode into the yard. I caught his look of surprise when he saw me, but I didn't give him a chance to comment.

I stormed over to him, dragging the canoe paddle behind me. "Make one crack, just one crack, about me finding myself in trouble again, and I won't be responsible for what I do with this."

Rick raised his hands in a placating gesture and took a step back. "Don't worry, Mayor. I wasn't going to say anything. Just that I'd best call Jim. He likes to handle the cases himself when you're involved."

"I'm not involved, Rick. I hate it when people say I'm involved."

Rick looked as if he wanted to cut and run, but he held his ground. "I didn't mean involved exactly. I just meant you were on the premises, that's all."

"I was invited for dinner. That's why I'm here. I looked down by the dock and saw two men beating up Don."

Rick slipped into deputy mode. "Two men? Did you recognize either of them?"

"No. One of them looked straight at me, too. I'd never seen him before. The other guy was holding Don while the first one hit him. I only saw part of his face, but I didn't recognize him, either."

"Jim will want to hear this himself. Let me get word to

him. You'll want to talk with him anyway." He waited just long enough to be sure I wasn't going to flare up again, then eased back toward his car.

The emergency squad members were still examining Don, checking and rechecking his vital signs, trying to determine if he could be transported safely. "We'll be taking him to Glens Falls to the hospital, but we want to make sure it's all right to move him," one of them explained.

My mind was churning, but I calmed down enough to consider what Don might need with him at the hospital. I made a mental list as I went back into the house—health insurance information, identification, his wallet. I picked up a book lying open next to his chair; he might want something to read when he woke up. Hold that thought, a little voice in my head reminded me, not if he wakes up, but when. I located a kit for toiletries in the downstairs bathroom and swept his toothbrush and a tube of toothpaste into it.

The food—I'd forgotten about the dinner preparations. I checked the kitchen. The spaghetti sauce was too hot for the refrigerator, but I covered it and stuck it in there anyway. The second pot contained nothing but water for the pasta. I made sure both burners were turned off and left the pot where it was.

After a minute's hesitation, I closed and locked all the windows. The house would be stifling when Don got home, but if the men came back for any reason, they'd find it harder to get in. Then I rummaged through Don's desk until I found his telephone book with his brother's number in Albany. I'd have to call Stephen and Elaine and tell them what had happened.

Before I could make the call, Jim Thompson shoved

open the back door. "Are you all right, Mayor? You took quite a chance going after those guys, if what Don's neighbor tells me is true."

I took a deep breath and tried not to bristle. "Jim, I know. I realized that right after I did it. When I saw how they were beating on Don, I didn't stop to think."

Jim clenched his teeth, but didn't comment further. Rick had probably told him I was in no mood for lectures. "The two men. Now, take your time. Describe them as carefully as you can."

I did my best. Their grotesque shapes were imprinted on my memory, accompanied by the dull thuds of the man's fists and the sight of Don's unconscious form sagging under the torrent of blows.

I shuddered as I relived the scene. Someone hated Don a lot to want that kind of punishment inflicted on him. I couldn't shake the feeling I knew exactly who that person was.

TWENTY-THREE

An hour later I paced anxiously outside one of the cubicles in the Glens Falls Hospital Emergency Room while Don underwent a thorough examination and a battery of tests. Once he'd been evaluated, I accompanied his gurney as he was wheeled, still unconscious, through silent, empty halls to the Intensive Care Unit.

As soon as he was settled in bed, I telephoned his brother Stephen and gave him directions to the hospital. I was dozing in the ICU visitors' lounge when I heard his voice.

"Loren, is there any change?"

I jumped up, my heart pounding as I came awake. Stephen had apparently taken time to shave, shower and break out a fresh shirt. I glanced at my watch. It wasn't four o'clock yet, but Stephen was dressed for a day at the office.

"Sorry. You probably just got a chance to close your eyes. These things always take so long."

"He's still unconscious. They've promised to tell me if he wakes up," I said.

Stephen sat down on the couch next to me. "Don called me a few days ago. He said he wanted to talk to me, but he insisted he couldn't do it on the phone. Urged me to meet him. Busy time for me with one of our clients. I told him it would have to wait a few days. Then he called back yesterday, said things were getting urgent."

"Do you have any idea what he wanted to talk about?"

"No, and I can't drop everything and take off just because he wants me to." His voice took on a petulant tone.

"Take off? He asked you to come up here?"

"He wanted me to meet him in Lake Luzerne. I couldn't make it a priority, not right now."

Lake Luzerne. The place did have a way of cropping up. I waited, hoping for a hint of what wasn't being said.

"But I'm here now. Tell me exactly what happened."

"Stephen, it was a terrible thing to see. Those men wanted to hurt him bad, maybe even kill him." My stomach started doing flip-flops again as I described the scene in Don's yard, but I wouldn't let myself stop. His brother had a right to know. I told him exactly what I'd seen.

As I described the beating, the color drained from Stephen's face. Twice he started to question me further, but stumbled over the words.

When I finished my account, he found his voice. "God. This is awful. They could have killed him."

"Yes. It looked like that was exactly what they were trying to do."

He shuddered. "Awful. This is awful," he said again.

I waited for the questions I felt sure he'd ask. Why had this happened? Who would do this to Don? Did he have enemies at the lake?

He didn't ask any of them. Instead he jumped to his feet and started for the door. "I've got to talk to his doctors."

I couldn't have moved that fast on a bet. My back ached like someone had stuck a knife in it and my right leg had fallen asleep. But, if Stephen was demanding an update on Don's condition, I wanted to hear it. I struggled to my feet and limped after him into the ICU.

By the time I reached there, Stephen had zeroed in on the nearest nurse and was bombarding her with questions in his top executive style.

She raised her eyebrows just enough to let him know she wasn't intimidated by the steamroller approach. "Mary's his nurse tonight. I'll ask her if she can step out and talk with you," she said.

Stephen shifted from one foot to another until a nurse emerged from Don's cubicle. She gave me a sympathetic smile as she patted my arm. "A long night, isn't it, Mayor Graham? Can you get any rest out there?"

Before I could answer, Stephen unleashed his barrage.

Mary listened politely, then repeated the same information she'd given me earlier. "You can go in for a minute if you want to, Mr. Morrison, but you'll need to prepare yourself. His face is bruised and swollen, and he won't know you're there. As I told Mayor Graham, he's still unconscious. We just have to wait and see."

"Yes. I should go in, I suppose." Stephen hesitated, then squared his shoulders and marched into Don's cubicle.

Mary and I waited patiently at first, then with mounting concern as the minutes ticked by.

"Maybe I shouldn't have let him go in there alone. I'd better make sure he's all right," Mary said finally. She slipped back into the cubicle.

Stephen emerged a few seconds later, visibly shaken, even paler than he had been earlier. Mary rushed out behind him and snatched up the phone at the nurse's station. Although I couldn't make out her words, the urgency in her voice frightened me.

My heart began pounding again the way it had in Don's yard. "Oh no. Something's happened."

Stephen sank down on a narrow bench near the door. "I was just leaving when an alarm went off."

A young man in surgical green came barreling through the swinging doors into the unit. "Sorry, but you can't be in here. Go sit outside and someone will come and talk with you there."

Back in the waiting room, Stephen and I each chose a couch and tried to get comfortable. I couldn't relax. Something must have gone wrong, terribly wrong.

"I know you told me on the phone, but tell me again so I can be sure I heard you right. When you got to Don's house, you saw men beating him up. You actually saw that happening?" Stephen asked.

The nausea hit me again as the scene in Don's yard came rushing back. "Yes. Two men—big men—strangers to me. One man held him and the other kept hitting him again and again, deliberately, methodically, even though he was unconscious. Nothing like a bar fight, or some kind of street brawl. They wanted to hurt him."

Stephen swallowed hard. My description of the scene appeared to make him sick, too. "Could Ted Hathaway have been one of them?"

"No. I didn't recognize either of them, but I'm sure the man hitting Don wasn't anybody I've ever seen before. The one holding him—I didn't get a good look at his face, but he was twice the size of Ted. Why do you ask?"

He hesitated, as if trying to decide how much to reveal. "Just that he might have it in for Don."

"You know then? Or you've heard the rumors?"

"Rumors?"

I was in no state for verbal fencing. "Stephen, I have a

suggestion. You and I are caught up in something serious here. Let's not play games. You mentioned Ted Hathaway. Everyone in town knows Madeline and Don were having an affair."

He swung around to face me, his mouth open in surprise. "People are saying that? Madeline Hathaway and Don?"

Why was he pretending he didn't know? Hadn't he just said Ted might have it in for Don? "Yes, that's what people are saying. And I'm sure you know that. Are you thinking Ted arranged for someone to beat Don up, maybe even kill him as revenge for an affair with his wife?"

Stephen wiped his hand across his face. I could see beads of sweat dotting his forehead. "Even worse. Maybe Ted killed her himself and now he wants to kill the man who was doin' her."

I shuddered. His phrasing sounded so crass. If Don had been seeing Madeline, I wanted to believe there was love involved…mutual affection and respect. I couldn't think of Don as doin' any woman. Still, an illicit rendezvous in Boone's third-rate motel was hardly the stuff of great romance.

I considered how to reply. "Ted isn't very likeable, I'll grant you that, and people insist he's ruthless in his business dealings, but I'm not ready to believe he's a murderer. Unless…" My thoughts spun off in a new direction. "Wait a minute. What if he didn't kill Madeline; what if he thinks Don murdered her?"

"Don couldn't have murdered her. Anybody who knows him would realize that. He's too laid back. He's a wuss really."

A compliment with a barb. A funny assessment to come from a younger brother. Weren't family personality traits supposed to line up the other way around? Hard-charging first born, then easygoing younger brother? This family seemed to have done a flip-flop. I found Stephen's word choices offensive, but that didn't mean there wasn't truth in what he said.

"I certainly don't see Don as a wuss," I said, stung into leaping to his defense, "but I suppose Ted could suspect him of killing her. He probably doesn't have any idea what Don is like. Madeline handled everything in their social life, made the friends, planned the activities, did whatever was needed in the way of civic responsibilities. Then, when all the work was done and success was guaranteed, he rode up on his charger to bask in the glory."

"You're saying he provided the money and she did everything else?"

"That's what people think. His contribution was to foot the bills as required."

Stephen shrugged. "Actually, that's how my wife and I do it. She's that same type. Probably couldn't earn a dime if she had to, but handles all the peripheral stuff real well. Wants to keep moving up socially. She's a climber. A lot like Maddy, I guess."

Two AND TWO came charging in from different parts of my brain, brought to life like those numbers in first grade arithmetic workbooks, begging to be put together. Maddy. Stephen had said Maddy. People in Luzerne said Maddy. Nobody around here called Madeline that. Maddy was the old name, the childhood name, the name cast aside as she moved up the social ladder. Don had asked Stephen to meet him at Lake Luzerne. Madeline was still Maddy over there.

How could this matter? Stephen hadn't gone to meet

him there; at least he said he hadn't. Was I reading too much into his use of the nickname? Or had he just told me something that would throw light on a whole new aspect of Madeline Hathaway's life and death?

TWENTY-FOUR

SHORTLY AFTER SEVEN the following morning, Stephen and I got the answers we'd been waiting for—at least some of them. After the day shift had heard reports and examined the patients, the nurse in charge called us to the desk for an update on Don's condition. The doctor had examined him again in the last hour, she told us, and although he was still unconscious, he was stabilized, even slightly improved. She thought it would be safe for us to leave. Although I wasn't a relative, I'd been cleared to get periodic updates on his condition.

Stephen gave her two phone numbers—his cell and a private work number—and made a copy of them for me. "If you hear anything, anything at all, be sure to call," he told me as we said our goodbyes.

By this time it was after eight. I considered making a stop at the sheriff's office to find out if Jim Thompson had any new information, but I was so tired I decided against it. Instead, I drove directly to Emerald Point and opened my office. After a quick appraisal of what needed to be done that day, I called Pauline with a request to come in early.

She was breathless when she dashed through the door less than an hour later. "Loren, I don't believe this. You went to Don's house and found two men beating him up? Were they anyone you know? Weren't you scared to death? What in the world did you do?"

"If you promise not to lecture me, I'll tell you."

Pauline made a zipping motion across her lips and dropped into the chair next to my desk. She listened wide-eyed as I described the scene on Don's lawn.

By the time I'd finished, she was close to bursting. "Can I say something if it's not lecturing?" she asked.

"Sure. I'd like to get your reaction. Do those guys sound like anyone you ever saw? You know a lot more people on the lake than I do."

"I can't think who they'd be. But don't you suppose Ted Hathaway is behind this?"

I had to agree. The day before, I'd admitted to Pauline that I finally knew the secret everyone was buzzing about—Don Morrison had been the mystery man in Madeline Hathaway's life. Now I asked the question foremost in my mind. "So, what does this mean? If Ted was behind the beating, is he taking revenge on Don for the affair, or does he think Don killed her?" I said.

"Wouldn't matter," Pauline insisted. "That Ted Hathaway is capable of just about anything. Or maybe he has other reasons for hating Don, something we don't even know about yet."

"You could be right," I told her. But I couldn't speculate about it anymore. I was shaking from exhaustion as both my body and brain sent frantic messages that they needed sleep. I took off for home.

Before I collapsed into bed, I fished Don's telephone book out of my pocket, intending to add the numbers from the slip of paper Stephen had given me. The book fell open a few pages before Stephen Morrison's listing. To my surprise, I was looking at Connie Leland's name.

Connie Leland. Don had entered Connie's name and

telephone number in his book. Had Madeline brought Don to Luzerne and introduced him to Connie and her uncle? Had he been the man the waitress had seen with Maddy at the diner, the man with the excellent manners? Possible, of course. But usually the first thing people noticed about Don was his thick, dark blond hair and beard. The waitress hadn't mentioned them. I'll think about this the minute I wake up, I promised myself, as I closed my eyes and drifted off.

I came awake at one in the afternoon, not exactly rested but too keyed up to sleep any longer. I called the ICU for a report on Don's condition. Stable, but no real change. With an empty afternoon looming ahead, I decided to drive over to Lake Luzerne. Perfect timing for lunch at the diner.

Jane the waitress greeted me with a smile as she arranged a place mat and silverware in front of me on the counter. "Well, hello there. You back already?

"And hungry for another egg salad sandwich," I said.

She gave me a thumbs-up.

As we waited for my sandwich to come from the kitchen, we discussed the lunch business, the weather and my appreciation of Dave's cooking. Then she asked the question I was waiting for, "Anything new on Maddy's death?"

I had my answer ready. "Nothing new on her death, but a guy in Lake George was beaten up last night. You mentioned she used to come here with a male friend. I wondered if he could have been that guy who came here with her."

"You don't say. Dave, you better come listen to this. This lady's got some news you might want to hear."

Dave rolled toward us, wiping his hands on his apron.

"A man got beat up last night over at Lake George. This

lady thinks he might have been that friend of Maddy's," Jane told him.

Dave nodded as he thought over what she'd said. "Could be, I suppose. 'Sow the wind, reap the whirlwind,' I always say."

"I was thinking he might be the guy Maddy brought over here sometimes. Big man, dark blond hair and beard," I said.

"You saying he had a beard? Nope. Couldn't be the guy came in here with her. You ever see her with anybody like that, Jane?"

Jane, visibly disappointed, shook her head. "No. I would have remembered somebody like that. The guy she's brought here was dark haired, not big exactly, but reasonable size, good looking, I guess, but definitely no beard."

So Don was ruled out. Madeline must have had another man in her life or else—why not give her the benefit of the doubt?—maybe this was a relative. If she had an uncle living here, why not a cousin as well?

So I asked. "Could it have been a relative maybe?"

"Not anybody from around here. I know 'em all," Jane said.

We chatted about other matters as I ate my sandwich, but my mind was racing. I thought I'd been on the verge of learning something about Madeline's secret life, but I was wrong. Fortunately, I knew somewhere else I could ask questions.

I PULLED OUT of the diner parking lot and headed down the road to Boone's Motel.

"I might need a room for some night next week," I told the woman behind the desk. I assumed this was the mother of the young man I'd spoken to before.

"Do you want to see a room while you're here?" the woman asked.

I nodded, hoping there'd be more chance for conversation if I took her up on the offer. She escorted me out of the office and down the covered walkway to the same room her son had showed me.

"A friend of mine stayed here sometimes. Madeline Hathaway." I spun out the story.

"Yes, she stayed here," she acknowledged. No warmth in her voice. No further comment.

Oops. Best not to pursue that topic.

After she'd showed me the room and we were walking back to the office, she stopped and turned to me. "You say you were a friend of Madeline's?"

"Yes. She did a lot of work on the new community center we've just opened in Emerald Point. We all feel terrible about her death."

The woman paused in the doorway, as if mulling over what I'd said. "If you were Madeline's friend, maybe I could give you something she left here. I really don't feel right hanging on to things that belonged to her and I don't think I should give them to her husband."

"Something she left here?" I still couldn't imagine Madeline staying in a place like this, much less leaving something behind.

The woman unlocked a door next to the office. She reached past an assortment of cleaning supplies and pulled out a black canvas duffel bag. After she dropped the bag on the walk in front of me, she stepped back fast as if she expected it to burst into flames. "You'd be doing me a favor if you took this. I don't want it around here. Don't want my boy seeing it."

"But shouldn't it be turned over to the authorities?"

"I'm not going to get involved with the sheriff's office over it. Just take it off my hands, will you?"

"But what do you want me to do with it?"

"Anything you want. You were a friend of hers, you said. Just take it and then you can figure out what to do about it." She shoved the bag toward me with her foot. As soon as I reached down to pick it up, she whirled around and, without another word, disappeared into the office.

I opened the trunk of my Saab and hoisted the duffel bag into it. It wasn't large enough to contain a body, I was relieved to find, but it was heavy and stuffed surprisingly full. I realized the woman didn't want me to check the contents then, just get it the hell out of there. So even though I was bursting with curiosity, I slammed the trunk closed, climbed into the front seat and took off.

TWENTY-FIVE

THE DRIVE TO my house seemed to take forever. One after another, I considered—and rejected—all the possible actions I might take with the duffel bag. I watched for places along the road where I could stop and check its contents. Too public. What if people came by, curious people who might see something I wouldn't want them to see?

With the possibility of stopping ruled out, I toyed with the idea of calling Don's brother to report the find. Too soon, I decided. Better find out first what the bag contained.

Of course, common sense told me to drive to the Municipal Center and turn the bag over to Jim Thompson. But the woman had entrusted the bag to me, hadn't she? Besides, Jim might be gone for the day by this time anyway. I'd leave a businesslike message on his voice mail with the promise "to stop by in the morning to turn in something of Madeline's." That should be enough.

If any passers-by were watching me unload the duffel bag in my driveway, they probably suspected me guilty of a heinous crime. I tugged the bag forward in the trunk until I could lift it out, then half dragged, half carried it into the kitchen. For anyone with an imagination, it could easily have contained a dismembered body. I locked the back door behind me, but I needed more privacy than the kitchen provided. I maneuvered the bag up the stairs and deposited it on my bedroom floor.

I didn't bother with gloves. I didn't think canvas would show prints and I'd admit to opening the bag if Jim asked me. I untied and loosened the cord in the neck and pulled the top layer of the contents onto my bed. Sheets. Sheets in a rich ivory color had been folded neatly at the top of the bag. I smoothed them with the tips of my fingers. They felt exquisitely soft, silky, luxurious, the thread count obviously off the charts. Elegant sheets for someone with no intention of making do with the offerings of a third-rate motel. I'd read that the Kennedy women brought their own special sheets when they were hospitalized. But these sheets weren't brought along to provide comfort during a hospital stay. A series of erotic images flashed unbidden into my mind. These sheets were used for romantic encounters with Don Morrison.

Damn him. If somebody hadn't already beaten him senseless, I'd charge back into that hospital and do it myself. A nice percale wasn't good enough for him. My beautiful bedroom with its windows overlooking the lake wasn't good enough for him. I wasn't good enough. Suddenly, I was fifteen again, watching Petey Mitchell stroll off with that slutty Nina Karpinski. If I didn't get a grip on myself, I'd start bawling my eyes out.

The chime of the doorbell echoing through the house set my heart pounding even harder, but it broke the spell. I raced downstairs to find Kate Donohue at the back door.

"You're locked up early. Those big-city ways die hard." She gave me a hug, then set a foil-wrapped package on the kitchen table.

"What's this?" I asked, grateful for the distraction.

"Manicotti. I know you like it. Have you spent all day at the hospital?"

I stared at her, trying to decide how much to tell her. If I wanted to confide in someone, close-mouthed Kate would be the logical choice. But did I really want to pull her into this mess?

"Loren, what's the matter? Are you all right? You haven't had bad news about Don, have you?"

Bad news, yes. Just not the kind she meant. I made my decision. "Kate, come upstairs with me. I want to show you something."

When we reached my bedroom, I motioned Kate to sit on the bed as I told her how the motel owner had given me Madeline's belongings. I showed her the sheets, then wrapped a small guest towel around my hand, reached into the canvas bag and slowly retrieved the other items.

My shtick might have been overly melodramatic, but it was effective. Kate stared wide-eyed. I pulled out pillow cases in the same elegant material as the sheets, edged with delicate crochet. Next came an assortment of neatly folded silk scarves, fragile, diaphanous, shimmering in shades of pink and rose.

"What do you think she did with the scarves?" Kate asked, as I tumbled them onto the bed.

"See, that's why you and I aren't getting much action. Cosmo girls know these are a must for romantic trysts. You fling them over the lamps to create a romantic glow, the proper ambiance, you call it."

"Don't they catch on fire?"

I shook my head in mock disgust. "Kate, Kate, we're talking about a different kind of fire here."

"Okay, so I'm really out of it. But can you see Josie's

face if I brought a guy home and she saw that I'd hung these over the lamps in my room?" She giggled at the thought.

"Maybe this stuff comes in a kit. Enchanted evening staples, everything supplied but the man." I could joke now with Kate beside me. If I kept my wits about me, I didn't have to picture any particular man.

I dug deeper into the bag. I lifted out an oblong box padded with a luxurious hand towel. Inside I found delicate crystal wine glasses wrapped in tissue paper. Another box held a corkscrew and silverware, a third, pink light bulbs.

"I had pink light bulbs when I first moved to New York," I told Kate. "I'd almost forgotten. Everything looks better with pink light bulbs, unless, of course, you're sunburned. Now that I think of it, that's why I stopped using them."

"Wow. This is an education in itself. Is there more?"

"A couple small items wrapped in tissue paper." I was digging into the bag after them when the ring of my bedside phone made us both jump.

"Loren." Stephen Morrison cleared his throat and hesitated, as if he were preparing to convey bad news.

I froze, mouthed his name to Kate. "Yes?"

"Well, he's awake, if you could call it that. He seems to have regained consciousness, but he keeps dozing off. He's in pretty bad shape. He's muttered your name several times. I think he wants to see you."

Relief flooded through me. "I'll be right down."

"I'm glad you're coming. He's still in the ICU, of course. Take a deep breath before you go in."

Kate helped me repack Madeline's bag and we were out the door in a matter of minutes.

In less than a half hour, I skidded full speed through the

unit's swinging doors and into Don's cubicle. Stephen had tried to warn me, but no words could have prepared me for the sight of Don's face. I'd been horrified by his appearance the night before, but now he looked infinitely worse. One quick glance and the churning nausea I'd experienced in his yard swept over me again. I had to turn away.

If I hadn't known this was Don's cubicle, I wouldn't have recognized him. He lay motionless, flat on his back, eyes closed. His body under the tightly-pulled white coverlet seemed to have shrunk to half its size. I focused on the equipment around him, the lines he was hooked to, the tangle of cords and wires coiling out from the bed. I studied the monitor on a pole next to him even though the green numbers and zigzag lines meant nothing to me. Anything to avoid looking at his face. But I couldn't hold off forever.

When I finally forced myself to lift my eyes to his head, I saw a swollen, lopsided mass, a tapestry of blue, red and purple bruises, mottled with patches of yellow and white. One eye was glued shut; his lips were puffed into a grotesque caricature of a mouth. The thick, dark-blond hair, always his distinctive characteristic, lay against the white pillowcase like a stain of brown sludge. When I'd come on the men beating him, they'd been concentrating on his body. If his face looked like this, I couldn't imagine what damage they'd inflicted on the rest of him.

"Don," I said quietly, leaning over him.

The good eye, if you could call it that, opened a crack. He groaned, seemed to realize I was there. He spoke haltingly, his words so low they were little more than a gasp. "…awake."

"How much pain are you in? What can I do to help you? Do you want me to ask your nurse to come in?" I knew I was bombarding him with questions, but I couldn't stop myself.

He struggled to speak. "Loren. Not… what you think."

"Last night. I came to your house for dinner. Remember? I saw those two men beating you. I thought Ted must have sent them."

He mumbled something I didn't understand.

"Are you trying to tell me Ted Hathaway wasn't behind this?"

Again, a faint sound, scarcely more than an exhaled breath.

I was bending over Don, trying to make out his words when Stephen Morrison entered the cubicle with Elaine at his side. "Loren, you got here fast. We went down to the cafeteria for coffee and a bite to eat. I tried to warn you, but I doubt you were prepared for this."

Don shifted his head slightly. I could tell he was struggling to focus on his brother. I wondered how much he could see or understand.

Before I could ask Stephen what he'd been told today about Don's condition, a nurse bustled into the cubicle. "I thought you understood he's allowed only one visitor at a time. Two of you need to wait in the lounge."

Stephen took charge at once. "Loren, why don't you and Elaine step out for a minute while I say a quick goodbye? I have an appointment for a late business meeting up here. I'll be leaving, and then you can stay with him as long as you like."

Didn't this guy ever stop working? Once again, Stephen's work ethic and his take-charge style—so at odds with Don's laid-back manner—didn't mesh with my idea of a younger brother's personality.

As soon as Elaine and I reached the empty waiting

room, she settled herself on one of the couches. Even for a trip to a hospital ICU, Elaine dressed fashionably. Tonight she was wearing an elegant summer suit in a soft lavender shade, perfect with her dark hair, and eye-catching silver jewelry. Conscious of my tousled hair and wrinkled slacks, I pulled up a chair across from her.

She gave me a sympathetic smile. "Loren, coming here must be so difficult for you."

I bit down on my lip, feeling close to tears. "I'd hoped when I got here tonight I'd find him more like himself. But he's still so helpless. It's hard seeing him like this, watching him struggle to speak."

"Of course, I'm sure it is. But, actually, I was referring to the circumstances. I thought you and Don were committed to one another. This turn of events must have come as a terrible shock to you."

"I still see those men beating him. It was horrifying."

"It must have been." She reached across the space between us and patted my hand. "I don't understand why people insist on playing such dangerous games without acknowledging the possible consequences."

A familiar theme. I half expected Dave from the diner to pop in with a chorus of "Sow the wind, reap the whirlwind." I made the low noise in my throat I'd perfected for Common Council meetings when I wanted to appear neutral.

"You don't agree?"

"I'm trying not to jump to conclusions until I can talk with Don." Not exactly the truth, but I wasn't ready to share my feelings with her.

"I'm sorry if I'm out of line here. I'll understand if you don't want to pursue the topic."

So Elaine had known about Don's affair with Madeline.

I really didn't want to pursue the topic—she was right about that—but if Stephen and Elaine had learned something this afternoon about Don's attackers, I was anxious to hear it.

I bumped our exchange up a notch. "If you're thinking Ted Hathaway may be responsible for Don's beating, I can't tell you whether I agree or not. Has the sheriff's investigator given you and Stephen any reason to think Ted was involved?"

"He spoke to Stephen. Perhaps he'll share what he learned with you. He's said very little to me. Seeing his brother in this condition has been very unsettling for him."

Unsettling was hardly the word for it. "I would think so."

"You've probably noticed how Don stays under the radar most of the time," she continued. "He's not the type to make enemies. But he's apparently managed to acquire a formidable one." She delivered this pronouncement in such a matter-of-fact way, I was surprised to notice her hand plucking nervously at the couch next to her.

I nodded. I wasn't about to discuss Don's faults with his sister-in-law, although I sometimes found his laid-back style irritating myself. More than once I'd wanted to shake him. I knew I sometimes took advantage of his good nature, confident he'd accept whatever I said or did at face value. Like the evening I'd left him and gone back to check the center—why hadn't he pushed harder to come home with me that night? That would have been our usual pattern.

If Don hadn't been so damn agreeable, I wouldn't have driven to the center, wouldn't have seen the body in the display case, wouldn't have been puzzling ever since over what had happened to it. I'd changed our routine that night and everything had gone wrong since. Of course, maybe he'd been delighted I'd put him off, glad for the chance to leave me and rush straight to Madeline. Maybe I was nothing more than the designated understudy when she wasn't available.

Don had whispered the words, "not what you think," but those words didn't sugarcoat his relationship with Madeline for me. No matter how much they cared for one other, no matter how much romantic paraphernalia she brought to a rendezvous, the fact remained she was a married woman cheating on her husband. As for Don—well I couldn't even think about that right now.

After Stephen and Elaine left the hospital that night, I did a fast postmortem on my conversation with Don's sister-in-law. Why, I asked myself, had I let it start my thoughts racing, push me into a whole downward spiral of regret? Once Don was out of danger, I'd have time for second guessing on my own. I didn't have to start tonight.

TWENTY-SIX

DON'S ICU NURSE let me sit with him for a while, but he gave no sign of realizing I was there. Shortly after eight, when she asked me to step out while she readied him for the night, I decided not to hang around any longer.

Once home, I spent some time on my front porch for my favorite therapy—staring at the lake. The last traces of daylight had vanished and the sweep of stars across the night sky frosted the dark water. A waning moon rose over the east shore and started its climb. As always, the soft night sounds coupled with the lake's gentle murmuring calmed me. I went back inside and checked for messages on my answering machine, then fixed myself a cold drink and a supper of Kate's leftover manicotti.

I considered examining the rest of the items in Madeline's bag—the two or three small wrapped packages left at the bottom—but decided against it. The day ranked high enough on the aggravation meter already. A good night's sleep was what I needed most. As I turned off my bedside lamp and slid beneath the cool cotton sheets, I felt as if I were sinking into a cloud.

When the phone rang at five-thirty, I bolted upright, blood pounding in my ears. In the half-light of early morning the disembodied voice could have come straight from a horror movie. "Loren, it's Stephen Morrison. I've just been notified that Don's going into surgery."

I squeaked out a response. "You mean now? At this hour?"

"That's right. They'll be taking him to an operating room in a few minutes. You knew the doctor expressed concern about a clot behind his eye. He's decided not to wait any longer."

Actually, I hadn't known that. A hundred questions tumbled around in my brain, but I couldn't get them out. Which eye? Could he lose sight in it? How much danger was he in? I didn't take time to shower. I threw on a sweater and slacks and took off for the hospital.

When I charged into the surgical waiting room a half hour later, I found Don's procedure had been completed and he'd been transferred back to the same cubicle in the ICU. I rushed to the unit. "What's happened? How is he?" I asked the nurse on duty.

"I just hung up from talking to his brother," she said. "As I told him, Mr. Morrison's come through the surgery without incident. He's still unconscious, but the doctor thinks his general condition is somewhat improved."

I pestered her with a few more questions, most of which she couldn't answer, sat with Don for a few minutes and took off. As I drove home, I concocted a new plan for the day. I'd go back to my house, shower, change clothes and check out the remaining items in Madeline's bag. Then, before I went to the office, I'd deliver the bag to Jim Thompson and be done with it.

I paused in the kitchen just long enough to start the coffee maker and took the stairs two at a time. As I shoved open my bedroom door, I pulled up short and stared into the room in horror. I could scarcely register what I was seeing. My beautiful room lay in shambles—drawers dumped, closet emptied, clothes heaped in tangled piles on the floor. And the bed, the bed had been literally torn to pieces: the sheets and coverlet ripped off, the mattress shoved from the box spring onto the floor. I glanced toward the corner where I'd left Madeline's duffel bag. The bag was gone.

I knew not to go into the room. I hurried downstairs and put in a call to Deputy Sheriff Rick Cronin.

When he came on the line, I fought hard to keep my voice steady. "Tossed. My bedroom's been tossed, Rick. Isn't that what they call it in detective stories?"

"Mayor Graham, take a deep breath. Are you sure there's no one in the house now? Stay on the phone while you look around."

A few minutes later, after I'd peered into all the rooms, I reported back. "Nobody here now, Rick. Whoever did this is gone."

"Jim's in a meeting this morning, but I'll be there in ten minutes. Don't touch anything. And stay out of the bedroom."

He didn't have to tell me that. The last thing I wanted to do was go into that room. Just the view from the doorway had made me want to cry. My personal space, the haven I'd fixed up so lovingly, my sanctuary, my favorite spot in the whole world torn apart, desecrated. I retreated to the kitchen and poured myself a cup of coffee.

Rick, as good as his word, knocked on the screen door ten minutes later. Without wasting time on questions, he led the way upstairs.

"Stand here," he said as he surveyed the damage from the hall.

I bit down hard on my lip. "I don't believe it. Who could have done something like this?"

"We'll get to that. Let's concentrate on the room. Think a minute. Is anything missing?"

"Madeline Hathaway's duffel bag. I called it her bag of tricks. A woman at the motel where Madeline stayed in Lake Luzerne said she didn't like having it left there, so she gave it to me." I launched into an explanation of why I felt I couldn't refuse to accept the bag and listed some of the articles Kate and I had pulled out of it.

Rick didn't seem to understand. "I don't get it. Why would Mrs. Hathaway have left things like that at the motel?"

"Rick, they were things to have an affair with. I don't know how else to put it."

He swallowed hard. His normally pink cheeks flushed a vivid shade of scarlet. "We need to let Jim know about this," he said gruffly. "You'll have to talk to him the minute he gets out of that meeting."

While we waited for the fingerprint crew, Rick agreed I could grab a quick shower and exchange the old sweats I'd thrown on earlier for slacks and a sweater from the hall closet. Then I left him to continue his investigation and took off for the Municipal Center, hoping to catch Jim the minute he came out of his meeting.

I didn't look forward to our confrontation. I was the victim here, I told myself as I drove south, but I knew Jim well enough to predict his reaction. He'd focus on the bottom line: I'd accepted evidence in a murder investigation. I'd delayed turning it in. Now it had disappeared.

On the plus side, I thanked whatever stroke of luck or genius had led me to leave a message on his answering machine the evening before. In it, I'd assured him I'd taken the bag with reluctance and promised to drop it off in the morning. Drop it off—that was the way I'd phrased it— the way I might drop off a box of donuts or tickets to an Emerald Point clambake, not possible evidence in a murder investigation.

The donut metaphor gave me an idea. I swung off the Northway two exits before the Municipal Center. Since I still hadn't managed any breakfast, I picked up two hot cups of coffee and a dozen assorted dunkers, with Jim's declared favorites, Boston crème pie donuts, heavily represented.

Even though I considered myself the wronged party in the case, my hand shook more than I liked when I tapped on Jim's office door.

"Yes, Mayor Graham. Come right in. Rick tells me you picked up evidence for us, evidence which has now gone missing." He appeared deceptively calm, but I heard the swoosh of anger under his words.

"Understand I didn't know at the time it might be evidence, Jim. The woman at the motel insisted I take it, told me several times over she wouldn't turn it in herself."

"And, of course, you wanted to be obliging."

While he revved up the sarcasm, I set out the two over-size containers of coffee, flanked by creams and sugars, on the side of his desk.

I wasn't really surprised at his attitude. I knew from past experience that law enforcement personnel, Jim especially, sometimes harbored suspicions of citizens doing good deeds.

"I didn't think you'd want me to refuse." I opened the box of donuts and positioned it with the Boston crèmes nearest him.

"But, as I understand it, that evidence has now disappeared," he said.

"Stolen. Right out of my house sometime early this morning."

"Stolen? You're sure about that?"

"Well, somebody tore my bedroom apart and the bag's gone." I pushed one of the coffees toward him.

"And you're assuming the reason someone broke into your house was to get these articles you picked up at the motel? What did Rick say you called the evidence—Madeline Hathaway's bag of tricks?"

"Yes. At least, I think whoever took it had to break into my house to get it. I thought I locked the door, but I did rush out fast. I can't swear to it."

Jim's eyes took on an unfortunate glint, probably the same way Jack the Ripper's eyes sparked as he moved in for a kill. The color drained from his face. "You picked up evidence in a murder investigation and not only didn't turn it in right away, you didn't lock your house?"

Tactical error. "Oh, I think I locked the house. I always do. I'm just trying to be totally honest here."

"Totally honest? How about totally non-butt-in-ski, totally let-me-stick-to-my-own-job-and-stay-out-of-sheriff's-department-business? We could have sent a deputy to Lake Luzerne to pick up that bag. That would have been a refreshing change for both of us. At least, I'm damn sure it would have been for me." He slammed his hand down, sending his coffee splashing onto his desk.

I nodded as if I agreed with every scathing word.

"Or, here's another idea. If you insist on helping us with our work in the future, you could turn evidence in immediately instead of taking it home with you."

Again, a nod seemed the preferable course of action.

"And of course, you probably know exactly what was in this bag of tricks, as you call it. Perhaps you'll be kind enough to share that information with me." The emotion behind those growls made me wish I'd left the bag back in that storage closet in Luzerne.

"I opened the bag, I admit it." I lowered my gaze. I even threw in an apologetic murmur, a submissive noise like wolves are said to make when bigger, more powerful wolves threaten them. Hey, I thought, it works for them.

During the next fifteen minutes, Jim paced around his office as I listed everything I remembered taking from Madeline's bag. When I mentioned I'd left two or three small wrapped packages unopened at the bottom of the sack, I steeled myself for another explosion. Jim didn't disappoint me. My eardrums vibrated from his roars. I weighed making an attempt at further explanation, but silence seemed the safest course of action.

When I couldn't hold my tongue any longer, I asked the question foremost in my mind. "Why, Jim? Why would someone want that bag bad enough to break into my house for it?"

He calmed down enough to answer me. "Too soon to say. Those small packages could be key. Or, maybe the perp was looking for something supposed to be in it. Let's go through this again. When the motel owner gave you the bag, did she give you anything else?"

I shook my head.

"Think about it. Are you sure?"

"Jim, for God's sake. I'm sure." Now I was the one getting testy.

"You carried the bag upstairs to your bedroom. You

took out most of the contents. Kate saw them. We'll get confirmation from her. Maybe she'll remember something you're not thinking of. Then, before you left for the hospital last night, you put everything back into the bag. Could you have set anything aside, maybe stuck it on a dresser or nightstand?"

"Not unless I overlooked something. I don't think I did, but I was hurrying."

I expected that remark to set him off again, but he held steady. He picked up the phone. "That could be it. Let's see if Kate remembers something that can help us."

Kate, unfortunately, had just left the coffee shop to deliver pastries to a breakfast meeting. Jim's mood darkened again. Any notion that I was the wronged party in this incident had been shoved to the back burner.

Escape looked like my best option. I promised to stay out of the house until Rick and the fingerprint crew finished their work and to call immediately if I thought of anything more. As I stood up to leave, I glanced toward the full box of donuts on Jim's desk. I still hadn't had breakfast. My mouth watered as I thought about grabbing a donut to take with me, but a final glance at Jim's face told me what a really bad idea that would be. I tore full speed ahead out of the Municipal Center without looking back.

TWENTY-SEVEN

AT THE OFFICE, I cleared up all unfinished business and struggled through a twelve-page report on water purity in Spencer's Bay, a mile north of Emerald Point. On an average day I would have found the report excruciatingly dull but, after my experiences that morning, I welcomed the mind-numbing diversion it offered. I couldn't dwell for one more minute on the burglary at my house or its possible connection to Madeline Hathaway's murder or Don Morrison's savage beating. Water purity seemed like such a nice clean topic—who could fault it?

When the phone rang, I held my breath waiting for more bad news. But this time it was only Rick Cronin telling me the crime scene crew had finished their work at my house and I could go home. As soon as Pauline came in for the afternoon, I did just that.

When I pulled into my driveway, I found Kate and Josie waiting for me in the catering van. Kate jumped out at once and gave me a hug. "Loren, we've come to help. I called your office and Pauline said you were on your way."

"Did Jim reach you?" I asked as I unlocked the back door.

"I had a message to call him when I got back to the coffee shop. I told him what we took out of the bag and he said you'd listed the same things."

"And the items left at the bottom. Did you mention them?"

"I said there were two or three things we didn't get to, looked like parcels wrapped in white paper. I thought they could have been documents of some kind, but I couldn't tell."

"Good. At least we remembered the same things." I led the way upstairs.

As we reached the door to my bedroom, Josie let out a long, shrill whistle. "Yikes, and my mother calls me a slob."

Kate surveyed the room, then stared at me in disbelief. "Your beautiful room, Loren. This is terrible, but at least they didn't slash open the pillows and mattress. We can whip this into shape in no time."

The three of us grabbed hold of the mattress and wrestled it back onto the bed. As I pulled a fresh mattress pad and clean sheets and pillowcases from the linen closet, Kate outlined her plan of attack for Josie and me.

"We'll start with the bed. Loren, you'll want to wash all this bedding in good hot water. After we make up the bed with clean sheets, we'll move counterclockwise around the room. We'll tackle the dresser next. When we get to the clothes on the floor, Josie and I will put them on hangers and hand them to you to put in the closet. You can decide later about laundering or dry cleaning."

To my surprise, the clean-up progressed rapidly. Even Josie dashed around, following her mother's instructions quickly and efficiently. Kate insisted we wipe down the furniture, even the doors and windowsills, with disinfectant and mop the floor. In an hour the room was spotless.

As soon as we'd finished our cleaning, Kate—still in take charge mode—insisted I come home with her and bring what I needed to spend at least one night at her house. I didn't refuse. Jim had implied the intruder had been looking for something besides the duffel bag. How could I be sure he wouldn't come back to search again?

THAT EVENING as Josie and I flopped down in chairs in front of the television, I ran an idea by her. "I'm thinking of going somewhere after work tomorrow. I thought maybe you'd join me."

"Not if it involves cleaning another trashed room," she said.

"It doesn't. You were a big help on that and I owe you. I'm taking a ride over to Lake Luzerne to talk to Connie Leland. She's that cousin of Madeline Hathaway's I told you about, the one who'd like a summer job over here. She's about your age. Maybe you could give her some ideas."

"You got the wrong girl, Lor. I know zip about summer jobs. My mother's making me work for her this year."

"Ride over with me anyway. I think you'll like this kid."

"I doubt it. I'm not big on meeting new people."

"I'll treat you to lunch."

A shrug.

"Might even let you borrow my denim jacket this weekend."

"The new one you just got? The one with the studs? You serious?"

I nodded.

Josie threw me a suspicious glance, but the jacket's lure was too strong to resist. "I suppose it won't hurt me to go. What's this kid got—two heads or something?"

"Nothing like that." I did have a hidden agenda, but I wasn't about to confide in Josie. Connie could use a friend. In the bargain, I might find out a little more about Madeline Hathaway's double life.

THE NEXT DAY I squeezed in a run, spent four hours at the office and arrived back at Kate's just as Josie was rolling out of bed. She'd finagled a day off from her mother by agreeing to accompany me. Then, by not being too specific about the time we'd be leaving, she'd racked up what in my far off adolescence were known as extra Z's.

I'd weighed the pros and cons of contacting Connie in advance and decided to take a chance on surprising her. We found her at home, sprawled in the battered hammock on the porch. I chatted with Uncle Dwight for a few minutes while Josie and Connie eyed each other warily.

"I thought I'd invite Connie out to lunch, Mr. Tanner. Why don't you join us?" I asked him.

"Dwight, please. Call me Dwight. And thank you, no. You young folks run along. You don't need an old codger like me cramping your style."

Josie took my inclusion in the young folk's designation in stride; Connie accepted my invitation; and we headed to the diner for a late lunch—actually a very late breakfast for at least one of our group.

Jane the waitress beamed as she plodded over to our booth to take our order. "Good to see you, Connie. This a new bud?"

Both girls looked stunned by her use of out-of-date slang, so I jumped in with an introduction. "Josie here has some ideas about summer jobs for Connie," I said.

Josie tossed me a withering glance, but stopped short of denouncing me as a liar. Then, as soon as Jane finished taking our order, she set the record straight. "I never said I knew squat about jobs. Waiting tables is great, but they want you to be eighteen. I guess the campgrounds hire younger. You can pitch a tent and stay right there, cook your own food, save a ton of money that way."

Connie brightened at the idea. "But don't I need a car to do that?"

"Yeah, but maybe if someone you know got a job there too, somebody who'd give you a ride…"

I gave her a fast kick under the table and earned another dirty look. I glared right back. The last thing I wanted to do was promote joint summer employment for Connie and Jordan.

As we gobbled our burgers and fries—I'd reluctantly passed on the egg salad this time—the girls slid into an easy exchange. I was congratulating myself on a great idea when the front door of the diner squeaked open and Jordan himself poked his head in. He spotted Connie and took a few steps toward our booth.

Dave let out a roar. "Hey, you. What'd I tell you?"

"Not staying, Dave. Just need a minute or two to talk to Connie." Jordan stopped short, testing Dave's reaction.

"No way. Even a minute's too long. I told you to stay out of here." Dave might have been grossly overweight, but he moved fast. He swung out from behind the counter, brandishing a sawed-off baseball bat he'd picked up en route. Two customers—large, muscular, unsmiling guys—slid off their stools at the counter, ready to jump in as Dave's back-up.

Before Jordan could decide how fast to cut and run, Connie leaped to her feet and grabbed his arm. She shoved him toward the door. "Come on, Jordan, don't be stupid. Do what he says."

As Josie and I stared after them, she opened the door and pushed him through. "Give me a minute," she called back to us over her shoulder.

Josie and I finished our burgers and I ordered a corned beef sandwich to take to Dwight. Through a side window we could see Connie and Jordan, heads together, talking earnestly.

"What are they gonna do—take all day?" Josie tapped her foot to let me know her patience was wearing thin.

When Dwight's sandwich was ready, I asked Jane to wrap the remaining half of Connie's burger and paid the check.

As we walked out, I caught Connie's eye. "We have to get going. Are you about ready?"

It was obvious she wasn't, but she turned away from Jordan and got into my car. She didn't volunteer any information about what he'd wanted, and neither of us asked.

When we reached the house, Connie and Josie dropped down on the shabby old hammock and picked up their conversation. I tapped on the screen door, pushed it open and stuck my head into the living room.

Dwight was huddled in a battered recliner in front of a small television, watching what looked like a baseball game being played in a snowstorm. He took forever opening the Styrofoam container I handed him.

"Why that's right kind of you, Missus. Is this a corned beef sandwich? Dave serves a nice one."

"Can I get you a drink of something, Dwight?" I asked, wishing I'd thought to bring soda or coffee to go with the impromptu lunch.

"A glass of water will be fine. And maybe bring a fork for this potato salad. Dave does a good job with his salads, too."

I scrounged around the shabby little kitchen until I located what he wanted, then added a paper napkin from a holder on the kitchen table.

"This is a real special treat, Missus. Can't thank you

enough. I've got something to give you, too, if you can wait a minute."

I flashed on how long it had taken Dwight to eat his cereal at my house, but this time he didn't delay. He set the container on the table next to him, pushed himself up from the chair and padded off down the hall.

When he returned a few minutes later, he handed me a packet of papers, secured with a rubber band. I hadn't got a close look at what was in the bottom of Madeline's sack, but this packet looked eerily familiar.

"What's this?" I held the papers away from me, reluctant to accept them. Since Madeline's duffel bag had disappeared so fast, I probably shouldn't accept anything else from over here.

"Concerns Connie. Just stick that in your handbag and take it with you. You can look through it at your leisure and we can talk about what to do." He settled back down in his chair and picked up his sandwich.

"But Dwight, are you sure you want to give this to me? Isn't there someone else who should have it?"

"Connie needs a decent person to take an interest in her. You seem willing to do it. Both her parents are gone now, and I'm not going to be around forever."

I didn't jump in with platitudes. I couldn't deny the truth of what he'd said. Connie had lost both of her parents. Now Madeline Hathaway, another adult who'd been kind to her, was gone, too. The girl did need someone to take an interest in her. I just wasn't sure I wanted to be the one to do it.

TWENTY-EIGHT

ON THE WAY BACK to Emerald Point, I pulled off the road and called the hospital on my cell. Don had been awake for longer periods, the ICU nurse told me. He seemed clearer, more focused and he'd asked for me several times. And no, as far as she knew, his brother hadn't been there.

It was almost five when I dropped Josie off. "Tell your mother I'll stay at my own house tonight. I'll call her later."

"I don't think she'll be here. She's doing a party on one of the boats. She'll probably be late."

"What about you? Are you supposed to work tonight, too?" I hadn't thought to ask earlier.

"Yeah. I guess."

"Josie, you should have told me. We could have been back before this."

"No problem. Plenty of time."

"You told me you had the day off. I didn't think about the evening." Kate had probably set a time for Josie to be home, and she hadn't bothered to mention it.

"Lor, it's okay. Don't sweat it." She shoved the car door open and slid out.

I didn't want to take Kate's time then with an apology, but I probably owed her one. The parties and wedding receptions she catered on the lake steamers brought in a big portion of her annual income. Josie should have been helping with the prep work instead of traipsing around with me. Teenagers—I didn't know if they were all so exasperating or if Josie had cornered the market on irresponsible behavior. Connie came across as a conscientious youngster, always concerned about her uncle. Or, was I only seeing part of the picture?

On the drive to Glens Falls, I continued sputtering to myself about Josie. Dwight Tanner's packet remained tucked in my pocketbook. I was in no rush to open it. I'd learned something about old people's treasures when I cleaned out my grandfather's house after he died. Several times I thought I'd stumbled on important documents only to realize my grandfather had saved things for reasons I couldn't discern. My first priority tonight was to check on Don at the hospital. Dwight's papers—whatever they were—could wait until later.

I steeled myself when I tiptoed into Don's ICU cubicle. Once again, the sight of him unnerved me. In the soft light of early evening, the bruises on his face appeared as garish as they had the night before, but he turned his head toward me with an expectant look. His dark eyes, brighter and more alert, flashed a look of recognition. He even managed a crooked half smile.

He knew me. I smiled down at him and took his hand. "You seem better today."

Another attempt at a smile.

"How do you feel?"

He struggled to speak, finally managed a hoarse whisper. "I made dinner."

I groped for a response. "Dinner?"

"The sauce…cooked longer…like how it turned out."

I pulled a chair next to his bed and sat down close to him.

"Don, do you know you're in the hospital?"

He glanced around the room. His voice was no more than a wisp of sound. "Good to me here."

"Do you know why you're here? Do you remember those guys beating you?"

"Stephen. They...beat...Stephen."

I could hardly make out the words. "Wait. What are you saying? Is that why Stephen isn't here?"

Don didn't answer. He grabbed my wrist. His eyes didn't focus the way they should.

With my free hand I reached for the buzzer and pressed it. "It's all right, Don. Don't try to talk."

Again he could barely get out the words. "...Stephen."

The nurse's voice crackled from the intercom. "Yes. Can I help you?"

"Could you come in, please? Right away?"

She arrived in seconds. I stepped back away from the bed and whispered to her. "He's talking about his brother and what he's saying doesn't make much sense. He's very agitated. I don't know why."

The nurse moved close to him. "Mr. Morrison, you don't look very comfortable. Let's see if I can fix your bed a little."

"What's wrong?" I asked her.

"Maybe it will help if I sponge him off."

I retired to the doorway while she repositioned Don in the bed and filled a basin with water. With quick, deft movements she turned him onto his side. She bathed him gently, changed the sheet under him, then substituted a fresh gown for the rumpled one he was wearing. As she worked, she spoke quietly to him. He grew calmer, his breathing slowed, became deeper, more regular. I could almost see his body relax.

"I'll wait outside," I told her. As I was entering the waiting area, Stephen and Elaine stepped off the elevator. "Stephen, Don seemed worried about you. Is everything all right?" I said.

"What's happened? Is he worse?"

"I don't know. I thought he looked better, but then he became very agitated. He acted very confused."

Elaine touched my arm. "Let's go to the waiting room for a minute. Stephen can check on him."

"He tried to tell me something, but he couldn't get the words out," I said as I followed her into the waiting room and sat down on the couch.

Elaine sat across from me, just as she had the evening before. This time she leaned in even closer and took my hand. "And it's upset you. I can see that. Do you think he's worse tonight? Is that what's bothering you?"

Her sympathetic tone loosened some of the knots inside me. "I don't know. He acts so confused. It's hard seeing him like this, so hurt and bruised, so different from his usual self."

She patted my hand. "I'm not sure why you put yourself through this. Aren't you furious at him? I thought you two had something good together."

"I thought so, too," I admitted.

"I admire your loyalty, but you could spare yourself a little. Stephen will be here every night."

Was there something she wasn't saying? "Do you think I upset him?"

"You can understand why you might, can't you? He's bound to feel guilty about what's happened."

"I don't know how he feels. He hasn't been able to tell

me." I pulled my hand away. Was she suggesting my visits made Don worse?

"Think about it, Loren, why don't you? Give yourself a little time."

Elaine had hit a nerve, but that didn't make her wrong. "You may be right. I could ask his nurse what she thinks."

She grimaced. "Don't expect her to tell you. Nurses never say anything definite. People have to make their own decisions in matters like this."

At that moment, I didn't want to decide anything. I wanted to get away as fast as I could. I stood up. "I'm ready to leave anyway."

Before Elaine could respond, I hurried out of the waiting room and back into the unit. Don's nurse emerged from his cubicle. "He's asleep, Loren. His brother plans to sit with him for a while. You look tired. Why don't you go along?"

Elaine's thought exactly, although the nurse had expressed it more gently. I turned on my heel and marched out.

On the ride home I calmed down enough to re-examine the situation. Elaine had meant well, even if I wasn't ready to accept her advice. I might not like hearing what she had to say, but that didn't make her wrong. Even the nurse had urged me to leave. Was it easier for me to forgive than for Don to be forgiven? Could I really be doing him more harm than good by going there?

I got the picture. I'd been designated persona non grata and I wasn't sure why.

TWENTY-NINE

When I pulled into Emerald Point that night, I couldn't face going home.

What I needed was a cheerful place to hang out, if only for an hour or two. But where? I didn't miss New York's night life much any more until occasions like this made me realize how limited my options were now. Kate would be tied up at her party; I hadn't reached the desperation level I needed for Thursday night bingo; and a solitary pizza at Mario's wasn't much better than a lonely supper at home.

Luckily, I had an idea. Diane, as part of a foreign film festival she'd organized, was showing an Italian comedy at the community center. I could still catch the last reel. The subtitles would force me to pay attention. I couldn't watch the screen, read dialogue and consider what to do about Don all at the same time

At nine o'clock I slipped though the unlocked front door of the center and headed for the stairs leading down to the auditorium. The exhibit area, illuminated only by the light from the hall, lay in shadow. I glanced quickly toward the display case. No body there tonight. Rogers and his Rangers, unperturbed by dangers past or present, stood their ground, their muskets pointed into the trees at an invisible enemy. As far as I knew, the man I'd seen in the case still hadn't been identified. Perhaps the disappearing body and Madeline Hathaway's murder were destined to remain our town's unsolved mysteries.

Downstairs, I slid into a seat at the rear of the auditorium and tried to pick up a sense of the film. Five minutes later the credits began to roll and the half-dozen people in the audience got to their feet and filed out. The speed of their departure didn't speak well for Diane's selection.

"How much of it did you catch?" Diane asked as soon as she spied me.

"Sorry. Just got here."

"I don't know that you should be sorry. That was only half the crowd. The rest didn't stick it out 'til the end— always a bad sign."

"Well, it is a workday tomorrow." I picked up some of the dirty coffee cups from a side table and carried them into the little kitchen.

"For some, maybe, but we had a group of seniors who don't have that problem. They were out of here in the first half-hour. I swear they only came for the cookies."

"Did you hide any? I'm starving."

"Sorry. All gone. How about we grab a bite at Mario's?"

"I thought you'd never ask."

Our shared pizza at Mario's proved to be the antidote we both needed. After I'd bolstered Diane's confidence in her film selecting abilities, she listened to my report on Don's condition and Elaine Morrison's suggestion that I not visit him for a while.

Listened and, like the good friend she'd become, landed squarely on my side. "You have to do what you think best, Loren. Didn't you tell me Don doesn't see that much of her and his brother anyway? How can she be so sure what's right for him?"

"Still, I do seem to upset him."

"Guilty conscience. He should be upset. Never mind what anybody else says. Make your own decision."

I left the restaurant in much better spirits, but I still had another hurdle to jump. Walking into my house a half hour before midnight would present a challenge, but I had to face it. As I unlocked the kitchen door and switched on the light, I braced myself for signs of another break-in. Nothing out of order. One by one I turned on the down-stairs lights and double-checked the doors. So far so good, I told myself as I headed upstairs. My bedroom, to my relief, looked exactly the way Kate, Josie and I had left it—fit for the cover of House Beautiful.

For the first time that day, I felt the tension drain away. As I undressed for bed, I heard the familiar putt-putt of the little outboard going past on its nightly run. The sound drifted in through my windows, familiar and comforting. I never thought about how late it was for someone to be out on the lake.

THE NEXT MORNING while I drank my coffee, I leafed through the papers Dwight Tanner had given me. As I'd suspected, they looked to be family keepsakes—old, but valuable only for sentimental reasons. I riffled through them quickly, my curiosity dulling as I went along. I'd check them all over, I decided, then stick them in a drawer and be done with them.

I picked up the final document. The paper, heavier than the rest and folded into squares, had an official look. I unfolded it carefully and smoothed the creases. My mind reeled as I skimmed through it. I read it again slowly, struggling to digest the information it contained, trying to relate it to the events of the last few days. That one little piece of paper changed everything.

Now, I viewed everything which had happened in a different light. The circumstances surrounding Madeline's life and death—her affair, her murder, the appearance of her relatives at the memorial service, Don's beating—everything had to be reconsidered, reexamined in light of this new information.

I didn't want Dwight's papers to meet the same fate as the duffel bag. When I left for work, I locked them in the glove compartment of my car and parked the car under my office window where I could keep an eye on it. That afternoon I checked to be sure they were still there before I rushed to the ICU. My mind whirled with new questions, questions I hoped Don could answer once his thinking became clearer.

When I entered the cubicle, he turned toward me, smiling as if he actually recognized me. Still, I reminded myself, I'd thought that before. Was this another case of wishful thinking on my part? But his smile seemed more genuine, his color better. His eyes looked different, too—brighter, more alert. Even the bruises on his face had faded to a less shocking color.

"You look more like yourself today." I smiled as I approached the bed.

He reached out his hand to me and whispered my name. He spoke slowly, his words still no more than puffs of sound. "Here every day…they said. Sorry…out of it."

Relief flooded through me. I softly touched his hand on the one spot which wasn't black and blue. "You don't have to apologize to me. I know more now about what's been going on. I'm the one who owes you an apology."

"Stupid…poor choices…got called on them…" His words, though halting and indistinct, made sense.

I leaned closer. "Haven't they told you not to talk? You sound like your vocal chords are strained."

"Got to…tell you."

I pulled up a chair and sat down. I lowered my head and put my ear a few inches from his mouth. "Only if you can do it in twenty-five words or less. That's all I'm allowing you."

He almost managed it.

THIRTY

WHEN I LEFT the hospital that afternoon, I knew exactly what I had to do. I drove directly to the Northway, but instead of turning north toward Emerald Point, I swung left onto the southbound ramp. The fifty-minute trip to Albany rushed by in a blur as I sorted through the facts Don had given me and filled in the blanks as best I could. At the last exit, I followed Western Avenue past the New York State University campus and headed downtown. In one of our conversations, Stephen had told me where his engineering firm was located, and in his usual scientific manner, he'd provided explicit directions.

Cars and buses jammed the Albany streets; sidewalks overflowed with pedestrians. Emerald Point never experienced congestion like this. Would we want it, no matter how much business it promised? In spite of what people said at our meetings, I couldn't imagine what an influx like this would mean for our little town. Yet, even with the heavy traffic, I located Stephen's building easily and squeezed into the one remaining space in its parking lot.

I wasn't sure what I expected to find in the Morrison Engineering offices—blueprints and contour maps, maybe. Instead, I entered a waiting room as spacious and well-appointed as the lobby of a five-star hotel.

The receptionist behind the gleaming mahogany counter

eyed me with misgivings. My casual slacks and sweater rated a quick grimace of disapproval. I got the message— not properly dressed for a visit to the Morrison headquarters. Before I'd finished my request, she interrupted me. "I'm afraid Mr. Morrison will be tied up all afternoon. He can't be disturbed."

Too haughty for my taste. I mentioned that I was mayor of a nearby community and a personal acquaintance of the owner. I caught a flicker of doubt in her eyes, just enough uncertainty to get me passed on to Mr. Morrison's private secretary, who ratcheted the disdain level up another notch.

I pulled myself up to my full five feet and eight inches and tried to intimidate her with the withering look I'd perfected for troublemakers at Common Council meetings. "Please tell him the matter is urgent. I must see him right now."

She hesitated again.

No way was I backing down. "I'm quite sure if you tell him the urgent matter concerns his brother, he'll appreciate the interruption," I said.

That statement swayed her. She spoke into the intercom. In seconds Stephen Morrison, in a navy suit as elegant as his office, peered out a door at the far end of the room. He greeted me warily.

"Loren, has something more happened?"

When I didn't reply, he ushered me into an interior hallway without further comment. As soon as he'd closed his office door behind us, his face changed. "Oh God, have you come to tell me Don is dead?"

"No. No. In fact, he's a little better today."

"You've seen him today?"

"Yes, I have." I understood the reason for his wife's advice now. So I hadn't taken it. Too bad.

I perched on one of his visitor's chairs and studied his face while he sat down behind his desk. On the way from Glens Falls, I'd planned what I was going to say, but by this time I'd built up such a head of steam, I couldn't predict how my words would come out. I kept things simple. "Stephen, I know."

He tried for a puzzled look, but couldn't pull it off. "What do you know?"

"I know you were the one involved with Madeline."

"Don told you that?"

"He didn't have to. I saw the papers. You're Connie Leland's father."

His face registered a series of emotions, but he didn't speak.

Since he didn't ask, I didn't tell him how I'd happened to see the papers. "You dated Madeline sixteen years ago and you've been seeing her again. You used Don's truck when you drove to Lake Luzerne to be with her. Didn't you realize everyone, especially Ted, would think Don and Madeline were having an affair?"

He continued to stare at me, as if he couldn't process what I was saying.

"All the time you were the one she was involved with," I went on, my anger building with every word. "You let your own brother take the blame. Even after those men beat him up, almost killed him, you didn't admit to what you'd done. You must have suspected Ted Hathaway was behind that beating, and you still didn't tell anyone."

He dropped his head into his hands. "I know. I know. He had someone following Maddy and, because of the truck, it looked like she met Don at that motel. You can't be any more appalled about this than I am. I didn't plan it this way, you know."

I bit hard on my lip, choked back other accusations I could have made. Maybe he didn't plan what had happened, but did that make him any less responsible? Don had whispered the essential facts, but my mind still whirled with unanswered questions.

"I never thought somebody would come after Don," he insisted.

"Why not? You borrowed his truck and you parked it out behind that motel. That way if Ted tracked her, you'd be in the clear."

"No. That's not why I borrowed the truck. If I'd parked my Jag at that motel, everybody would have noticed it. I needed something less conspicuous. Maddy never thought Ted would follow her there. She went to Luzerne a lot to help out her uncle. Ted accepted that."

I kept pushing. "You knew Madeline years ago and she got pregnant. Isn't that how all this started?"

He took a deep breath, then blurted out the answer. "Yes, but I didn't know. I didn't know about the baby."

That surprised me. "You didn't stay in touch with her?"

"Loren, I was seventeen the summer I met her. I'd come up here from White Plains for a job as a counselor at a boys' camp near where she lived. We started going together—a summer romance. I was crazy about her, but I was still in high school. She was a couple of years older, beautiful. I couldn't believe she was interested in me. I spent every minute with her when I wasn't working. But we both knew it couldn't go anywhere. She'd leveled with me about that right from the beginning."

"Because you were so young?"

He nodded. "Exactly. Maddy spelled it out for me our first time together. She said she had to marry someone established…somebody who could take care of her."

"Take care of her?"

"Somebody with money. Her parents were losers. She was determined to make a better life for herself. Never made any secret of that."

The intercom buzzed. Stephen signaled for me not to speak while he answered. "Yes, yes. Put him in the conference room. Tell him I'll be right there."

I didn't let his words deter me. This was probably his standard procedure for getting rid of unwelcome visitors. I picked up the conversation where we'd left off. "You were saying she wanted a better life. Then she got pregnant?"

"Yes, but I didn't know it. That's the truth. I left at the end of the summer. If she knew then she was pregnant, she didn't tell me. And she'd insisted we couldn't stay in touch."

"Then when did you find out Connie was your child?"

He hesitated, then said, "Maddy contacted me. Last fall, I guess it was. She'd met Don at a party and realized he was my brother. She wanted to tell me about Connie. Her cousin and his wife had adopted her, and both of them had passed away. Except for her elderly uncle, the girl doesn't have anybody."

I was trying to understand. "Madeline put your baby up for adoption and you never knew?"

"Her cousins wanted a child. They couldn't have one of their own and they'd been trying to adopt. She let them have the baby."

"Stephen, are you sure this is your child?"

"Yes. Maddy insisted last fall I have some tests. Wanted me to be sure."

"But didn't you have to agree to the adoption, sign papers or something?"

"She got around that somehow. Told them the father had skipped out on her. I expect she already had her eye on Ted Hathaway. He used to come to the paper mill in Corinth on business. She never told him about the baby, not for a long time." His voice had steadied, but his hands shook as he pawed though the papers on his desk and slid several into a briefcase.

"You mean Ted himself only found out about Connie recently?" That possibility set my thoughts stampeding in a whole new direction. Had Ted killed Madeline in a rage when he learned about her illegitimate child?

"No. He knew when they bought the house on Emerald Point. He agreed to the move so Maddy could be near Connie but he made her promise she'd never tell people at the lake she was her mother. The adoptive parents were Maddy's cousins, remember, so it didn't seem strange that she'd keep an eye on the child after they died."

"But then how did you find out?" I was trying to understand.

"She met Don at a party and realized he was my brother. She asked him how to get in touch with me. Then she came to my office and told me about Connie, said her adoptive parents had died and she wanted me to know about her. That was all."

"All? How can you say that was all?"

"At first it was. Then we started feeling the same way we did years ago. We began seeing each other. We tried not to let anyone find out. She didn't want to hurt Ted. I felt the same way about Elaine. She stuck by me through some really rough times."

The intercom buzzed again.

He grabbed the briefcase and slid out from behind the desk. "Look. This will have to wait. I've got an important client scheduled. You've got to go."

"Fine. As long as you understand I'm going to make sure Investigator Thompson knows about this."

"I expect you'll find he already does know most of it. There's no reason for you to be involved in this, none whatsoever. I plan to straighten everything out." He stood next to my chair, waiting to escort me out.

The don't-get-involved advice reiterated what Elaine had said at the hospital. This time the meaning remained the same, but the words had a sharper edge. Butt out. Both Stephen and his wife wanted me out of their lives and they wanted to be sure I got the message.

I shoved back my chair and stood up, scowling, letting my face register how disgusted I was. "You'll straighten everything out? Great idea. You've managed things well so far. One person dead and another close to it."

To my amazement, he smiled down at me as he walked me to the door. "You seem to be blaming me for things that aren't my fault, Loren. Perhaps when you've had a chance to think this through…"

"And just how will that change anything? Can you tell me what possible difference that could make?" I wrenched open the door.

After our conversation, I was even angrier than I'd been when I arrived. Whatever sympathy I'd started to feel for Stephen had vanished. After his initial surprise that I'd learned his secret and his brief show of regret over his brother's beating, he'd retreated behind a supercilious manner which infuriated me. He hadn't expressed one word of sorrow over Madeline's death. These two people had loved one other, conceived a child together, separated, and then found each other again years later. What must it have meant to Madeline when Stephen came back into her life? Had she found the long-lost love she'd never forgotten or had she simply exchanged one cold, controlling man for another? Maybe Stephen Morrison wasn't so different from Ted Hathaway after all.

THIRTY-ONE

ON THE DRIVE HOME I calmed down enough to consider how this new information meshed with what I already knew. Madeline had been a poor girl who had wanted a better life. She'd given up her baby, hoping that decision would be the best thing for both of them. I couldn't fault her for that. She'd kept track of the child and when the adoptive parents died, she had moved nearby and found ways to be part of her daughter's life. To me, her actions seemed admirable.

The Madeline Hathaway I'd come to know over the last two years had been a vivacious woman, well-liked by everyone and quick to volunteer in community activities. Gossip had linked her to several local men, but no one could come up with any hard facts. If she'd used her committee work as a screen for extramarital affairs, she'd managed her deceptions well.

What I hadn't known until today was the role Stephen Morrison had played in her life. This afternoon in his office he'd confirmed what Don had whispered to me at the hospital. Last fall Madeline had met Don at a party and realized he was Stephen's brother. Through him, she'd been able to contact Stephen and tell him about his daughter. They'd met and, before long, their old feelings had come rushing back.

As the sheriff's investigator in charge of Madeline Hathaway's murder case, Jim Thompson probably knew more details, but did I want to talk to him right now? I couldn't very well stop at his office without turning over the packet Dwight Tanner had given me. Before I found the birth certificate, I'd thought the other papers unimportant. But maybe if I took more time...if I went through them again...

I passed the exit for the Municipal Center without a qualm.

By the time I pulled into my driveway, I was experiencing serious let-down from the day's events. After the theft of the duffel bag, I didn't want to take a chance by keeping Dwight's packet in the house. I'd leave it locked in the glove compartment, I decided, and go through it once more in the morning after a good night's sleep.

I grabbed a cold drink from the refrigerator and went straight to the porch for some badly needed decompression time. The lake lay tranquil, its surface a sheet of hammered silver under a darkening sky. Pink-tipped clouds, stacked above the mountains on the east side, clung to the last vestiges of sunset light. A perfect twilight, the kind Wordsworth eulogized. I had everything needed for serenity, but I was too restless to sit still. I wandered out to the kitchen and fixed a salad.

When I heard a knock at my back door fifteen minutes later, I rushed to it eagerly, delighted at the prospect of a guest. Ramona Dolley peered at me through the screen.

"Ramona, I'm so glad to see you. I need company, need it bad." I pulled her into the kitchen.

"I doubt you need the news I'm bringin' you, Loren, but I had to tell you. He's back."

I stared at her blankly. "Back? Who's back?"

Ramona settled herself at the kitchen table. "The fellow

who rented the cabin from me the night you saw that man in the display case. I just know it's the same guy you saw."

I slid into the chair across from her. I needed a minute to jump-start my memory. Finding the man in the case—upsetting as it had been—now seemed part of another lifetime; its importance paled in comparison to Madeline's murder and Don's savage beating.

A week had passed after I'd seen the man in the display case before Ramona told me about the stranger who'd rented her cabin the same night. At that point, I'd thought her suspicions a bit farfetched. When her mystery tenant moved out before I could take a look at him, I'd considered the problem solved.

"This time you've got to check him out," she insisted. "I couldn't believe my eyes when he knocked on my door. I wanted to tell him I didn't have anything to rent, but I was afraid he'd think I was on to him. I told him I didn't do breakfast any more, but he still took the cabin."

"Ramona, I don't know. I'm not sure I'd recognize him even if I looked him straight in the eye."

She held up her hand to stop me. "I've set things up so you can do that very thing. I told him to go to Kate's for breakfast and he asked if she'd be open by seven. I gave him the directions and I expect he'll be there."

"So all you want me to do is stop at the coffee shop tomorrow morning and see if he looks familiar? I guess I could do that." At least she wasn't asking me to peek in the cabin window.

"Call me the minute you get to your office and we'll figure out what to do next. I made him print out his name this time so I'd be sure of it. It's Leonard Westerhall." She pulled a scrap of paper out of her pocket and shoved it across the table.

I studied the name. "Westerhall. Any family by that name around here?"

"No. And I wish I knew why he's come back. I'm locking my door tonight, let me tell you."

After I'd walked Ramona to her car, I paced around the house, still on edge, It wouldn't hurt me to check out the guy, I told myself, even if I didn't expect to recognize him. Ramona would feel better if I did it, and maybe I would, too.

Not ready for bed, I stretched out in the hammock on the screened porch and leafed though a *Newsweek* in the circle of light cast by the old-fashioned bridge lamp, a rewired relic from my grandparents' time. I luxuriated in the cool breeze off the lake and the muted sounds of a summer evening—the slow wash of waves against the dock, the soft stir of leaves, the scurrying of a night creature in the yard. Even the ragged putt-putt of the little motor boat slipping by on its nightly trip added to the gentle symphony. I felt myself dozing off.

I CAME AWAKE with a jolt, my heart pounding. I'd heard a noise of some kind, but I couldn't tell where it was coming from. A voice whispered my name. The hammock creaked as I bolted up to a sitting position. I stared into the dark yard.

"Loren," the voice hissed again. A figure stood on the steps outside the door, a shadowy form silhouetted against the screen.

"What? Who is it? What do you want?"

"I didn't mean to startle you. I knocked on the back door, but you didn't hear me."

"Who is it?" I asked again. I tried to calculate how long it had been since Ramona had left. Wasn't it too late for company?

"It's Elaine, Elaine Morrison. I drove up for a meeting

near here. I took a chance you'd be up. I guess it's later than I thought."

"I must have fallen asleep," I said.

"I'm so sorry if I've disturbed you. I only meant to visit for a couple of minutes."

"What time is it?" I muttered, but I was waking up enough to be curious. "Are you here about Don? Is he worse tonight?"

"No. If anything, he's a little better. Come outside, why don't you? I bet you have a beautiful view down by the water and those chairs look comfortable. Can we sit there? I won't stay long."

I slid back the bolt on the screen door. Neither the bolt nor the door was sturdy, but now when I was alone at night I liked the feeling a locked door gave me.

Elaine spun around and floated down the slate steps toward the Adirondack chairs near the dock. The pearl gray silk of her tunic and slacks shimmered in the moonlight. Her dark hair hung loose over her shoulders. She didn't look back to see if I was following her.

She sank down effortlessly into one of the Adirondack chairs. "Don is awake. I guess you talked with him earlier today."

"Briefly. He could barely speak." I took the chair next to her.

"Fortunately, that's temporary. We had a long talk with his doctor." She launched into a rundown of Don's injuries and the problems he'd have to deal with during his convalescence.

What had happened to that promise of a short visit? "Elaine, I'm sorry, but I'm half asleep. Could we talk about this tomorrow?"

"Of course. But I want to apologize to you for something before I go. I misled you. I guess you know now Stephen had a thing with Madeline Hathaway."

Misled? A thing? I was too tired for word games. Why couldn't we speak the truth? I didn't reply.

"I'm really sorry we didn't keep you in the loop," she continued. "For a while Stephen thought the less said the better. I went along with him. I guess you know now he's Connie Leland's father."

"Has he admitted that to you?"

"Yes. I don't think there's any question about that. It happened a long time ago, before I knew him. I have no problem with it."

A long time ago? Didn't Elaine know Stephen and Madeline had been seeing each other again? Or now that Madeline was dead, had she decided to rewrite that part of their history? I didn't have a clue.

"We both want to help the child financially," she continued, "but we'd like to avoid any messy legal problems, anything public you might say."

"Such as...?" I shifted in the hard wooden chair. The breeze had more bite here by the lake. Elaine seemed oblivious of the chill, but I felt a shiver run through me.

"Who knows what Ted Hathaway is capable of?" she said. "Stephen wants to handle everything quietly by himself—if you'd just leave it to him."

"And not interfere, you mean?" The same message Stephen himself had given me in his office.

She nodded. "Well, I suppose you could put it that way. We see this as an extremely delicate matter, best left to Stephen's attorneys to deal with."

"And what about Don? He took a pretty hard hit in this thing. Does he agree with his brother?"

"Of course, he's in total agreement. You can talk this all over with him the next time you visit him."

"I'll do that." Maybe she did have a point. Maybe it would it be best to leave the matter to Stephen and his attorneys. Elaine had gone out of her way to drive up here to talk to me. I probably should give her the benefit of the doubt.

She sat quietly for a few more minutes, then stood up and gazed out at the water. "You have a spectacular location here, don't you? The lake is amazingly beautiful at night. You must enjoy it."

"Very much." Too tired for small talk, I left it at that.

"Well, good night. Sorry I woke you." Without further comment, she turned away and climbed the slate steps to the lawn. She cut across the grass to where her Mercedes was parked, paused and gave me a cheery wave. As I reached the porch, I heard her start the engine and pull away.

Once inside, I slipped the bolt on the porch door, stepped into the hall and locked the door to the house. The downstairs lay in shadow, illuminated only by a low light in the kitchen. For the second time that week, I stood staring into a familiar space in disbelief. This time it was my cozy living room which had been ripped apart, trashed even worse than the bedroom had been. Desktop swept clean; desk drawers dumped; papers and books scattered across the floor. Cushions from the couch and chairs were tossed around the room. Even the magazine rack was upended with my magazines and newspapers strewn about.

Another break-in. Another frantic search, apparently for something the intruder hadn't found in the canvas bag of Madeline's possessions or in my bedroom. But this invasion had happened within the last couple of hours, while I was home, either when I was dozing on the porch or when I'd walked down to the dock with Elaine. My intruder was growing much too bold. I reached for the phone.

THIRTY-TWO

A HALF HOUR LATER, Sheriff's Deputy Rick Cronin fired off a string of questions as he surveyed my living room. "You never left the premises all evening, Mayor? You say you spent most of the time on the porch and didn't hear a thing?"

"I can't believe it either," I told him. "A breeze came up after sunset and the waves were a little louder than usual, but I think I would have heard somebody dumping drawers and flinging stuff around in here."

"Your back door was locked. You're sure of that?"

"Yes. I've been double checking since the break-in."

"And you're sure you didn't hear anything, anything at all?"

"Nothing. Unless…"

Rick pulled his notebook out of his uniform pocket. "Unless what? Investigator Thompson isn't going to be over here until tomorrow morning, but he'll want me to have a full report on his desk when he gets to the office."

"I sat down by the dock for a short time with Elaine Morrison. She could have joined me on the porch, but she suggested we go down there."

"Are you implying she lured you away from the house?"

"Rick, I'm not sure what to think. I didn't understand why she came here so late in the first place."

"Lots of strange things happening to you these days, Mayor. Here we just get one of them figured out and something else happens."

"You figured something out?" I didn't mean to sound surprised by his disclosure, but I probably did.

"Didn't Jim tell you? We found out who set off that cherry bomb at your center opening. It was a kid named Jay Brown. Wanted to look cool in front of Josie Donohue, I guess."

"Jay Brown, the one with the contour map?"

"Yeah. He's not a bad kid. Jim gave him a talking to, scared the daylights out of him."

"Well maybe Jim should try the same thing with Elaine Morrison, see what might come out of that. She claimed I didn't hear her knocking on the back door, so she came around to the front. But I wonder how she knew I was on the porch? She couldn't have seen me from out back."

"Look, why don't you let me take you to a friend's house for the night. You don't want to stay here alone and you don't want to touch anything until the crime scene crew gets here tomorrow to check for prints and such."

Twelve-thirty in the morning wasn't a great time to drop in on people, but I did have a place to go. Goodhearted Kate had issued a standing invitation for me to come back any time, take the key out of the mailbox and sleep on her couch.

After Rick and I checked upstairs and found nothing disturbed, I thanked him for his offer of a lift but insisted on driving myself to Kate's. With the envelope Dwight Tanner had given me still locked in my glove compartment, I figured I'd better keep my car close by.

SHORTLY AFTER NINE the next morning, I pulled into my driveway and found Sheriff's Investigator Jim Thompson leaning on his car waiting for me.

The sight of him threatened to send me over the edge. His hair glistened, still damp from the shower; his slacks displayed the usual knife-edge creases; his shoes shone with fresh polish. I was un-showered, un-pressed and un-rested after hours spent tossing on Kate's lumpy sofa. Then, to add to my wretched state, I'd fallen asleep at dawn and awakened too late to stop for coffee and still get back here by the time Rick had set.

"Damn it, Jim, this is too much," I said as I stomped over to him.

"I couldn't agree more." Jim might look picture-perfect, but his irritability quotient—thanks to this new development—was threatening to spiral off the charts. The twitching in his jaw signaled an explosion was imminent.

Okay. I'd light the fuse. I pulled the papers Connie's uncle had given me out of my glove compartment and shoved them at him. "I suppose these are what the burglar was searching for. Dwight Tanner gave them to me, insisted I take them."

As Jim flipped through the bundle, the twitching increased at an alarming rate. "Maybe if you'd showed me these right away…"

Not the best response to someone in my state of mind. "What? Stephen Morrison claims you knew he was Connie's father anyway. And so did everyone else involved. Why would the papers be such a big deal that someone would break into my house looking for them?"

Jim's jaw movements accelerated into super-sized

spasms of clenching. "Maybe if you'd quit figuring and leave the police work to the professionals..."

"What? What would happen?" My voice rose half an octave higher, but I couldn't calm down. "As far as I can see, you're getting nowhere. My house has been burglarized twice, and somehow it's all my fault. That's a pretty clear-cut case of blaming the victim, isn't it?"

Jim's eyes glinted like two chunks of black ice. His jaw clenching subsided, probably an even worse sign.

Luckily, Rick Cronin picked that exact moment to come bounding out my kitchen door. "Mind if I borrow her for a minute, Jim?" he asked.

Jim did a masterful job of recovering his cool.

"Be my guest. Keep her as long as you like...give me time to go through these papers."

Rick and I examined my trashed living room one more time. The crime scene guys lifted some fingerprints—probably mine—and we called it a day. This time Kate wasn't on hand to help deal with the mess and I wasn't going for a Homemaker of the Year Award. I tidied up just enough to clear a path through the living room and left it at that. I knew exactly what I was going to do next.

THE MINUTE JIM, Rick and the fingerprint crew left, I brewed a pot of coffee, guzzled down enough of it to activate my sleep-deprived brain cells and stood in the shower until the hot water ran out. Once I felt semi-human, I made a careful reexamination of what had happened.

Not only had I missed my chance to check out Ramona's tenant as I'd promised to do, I'd been ignoring what was right under my nose. I'd let myself be distracted by Don's beating, his brother's ties to Madeline and my growing feelings of sympathy for Connie and Uncle Dwight. For the root cause of this mess, I needed to go back to Ted Hathaway. What did he know about his wife's affair with Stephen Morrison and when did he know it? He'd been quick enough about approaching me for information after Madeline was killed. Why couldn't I ask him a few questions right now?

Despite my recent resolve not to impose on Pauline, I called her and asked her to cover the office that morning. I left an apologetic message on Ramona's answering machine, explaining why I hadn't been able to check out her tenant then drove to Ted's house. No phone call in advance. I didn't want him forewarned.

My plan got off to a good start. Ted's Lexus was parked under the portico and he answered the door himself. An auspicious beginning.

I didn't waste time on preliminaries. "Ted, I've been pulled into something I don't understand. I want to know what the hell is going on."

"Going on? I have no idea what you're talking about." He stiffened, glowered as if he were ready to slam the door in my face.

No way was I going to let that happen. I stepped over the threshold and squeezed past him into the foyer. "The young girl you referred to as Madeline's cousin—Connie Leland. I'd like to know more about her background."

"I'm not sure that's any of your concern."

Fighting words to a woman who had been awake most of the night. "Look, you asked me to find out what was going on with Madeline. The girl came to my house with her uncle the day of your reception. They were stuck without a ride home. I took them back to Luzerne."

"So?"

"So, that started me wondering about her connection to Madeline."

"And now you expect me to tell you?" His tone was wary, but he motioned me into the living room.

I took a deep breath, made an effort to hide my annoyance. "Ted, you asked me who Madeline was seeing, remember? You brought the subject up. I don't think it's unreasonable for me to ask you a question as well."

Ted gestured toward a chair and sat down in one next to it. "Consider the circumstances. At the time I asked you that question, Madeline had just been killed. I had no idea who'd done it. Surely you can understand my reaction."

"You admitted you quarreled with Madeline the night she was killed. It's not much of a stretch to conclude you were arguing about the man she was involved with."

"So you think I should explain?" Ted stood and walked quickly to a bar in the corner of the room. He poured himself a Scotch rocks and, without asking if I wanted a drink, filled another glass with wine.

"See how you like that," he said, thrusting the glass at me. "A French import. A new winery promoting it. Should earn a top rating."

The crystal glass sparkled in the sunlight. Like everything in the Hathaway home, it was elegant, expensive. Under different circumstances, I would have liked to try the wine, but not at eleven o'clock in the morning and under orders. I set the glass on the occasional table next to me. "You were about to explain something."

Ted tried a small, conspiratorial smile. "You're from the city. I expect you can understand this, whereas other people around here can't."

"Can't? I've found people here understand just about anything."

"Well, you never can be sure of small-town reactions. Madeline and I had an open marriage. Neither of us was against an occasional discreet affair. We both understood our arrangement perfectly, but we didn't advertise it."

I frowned, letting him see how much his remark puzzled me. "But Ted, I find that hard to believe. When you came to my house and asked me who Madeline was seeing, you were very upset."

"Place that conversation in context, Loren. Madeline had been murdered. I assumed the man she'd been seeing had killed her."

"And do you still think that?" I knew he wasn't telling the truth. What had Ellen Davies told me? Ted was jealous, obsessively so. Ellen didn't believe Ted and Madeline had anything close to an open marriage.

"Of course, that person would be a logical choice. Unfortunately, Jim Thompson refuses to acknowledge the possibility, at least to me."

Dead end there. I tried another question. "Ted, the girl who came to Madeline's memorial service—Connie Leland. Do you know who her parents were?"

His face darkened as he dropped his pretense of a cordial exchange. "Is this your way of telling me you do?"

I nodded. "I know she was Madeline's child."

"All right. It's not a secret. She was Madeline's child, fathered by some country bumpkin who worked at a summer camp near her home. A mess she cleaned up as best she could. She moved on."

"Moved on?" I said with surprise. "I understood she came back to the area because of Connie."

"The girl's circumstances changed and Madeline wanted to keep an eye on her, wanted to be sure she was all right. But that was all. No tearful reunion scenes, no round robin of gossip if people found out."

"Really." I resorted to one of Pauline's favorite words for probing. It gave nothing away and sometimes could elicit a lot.

Ted walked over to the bar and poured himself another drink.

He ignored mine. "I'm not sure how well you knew Madeline, really knew her. She created her life here exactly the way she wanted it. She enjoyed having money and the things it could buy. She was never meant to be poor, and she wanted social position almost as much as wealth. Trotting out an illegitimate child would have been disastrous."

"But times have changed. Maybe now…"

"Loren, think what you're saying. You know the Old Guard on the lake. Tell me they could handle a scandal like that and not close ranks."

I suspected he was right. If acceptance by the Old Guard was what Madeline wanted most, she'd probably judged the situation correctly. But, if she passed Connie off as a cousin, an orphan who needed her, why would anyone suspect anything else? Except that, even in Emerald Point, the truth had a way of coming out.

Ted got to his feet, giving a clear signal he expected me to leave. "You've apparently been asking questions, gathering information. Not the best approach for you to take. As a matter of fact, I don't understand why you are concerning yourself with any of this." The sharpness of his tone conveyed how angry I'd made him.

I stood up. "You've done quite a turnaround, Ted, since

the night you asked for my help." I felt my cheeks burn as I hurried out of the living room and into the hall.

I heard him behind me as I yanked open the massive side door. I whirled around to face him one more time. "Of course, if you'd paid more attention to how Connie and her uncle were going to get home that day after the memorial service, I wouldn't have been pulled into this at all."

I didn't give him a chance to answer. Without watching where I was going, I flung myself off the threshold onto the slate portico at the top of the outside stairs. I was moving fast, so fast I couldn't stop myself from crashing into the man with the shock of black hair standing a few feet from the door. He'd been waiting quietly, his face turned slightly away, his thumbs hooked into the pockets of his denim jacket. I banged into him hard, knocked him back several feet toward the top of the stairs. He staggered away from me, teetering off balance, arms flailing as he struggled to keep from falling.

I lunged forward and caught his sleeve. "I'm sorry. I'm really sorry. I didn't realize…"

My apology ground to a halt. I stared in disbelief as the man, still desperately trying to regain his footing, careened even closer to the outside edge of the portico. I knew who he was. I was one hundred per cent certain. The visitor waiting at Ted Hathaway's door was the man I'd seen lying unconscious in the Rogers' Rangers display case that night at the community center.

THIRTY-THREE

"WHOA THERE, MISSUS. Slow down." The man straightened up, still fighting to keep his balance.

"I'm so sorry. Are you all right? I could have pushed you down the steps." I babbled apologies as I cast around for some way to engage him in conversation.

Ted interrupted from the doorway behind me. "Come along in. Ms. Graham was just leaving."

Two years of common council meetings had taught me to think fast on my feet and if there was ever a time for that, this was it. Direct questioning was out. I couldn't picture myself asking a complete stranger how he'd happened to be knocked out and stuffed into a Rogers' Rangers display. But I couldn't let him get away without learning something about him.

I fell back on a technique I'd learned from a college roommate with a fail-proof strategy for picking up guys. I put on my brightest smile and pulled a name out of the blue. "Good heavens, I don't believe it. Henry Talbot." It was the first name I thought of. "What in the world are you doing here? I haven't seen you in what? Five years or more, I guess. I thought you moved to Cleveland."

The man I'd collided with stared at me as if I'd lost my mind. "I'm not…"

I didn't let him finish. "Henry, are you all right? We heard about your accident but nobody knew how to reach you."

"Listen, sister. You've got the wrong guy. I'm not who you think I am."

"Of course you are. I know it's been a long time, but..."

"Look, my name is Leonard Westerhall. Now please move and let me keep my appointment with Mr. Hathaway." He brushed past me and stepped into the hall. Ted slammed the door fast. I'd outworn my welcome with both of them, that was clear.

No problem. I'd learned what I'd wanted to know. My roommate would have been proud of me. As I followed 9N south along the lake, my mind struggled to assimilate these two new pieces of information and relate them to the events of the last two weeks.

Fact one: Ramona had been right all along. Leonard Westerhall, her mystery tenant, had been the man in the display case. Somehow he'd managed to get out of the center that night, find his way to her motel and rent one of her cabins. He'd holed up there for over a week, then disappeared before she decided to ask me to check him out. And perhaps even more important—my mind took off at a gallop as I pieced these facts together—he'd disappeared from Ramona's cabin the same night Madeline Hathaway was killed.

Fact two: Leonard Westerhall, the poorly dressed man who'd been locked in the display case, had then rented a cabin at Ramona's rundown little motel, now for some reason had an appointment with Ted Hathaway, one of our area's wealthiest businessmen. The realization gave rise to more questions. What business could Westerhall possibly have with Ted and was it connected in some way to Madeline's murder?

Once again, I found myself being pulled deeper into the

mystery surrounding Madeline Hathaway's death, even as more and more people urged me to butt out. Now I could add Ted to the MYOB list, a roster which already included Stephen and Elaine Morrison, Sheriff's Investigator Jim Thompson, Deputy Rick Cronin and—I'd bet money on it—Don Morrison as soon as he regained enough strength to manage a few more words. A solid half-dozen in all.

The number of people who wanted me involved, even marginally, stood at one, maybe two. Connie, if I could help her find a summer job, and Uncle Dwight, if I was willing to act as a responsible adult in his niece's life. And—with my curiosity itching me worse than a case of poison ivy—I'd have to count myself in that category. Make that three.

I needed more information. First step—I'd tell Ramona I'd seen her tenant and get her read on why he might have come back to Emerald Point. In fact, I'd do it now while he was tied up with Ted. I drove directly to her motel.

"You can't mean it," she exclaimed when I broke the news. "You actually ran into him!"

"Literally. Almost knocked him down Ted's outside stairs," I said.

"I wonder what he could have been doing there. I don't see him as a friend of Ted Hathaway's."

"My first thought, too, Ramona," I said. "Then I realized he wouldn't have to be a friend of his. He could be working for him in some capacity. And you know what else I was thinking as I drove over here? He can't be one of the men who beat up Don. This guy's nowhere near big enough."

"So now what? You'll tell Jim you saw him, of course." That was a done deal as far as Ramona was concerned.

"It's one possibility, I guess. I'd sort of like to talk to the man first myself."

"I don't know, Loren. Jim's not going to like that."

"Well, he doesn't like much of what I do anyway. Why don't you call me when Mr. Westerhall comes back? Maybe I'll take a ride over." Before she could say more, I swung around and headed for my car.

"You better give this more thought, young lady," she called after me, "a lot more thought."

I pretended I didn't hear her.

AT HOME, I started a fresh pot of coffee and tackled the mess still left in my downstairs. I'd picked up most of the books and papers still scattered across the living room floor when the phone rang.

Ramona got right to the point. "Well, he just pulled in, but I still don't like this scheme of yours, Loren."

"I'll see how it goes with him. I can always let Jim know after I talk with him."

Confident words from a woman who had no idea what she was going to say. Oh well, I thought, something will come to me when I get there.

Fifteen minutes later I knocked on the door of Ramona's cabin.

"Mr. Westerhall, may I speak with you a minute?" I called from the little porch.

He yanked the door half open. "Yeah? What do you want?"

"I want to apologize for the way I acted at Ted Hathaway's. I was trying to find out who you are. I'm the mayor here in Emerald Point and…" I pulled out my wallet and stuck my identification card through the opening.

"Fine, lady. You've apologized. Case closed." He pushed the door toward me.

I pushed back." Look. Give me a minute to explain. I

saw you lying in the display case at the community center one night a couple weeks ago."

"You what?"

I didn't blame him for doubting me. "This time I swear I'm telling the truth. I saw a light on and went into the center to check. That's when I saw you."

His expression changed. "Yeah? Where was I again?"

"Lying in the Rogers' Rangers display case. I tried to reach in and feel for your pulse but the case was locked. I knocked on the glass but you didn't move. I thought you were dead."

"Keep talking."

"You were unconscious, I guess. You probably don't remember."

"You talking about statues with some kind of uniforms on? I might remember more than you think."

"The case was locked. I couldn't open it. I ran to a house up the road and called for help. When the rescue squad got there, you were gone."

"Yeah, that was one weird experience, but you're tellin' it about right."

He'd started to believe me. I waited, determined not to rush him.

"I figured the place was open to the public," he said finally. "The door was unlocked. I went in. Nobody around. The next thing I know somebody slams me on the head from behind and I go down."

I held my breath. I couldn't believe my good fortune. He was telling me what I wanted to know. "You didn't know the center hadn't opened yet?"

"No. I had some business there. When I came to, like you say, I was in some sort of glass case with statues in it."

I nodded. I was almost choking on the questions I wanted to ask, but I followed his lead. "Somebody put you in that case?"

"Must have. I didn't climb into the damn thing myself, you know."

"Of course not. I didn't mean…" I clamped my mouth shut, gave him more time.

After a long pause, he said, "So maybe I did catch a glimpse of somebody trying to move the glass. Are you telling me that was you?"

"Yes. The glass was locked. I couldn't open it. So I went for help."

"Yeah, you ran out and I got the hell out through the back panel as fast as I could. I'd left my car hid behind the building."

I tried a couple of easy questions. "Did you say you were supposed to meet somebody? Are you sure you went to the right place?"

"Look, lady, I'm a private detective. I don't make rookie mistakes."

"A private detective? Really?" I couldn't hold back any longer. "Who do you work for?"

"Names of clients are confidential."

"Ted Hathaway? Do you work for him?"

"Told you—confidential."

"But I saw you at his house. You might as well admit to it."

"I may have been in his employ at one time, okay? I do a little wife surveillance sometimes, but I don't do rough stuff. That's not my thing. If clients want that, they have to hire somebody else. Let's leave things right there."

"Fine," I shot back. "But if you do any more work for

Ted Hathaway, I suggest you get your money up front. He asked me for help a while back. Now he wants to pretend it never happened."

"Sure. People will turn on anyone. You might want to give that a little thought yourself."

The remark startled me. "What? I don't know what you mean."

"You tried to help me out, so I'll return the favor. You're pushing buttons, riling things up. Somebody's keepin' a pretty close eye on you."

"On me?"

"Take my word for it. There's people interested in what you're up to."

I bristled. "I don't know how anybody can know what I'm up to. Are you saying somebody's keeping track of what I do?"

"Ted Hathaway had somebody keeping track of what his wife did, didn't he? So what makes you immune?"

The icy waves of nausea that had swept over me after the break-ins came pounding back. "Okay. I admit somebody broke into my house. Twice as a matter of fact."

"Didn't get what they wanted the first time, so they came back?"

"Maybe. But I don't think they got it the second time either. In fact, I'm not sure what they want."

"So that must tell you something, doesn't it?"

"But what? Are you implying Ted Hathaway was behind those break-ins?"

"Not implying anything. How about somebody spying on you from a boat? Ever think about that?"

"Boats go by all the time, but..."

"Ever hear a boat around your place at night? Starts up

sudden, like it's been out there for a while?" He stepped back and pushed the door toward me.

"Wait. Please wait. What are you telling me?"

"More than I should, lady. You figure it out." He shoved the door shut.

"Mr. Westerhall, please. Give me one more minute." I threw my weight against the door, but it didn't budge.

Even after I heard him ram the bolt across, I kept pounding and calling his name.

There was no response from inside the cabin.

THIRTY-FOUR

I DIDN'T STOP to report back to Ramona. As I dashed to my car, I gave her a casual wave and took off fast. I needed to get home to the quiet of my porch and think through everything Leonard Westerhall had told me.

My mind reeled. The motor boat I'd been hearing, the comforting putt-putt of the little outboard which lulled me to sleep, which soothed me into thinking a friendly presence shared the peaceful night—had that sound actually meant something ominous was lurking out of sight on the dark water?

I didn't believe that for a minute. Or did I? I re-examined the circumstances surrounding the two break-ins. Maybe the boat could have been involved in some way. The break-ins had taken place when my regular schedule was disrupted. The morning my bedroom was ransacked, I'd been called to the hospital for Don's unexpected surgery. Ordinarily, I wouldn't have left the house that early. And last night when I'd fallen asleep on the porch, and later, when I'd walked down to the dock with Elaine, I was departing from my usual routine. Was the timing of the break-ins only coincidence or had someone been watching me?

Now that I was forewarned, maybe I could find out for sure.

Tonight Diane was holding a short meeting to schedule

some upcoming center events. I'd attend that. Then when I came home, I'd leave my car down the street and sneak back into the house and watch for the boat.

Everything went off like clockwork. At seven o'clock I made a show of locking the doors and switching on the low light that I normally left burning when I went out at night. I took off in my car, carrying the briefcase I always brought along to meetings.

An hour and a half later, I parked the car a block away from the house. By that time, the soft evening twilight was fading to a dusky gray. I crept along in the shadows, moved quickly to the back door and slipped into the kitchen. No sign of a disturbance. No surprise. I hadn't expected the burglars to make their move this early.

I didn't turn on any lights, just hurried upstairs and pulled on a pair of dark slacks and a navy sweatshirt. I stuffed my cell phone in one pocket and a small flashlight in the other. Then I settled myself on the floor next to a bedroom window and took up my watch.

The main thing I'd failed to consider was the boredom. I hadn't given Leonard Westerhall and other detectives who did surveillance work enough credit. After fifteen minutes I was desperate enough to gather up loose socks from a dresser drawer and attempt to pair them in the dim light and cull out the singletons. Soon it was too dark even for that.

At nine-thirty when I still hadn't heard the motor, I patted my pockets to make sure I had my flashlight and cell phone and tiptoed down the stairs to the hall. The creaks and groans from the old house sounded like strings of firecrackers going off.

I sidled up to one of the narrow windows flanking the

front door and sneaked a quick peek at the lake. The night sky was overcast with no sign of the moon or stars. Masses of ominous clouds scudded low over the water. A storm was brewing. I couldn't believe anyone would stay out on the lake much longer.

There was still no sound of a boat. Maybe Leonard Westerhall had lied to me. Maybe no one was watching me tonight. I froze against the door jamb, forced myself to count to one hundred before I allowed myself another peek out.

I'd made several more counts when I finally saw what I was looking for. A small boat loomed up a short distance offshore, a ghostly apparition which started my heart racing. I didn't hear a motor, couldn't recognize the figures crouched low in the seats, but muffled splashes told me someone was rowing toward shore. And not just toward shore, but directly toward my dock.

My stomach churned; cold tendrils enveloped my limbs. I slipped through the dark house and eased open the kitchen door, lifting it to keep the hinges from squeaking. After a quick check of the back yard, I tiptoed out, flattening myself against the wall of the house, gliding quickly through the shadows cast by trees and shrubs. I'd already selected the best spot for my surveillance—near the front of the house, under my grandfather's pride and joy: a giant spruce with wide, low-slung branches and a hollow beneath it for a hiding place. As a child, I'd spent many happy hours in that imaginary playhouse. The trick now would be to squeeze my adult body into the space.

I dropped to the ground and wiggled backward into the cavity on the side of the tree facing the lake. Not quite as easy as I'd hoped. I twisted myself into strange contortions, wincing from the scrapes and jabs of once friendly branches, now turned surprisingly inhospitable. The cool earth gave off a heady odor of loam and decay.

From my vantage point I could see the boat as it slid close to my dock. I held my breath as the figure in front grabbed for a post. He threw out a rope and secured it. He was coming ashore. Now I could see another form silhouetted behind the first, a large shadowy mass. A flash of lightning illuminated the scene and I realized the men were frighteningly familiar.

I fished the cell phone out of my pocket and flipped it open.

One at a time, the men heaved themselves out of the boat. Their shapes, outlined against the dark water, loomed like apparitions from a nightmare. I struggled to distinguish identifying features. As they moved along the dock, another flash of lightning lit them like a spotlight. I knew for sure. They were the thugs who'd beaten Don so mercilessly.

I ducked my head inside my sweatshirt and shoved my cell up close to my mouth. My hand shook as I dialed 911. The rings seemed to go on forever. Finally, the operator's voice. I kept the message short and to the point. "It's Mayor Graham. Break-in…my house…38 Lakeside…two men. Send sheriff's car. No lights, no siren. Hurry." I whispered the words just loud enough to be heard. I tried to sound calm, but I couldn't muffle the tremor of panic in my voice.

The operator responded in even tones. "Stay on the line. Where are you?"

"Outside. Can't talk. Okay for now."

The men moved stealthily up the slate steps from the dock. They stopped and surveyed the front porch. Had they done this very thing the night before, seen me asleep in the hammock and still found a way to get into the house and ransack my living room?

The muscular guy I'd seen pummeling Don climbed the three steps to my porch and wrenched the door open with one pull. So much for my hook and eye lock. Why had that feeble excuse for a lock made me feel safer?

The men checked the porch and then started around the side of the house near where I was hiding. The operator's voice cut through the silence. "Car on the way. Give intruders' exact location."

The man nearest to me swung his massive head from side to side like one of the bulls in our summer rodeos getting ready to charge. "What the hell? I heard somebody."

I shoved the cell back down inside my sweatshirt, but I was too late. I'd tugged it out to listen to the operator and now the men were close enough to have heard her voice.

"Over there. Somebody's out here on this side of the house." Both men charged toward me, foregoing quiet for speed. The crashes of thunder, almost steady now, muffled the sound of their footsteps.

I shrank back under the branches, pressing my spine against the trunk, not sure if I was completely hidden. I stifled a gasp as my foot encountered a sharp root. I could tell the men were moving nearer. I saw the beam of a flashlight raking across the ground, sensed them zeroing in on my hiding place, caught glimpses of their legs and feet as they shoved branches aside, closing in on me.

Suddenly a big hand reached into the narrow aperture and seized my foot. "What the hell?" a harsh voice snarled as the hand yanked me out from under the tree.

"Easy, take it easy! What do you think you're doing?" I tried to sound indignant, struggled to keep fear out of my voice, as my back scraped along the rough ground.

"Just what we need. Another broad we gotta deal with," the man who'd grabbed me muttered.

My mind sifted through ways to explain what I was doing there, reasons an adult woman might be cowering under a tree at night. Would they believe I'd been sleeping outside? Searching for night crawlers? Hiding because I'd seen someone on my dock?

Ridiculous. They wouldn't buy any of those excuses. I struggled to my feet, weighed my chances of outrunning them.

I was making a big show of brushing dirt off my clothes when I caught the low purr of an engine up the street. I heard a car come closer, pull into the driveway at the opposite side of the house. No lights, no siren. It had to be a sheriff's car.

I spoke with assurance, but my knees buckled with relief. "Do you hear that? That's a sheriff's car pulling into the driveway. I called 911 when I saw you on my dock."

The men took me at my word. They whirled and charged down the hill. Once again I marveled at their speed as they pounded over the rough ground.

"Hold it right there!" It was Deputy Rick Cronin's voice. Other deputies had joined him.

I scrambled down the hill to the sounds of more shouted warnings. I could see the men on the dock, hands raised, their shapes outlined in the beams of the flashing red and white lights of a second sheriff's vehicle which had pulled into my yard.

The rain then began in earnest. The wind whipped it off the lake in sheets that stung my face and forced me to close my eyes. I sagged against a tree as the men were handcuffed and escorted to one of the cars.

Rick Cronin slammed the door shut behind the prisoners and watched the car disappear up the street. Then he hurried over to me. "Mayor, are you all right?"

Relief gave way to anger. "All right? How can I be? Three times now somebody's broken into my house. Three damn times, except this time they didn't make it past the front porch. I suppose that's progress though, right?"

"Hang on, Mayor. Let's go inside before we both get soaked. I know this is upsetting for you, but you're the one's got to tell us what these guys are looking for."

"Rick, I recognized them. They're the goons who beat up Don Morrison. I don't know what they're looking for. Don't you think I'd tell you if I did? Hell, if I could figure out what they wanted, I'd give it to them. I'd do it in a minute if I thought it would get them off my back."

Rick took hold of my arm. "Here, let me walk into the house with you, Mayor. They're out of your hair for now. We'll be able to hang on to 'em for tonight, anyway."

I stopped dead in my tracks. "Hang on to them for tonight? You mean you're not going to be able to keep them in jail?" I shouted.

"We'll try, but from what you say they're probably working for somebody. They'll probably make bail. Makes sense the person who hired them will want to get 'em out before they start telling what they know."

"Great. That's just great."

"You should get some rest, Mayor, and tomorrow think everything through. You picked up that bag of stuff from the motel, and then you got those papers from the girl's uncle. This has to be connected with one of those things, don't you think?"

"What I think, Rick, is that I'm sick and tired of this

whole stupid business." I wheeled around fast and made a dash for the house.

Rick hung in close behind me. He didn't say any more but, as I went through and switched on the lights, he followed me and checked out every room upstairs and down.

When he left, I didn't turn off the lights. Those two hooligans had scared me—I had to admit that—but I was hopping mad, too. I was fed up with being a victim, disgusted with the twists Rick and Jim kept putting on everything that happened, sick of the way they blamed me instead of getting to the bottom of what was going on.

I towel-dried my hair and changed into dry clothes. The storm raged on with a vengeance. The lights and TV flickered enough to start my heart pounding even harder, but the power didn't go off. I found a late-night movie and sat upright on the couch with my baseball bat and a big hunk of firewood within easy reach.

I kept hearing the guy's words as he yanked me out of my hiding place under the tree, "Just what we need—another broad we gotta deal with."

Did that mean they'd be coming back to "deal with me" as soon as they were free?

THIRTY-FIVE

AT SEVEN-FIFTEEN the next morning, I glanced out my kitchen window and saw Jim Thompson pacing around my yard. Good. I'd forced him to start his day earlier than he usually liked. Why should I be the only one losing sleep?

"Come in," I growled. I yanked open the door.

He wasn't in a mood for pleasantries either. "I got Rick's report. The intruders were after something. You've got to figure out what it is."

I gritted my teeth. "Obviously. What about that copy of Connie Leland's birth certificate? It was in that packet I gave you."

"No secret about that. Rick thought they must be after something else."

My hand shook as I poured coffee for us both. "That boy's turning into a real Sherlock Holmes, isn't he?"

"No need for sarcasm, Mayor. We're all on the same side here."

"Are we? Are we really?" I shoved the sugar and cream toward him.

He tried to appease me with a compliment. "You handled things fine last night. We've got those guys in jail, but we're only halfway there. The sooner we figure out what they're looking for, the sooner we'll get this matter resolved."

"They said something strange last night, Jim. At least

one of them did. When he was hauling me out from under that tree, he said, 'Great. Another broad to deal with.'"

"That was it? Nothing else?"

"I was more concerned then with how they planned to deal with me. But, when I thought about it afterward, I wondered if they were referring to Madeline, if that meant they were the ones who dealt with her."

"Possible, I suppose. We're checking them for priors. They're working for somebody, but they aren't admitting to it right now. Once they see we can build a case against them, they may be more cooperative."

I took a deep breath and settled down. "Okay. So what do you want me to do?"

"We called Don's neighbor. He rushed right down first thing this morning and identified the prisoners as the two men he saw assaulting Don last week. We'll need your identification, too. I'd like you to come in and see a lineup as soon as you can."

"I can do that this morning. The stronger the case you build against them, the better I'll like it."

"We have to determine what they were after. Must have been important to warrant three attempts to find it. And I don't suppose I need to point out…"

"Don't say it. I shouldn't have accepted your precious evidence in the first place. Don't you think I regret that myself without you telling me?"

I shouldn't have given him that opening, because I was about to break other news he wasn't going to like. "Don't answer that. I've got something else to tell you. You probably won't be happy about this either."

"What? For God's sake, now what?"

"There's another guy I think has been working for Ted

Hathaway. Remember the man I saw in the display case at the center? I've seen him again."

"Damn it, Loren. Have you been trying to find him?"

"No way. I ran into him by accident. I literally ran into him, almost sent him sprawling down Ted Hathaway's stone steps."

Jim hit the table so hard his coffee sloshed onto the place mat. "You went looking for him, didn't you? You're playing with fire, don't you realize that?"

I struggled to keep my voice steady. Now I really had to stay calm. "Jim, I did not go looking for him. I walked out of Ted's house and he was standing on the doorstep. His name is Leonard Westerhall. I think he works for Ted."

"For Ted Hathaway?"

"He told me those men Rick arrested last night had been watching me from a boat. That's how I happened to see them climbing onto my dock. Otherwise I would have been in bed asleep."

"Why? Why would he tell you that if he works for Ted?"

"I guess because I tried to help him that night at the center. He told me he's a private detective. He didn't want to be linked to the two guys who beat up Don. He's staying at Ramona's motel if you want to talk to him."

"I certainly do want to talk to him. In fact, I'll do that very thing right now." Without another word, he shoved back his chair and slammed out the door.

I breathed a sigh of relief. I hadn't mentioned—and he hadn't thought to ask—where my conversation with Leonard Westerhall had taken place.

TEN MINUTES AFTER Jim left, I looked out to see Ted Hathaway himself striding up to my kitchen door. One visitor before eight o'clock in the morning was bad enough; two threatened to push me over the edge.

"Loren," he said when I answered his knock, "I've stopped by to apologize for being in such a rush yesterday. I promised I'd catch up with you another time and…"

His unctuous manner set my teeth on edge, but I finished his sentence for him. "…and so here you are."

When I motioned him in, he didn't hesitate. He walked past me and took the chair Jim had just vacated. Déjà vu all over again, as a friend used to say. Ted was sitting in the same place he'd sat the night after Madeline's death when he questioned me about the man she was seeing.

"Okay if I sit?" he said, ignoring the fact he'd already done just that. He was dressed for work in his usual top-of-the-line business look—expensive suit, crisp white shirt, power tie—appropriate attire for the halls of commerce maybe, but I found it excessive for an early morning visit.

He glanced pointedly at the coffee pot. "I'll take some of that coffee if there's any left."

Fine. I'd play his game if he'd tell me what I wanted to know. I pulled a mug out of the cupboard and filled it.

He didn't waste time with the coffee, just drained the mug and set it down. "Loren, I need your help. You seem to have gotten friendly with Madeline's relatives in Lake Luzerne. There are important papers missing, papers my attorneys need to settle Madeline's estate. And I suspect I'm not the only one who's been looking for them."

I feigned ignorance. "Papers? What kind of papers?"

Ted didn't buy it. "I think you know what I'm talking about. Madeline wanted Connie Leland taken care of. I have no problem with that. But somebody else has been sticking their nose into this matter big time."

"Are you referring to me, Ted?"

"No, although that description may not be too far off the mark." He softened the crack with a twitch of a smile. "I'm trying to make you understand there are people involved who play a lot rougher than either you or I would."

"But…" I fumbled for a response.

"Look, I know you already turned some of Tanner's papers over to the sheriff's department—probably not the worst place for them. But there are more—important financial records, part of Madeline's estate, which my attorneys are handling in case you have any questions."

"I don't have any other papers, Ted, and I certainly don't want any. I don't know how I can convince you of that."

"All right, I'll tell you what will convince me. You ask Dwight Tanner to produce those records. He doesn't have to give them to me or my attorneys. He can give them to that sheriff's investigator friend of yours, if he wants to. He can't go on sitting on them indefinitely, especially if he wants that girl to get something."

I felt as if I were making a pact with the Devil, but I nodded in agreement. "I could discuss that with him, I guess. At least I can find out why he's put off doing it. I assume everything has to be made public eventually."

"Of course. That's the right decision, Loren." He started to get up.

"Wait. In return, you can level with me about something. You asked me if I knew the name of the man Madeline was seeing. Remember? You sat right there in that very chair and asked me?"

"Yes. Yes." He tried not to let his annoyance show, but it smoldered just beneath the surface.

I didn't care if I sent him into a rage. I plowed on. "I told you I didn't know. I realized afterward you suspected it was Don Morrison. That's why you asked me. You figured I'd be angry enough at him to confirm your suspicions."

"I did have my suspicions about him. You're right."

"And even when I didn't confirm them, you sent your goons to beat him almost to death. And he'd done nothing, nothing at all."

"Loren, you're wrong about so many things. Your friend wasn't totally innocent, remember. His brother was having an affair with my wife, and he colluded with him, loaned him a truck to help him hide his identity."

"Ted, that's a classic case of blaming the victim. Letting your brother use your truck is hardly collusion. And if what you told me about your open marriage is true, Stephen and Madeline weren't hiding from you. It was Elaine they were worried about."

He reared back in his chair, the unctuous manner gone. "All right. I'll agree somebody made an unfortunate mistake when they beat him up, but what makes you think I had something to do with it?"

I tamped down my temper, but it wasn't easy. "So, if those goons got the wrong man when they attacked Don, does that mean they picked the wrong house when they spied on me from the lake, or when they broke in and tore the place apart? Were those unfortunate mistakes, too?"

"You're jumping to conclusions, Loren. And you're losing sight of the most important aspect of this whole mess. Somebody killed my wife." He jumped to his feet and glowered at me across the table.

I glared up at him. "Sit down and knock it off, Ted. Calm yourself or get the hell out of my house."

To my surprise, he muttered a "sorry" under his breath

and sank back into his chair. "But don't you understand? Madeline is dead. Nothing else matters to me."

I faced him across the table. My words tumbled out of their own accord. "You know, Ted, I'm still not convinced you didn't kill her yourself. Maybe you didn't intend to, didn't want to even, but maybe she made you so jealous you lost control."

The color drained from his face. "No. No. You don't understand. I loved Madeline."

"But if she told you she was going to leave you…"

"Madeline wasn't going to leave me, Loren. You can take that to the bank. If there's one thing in this whole rotten mess any of us can be sure of, it's that." He shoved the chair back so violently it toppled over onto the floor. He kicked it aside and stormed out the door.

Not my idea of a good start for the day. If the stream of irate visitors kept up, I'd be lucky to have any furniture left. I unplugged the coffee maker and took off.

By the time I reached the office, I was racing against the clock. I left a note for Pauline, hung out an Open At 1:00 P.M. sign then drove to the jail. The deputy in charge made a couple of phone calls and an unnamed higher-up approved me for a private viewing.

Five men shuffled into the glass-enclosed area a short time later—the two men the deputies had arrested the night before on my dock and three other prisoners, apparently recruited for the line-up.

The guys I'd watched come ashore from the rowboat and rip open the screened door on my porch were definitely the same men who'd attacked Don. In the bright morning light they didn't appear quite as frightening as they had on those other occasions, but they still looked scary enough

to me. I shuddered as I recalled how they'd yanked me out
of my hiding place under the tree. What if the sheriff's car
hadn't arrived when it did?

"They're the ones," I said with conviction, secure in the
knowledge they couldn't see me through the one-way
glass. "They're the men who tried to break into my house
last night, the same ones who beat up Don Morrison. No
doubt about it."

I was relieved to have the glass between us—don't get
me wrong—but I wished I could have asked them what
they'd been looking for at my house. No matter what they'd
thought, I didn't have the—what did Alfred Hitchcock call
it?—the McGuffin. Wasn't that the thing everyone in his
films was searching for? I'd have to ask Diane, the film
buff. If I remembered correctly, the McGuffin was of little
or no value itself, like the Maltese Falcon, for example, but
it set everyone off on a race to find it. Was that what was
happening here? If there were only some way to let people
know I didn't have it, didn't know what it was and wouldn't
recognize it if I saw it.

THIRTY-SIX

WHAT I DID HAVE that morning was a plan of action, even if it was still bogged down in its preliminary stages. On my drive over the mountain to Lake Luzerne I fired up my brain and considered the best way to implement that plan. I stopped at the diner and picked up an assortment of breakfast treats—enough juice, food and coffee to feed Dwight and Connie for the entire day. As I swung onto the road which led to their place, I still hadn't figured out my approach, but I wasn't going to postpone my visit. The clock on my dash showed a few minutes before eleven o'clock when I pulled up to the shabby little cottage.

Dwight Tanner stared at me in bewilderment when he found me standing on his doorstep, loaded down with bags of food. He greeted me politely, but with no sign of recognition. "Yes?"

I said my name and reminded him about the papers he'd given me.

"Yes?" he said again. His confused look made me wonder if he had any idea who I was.

"All right if I come in, Dwight?" I asked finally.

"I guess." He pushed open the screen door and I stepped inside. Not an auspicious start, but at least he'd let me in.

"I brought some breakfast for us. Could we sit in the kitchen and eat while we talk?"

"Okay." He turned and shuffled ahead of me down the hall and into the kitchen.

"Let me get set up here." I slid the bags onto the kitchen table and took out the containers of coffee and juice and the packages of sweets.

"Did you want to see Connie?" Dwight lowered himself into a chair and eyed the assortment of Danish pastries I'd brought.

"Actually, I wanted to talk to you privately first."

"That's good, because she's not here. She's babysitting for the Passaic family. Started a couple days ago. She thought it would make a good summer job for her."

I opened coffee for both of us. Dwight accepted his eagerly and stirred sugar and cream from the little packets into it. I slid a paper plate with two of the pastries toward him and he gobbled them as he sipped the coffee. When he seemed comfortably full, I brought up the bag the motel owner had given me.

"A bag?" he asked.

"A black canvas duffel bag. It belonged to Madeline."

I saw no sign he understood what I was saying.

"Madeline Hathaway." I paused, waiting for him to assimilate what I'd said and offer a question or comment in return. Nothing.

"Madeline had left the bag at a motel, Dwight, and the motel owner wanted me to take it." I hesitated. Since he didn't seem curious, I didn't offer details about the bag's contents.

He nodded, as if he might be starting to understand.

"Madeline's bag? You have it now?"

"Dwight, someone stole that bag from my house. I'd planned to turn it over to the sheriff's department. The next thing I knew it was gone."

"Were the papers in it, the papers I gave you?"

Finally, we seemed to be connecting. "No, the papers are safe. But my house was broken into a second time. I thought the same people who stole the bag might have come back for the papers."

"I thought you'd put those papers where nobody could find them. Didn't you tuck 'em away somewhere safe?" he asked.

"Dwight, I've turned the papers over to the sheriff's department."

He gave me a startled look. "Why would you do that?"

"They may be evidence in a murder investigation. I really shouldn't have taken them in the first place. I should have turned in the bag from the motel, too."

"But the birth certificate. It's just a copy, you understand. Is that what you're worried about?"

"That and more, Dwight. The people who broke into my house must be after something really important to them… something they thought might be in Madeline's bag."

"Yeah, seems like everybody's lookin' for things Maddy maybe left here. Ted Hathaway's attorney called me, too."

"When was this, Dwight?"

Dwight bit down hard on his lower lip, trying to recall when he'd gotten the call. After a minute, he gave up. "Oh, hard to keep track of just when things happen. Phoned me a couple of times. A day or so ago. Maybe more."

"Dwight, I think the people who broke into my house came back because they thought you'd given me something else. But other than the birth certificate, I can't figure out what it could be. Can you?"

Dwight stirred his coffee. He didn't answer, didn't seem to notice the clatter of his spoon against the side of the cup. He bit down hard on his lip as if weighing pros and cons before a decision. Finally, he said, "I suppose I better tell you then."

I realized I could be making another mistake. Much as I wanted to hear what he had to say, I took the high road. "You know, Dwight, you probably should talk to the sheriff's investigator about this."

He didn't acknowledge the suggestion. He'd made his decision. "Well, there's some financial records Maddy left here—legal papers and a bank book meant for Connie, so she'll be able to claim money someday. Now with Maddy gone, maybe the time has come for Connie to do it."

"So where are these records, Dwight?"

More clattering with the spoon. "I did what Maddy told me to do with them."

"And what was that?"

"When Maddy gave 'em to me, she told me not to tell anyone, but now I don't know. With her gone, maybe I should tell."

I was close to bursting with curiosity. Jim would have insisted Dwight come to his office and present his information properly in an official setting. But would he be willing to do that? And what if the men came here looking for the papers before he did it?

"Dwight," I said. "I don't think you've got much choice at this point. Tell me what you did with the records. I'll help you any way I can."

He nodded. "All right. I'll show you. Maddy said if anything happened to her, I could give them to Stephen Morrison. She said I could trust him to do right by Connie. But I don't know if I want to do that."

"But...but..." I thought I understood what Madeline had been thinking. If Stephen was Connie's father, as the birth certificate indicated, he'd be the logical choice, wouldn't he? Was Dwight about to show me the McGuffin, the mysterious object the burglars had been looking for at my house?

"You're probably thinkin' maybe they should go to Mr. Hathaway," Dwight went on. "But you know what? He didn't bother much with Connie. Came here one or two times with Maddy. That was all. Didn't want us to go to that service at his house, you know. Like we was poor relations he needed to keep under wraps."

I murmured something sympathetic.

"I didn't mind for myself, that wasn't it. But t'weren't right to treat Connie that way. She'll grow up every bit as lovely as her mother, you mark my words. I won't live to see it, but you will and you just remember I said that."

I reached across the table and touched his hand. "Oh, Dwight. I can see that now. She's a beautiful girl. You've done a wonderful job taking care of her."

He got to his feet and shuffled down the hall toward his bedroom. When he came back, he set a battered, gray strong box on the kitchen table.

"Stuff's in here. I'll show you," he said.

"But only if you agree to go with me to the sheriff's investigator and turn over anything that belonged to Madeline. Whatever she left here could be evidence in a murder investigation, Dwight. You've got to let Investigator Thompson know about it."

Once again, Dwight didn't seem to hear me. He'd made up his mind. He laid out a bank book and a sheath of papers. "All this is for Connie. So she can have a college education and a chance in life. That's what Maddy wanted."

"And you want me to look through this?" I asked.

He nodded.

My hand shook as I opened the bank book. The pages recorded deposits to the account. I scanned the figures quickly. Varying amounts had been added over a period of ten—no, twelve—years. The size of the deposits varied from as little as one hundred dollars to as much as a thousand. There were no withdrawals. On the last pages the amounts swelled in size. I checked and double-checked the final balance several times over. Unless there'd been unrecorded withdrawals, the account contained over three hundred thousand dollars.

Stunned by what I saw, I skimmed back over the deposits.

This was serious money. Why would it be in a passbook account? How had Madeline obtained this money and why hadn't she invested it, put it into stocks or bonds, at least into money market certificates? I flipped back to the first page. The account was in Madeline's name—Madeline Tanner Hathaway, then the shocker—and/or survivor, followed by the name, Constance Mary Leland. No mention of Ted Hathaway or Stephen Morrison. As Dwight had said, this money was earmarked for Connie.

"Dwight? How long have you known about this?" I asked.

"About what?"

"That this account was intended for Connie if anything happened to Madeline."

"Maddy was generous, helped us out a lot."

"But this is a large amount of money, Dwight. How long have you had this bank book?"

"A while now. I don't remember. Maddy came over one

day and gave it to me. And these other papers, too. She told me to take good care of all of them."

I pulled the sheath of papers toward me. I was in too deep now to quit. "Okay if I look at these, too?"

"Yeah. But I need to get off of this hard chair. You sit here and look all you want. I gotta get someplace more comfortable." He leaned on the table, pushed himself slowly to his feet. His breathing became harsh, labored.

"Dwight, are you all right?"

"Just need to relax a few minutes," he said. He shuffled past me and disappeared into the living room. I heard the creak of his recliner as he pulled the lever and settled back.

By the time I'd followed him into the living room, his eyes were closed. I watched him for a minute or two while his breathing slowed. As soon as I sensed he'd fallen asleep, I went back to the kitchen table.

The sheath of papers more than doubled the size of Connie's inheritance. At some point, Madeline had apparently purchased Dwight Tanner's house and several acres of land surrounding it and she'd signed all of it over to Connie. An even bigger surprise—an insurance policy on Madeline's life for $500,000 with Connie as beneficiary. The policy had been taken out more than ten years ago. If the premiums had been paid, I couldn't see why there'd be any problem collecting it. Connie might not be living in luxury now, but she was about to become a wealthy young woman.

The implications here were mind-boggling. This kind of money would mean change, incredible change in Connie's life. I drifted a million miles away, speculating about how an inheritance of this size could affect a young woman who'd grown up with so little, wondering if Connie would make sensible choices, if her sudden wealth would lead to happiness or disaster.

A loud, insistent banging on the front door brought me crashing back down to earth.

THIRTY-SEVEN

MY HEART POUNDED as I shoved everything back into the strong box and grabbed a newspaper from the counter to drape over it. Not the best hiding place, but at least the financial records were tucked out of sight.

As if I wasn't already reeling with surprise at Dwight's disclosure, I got hit with another when I opened the front door. Elaine Morrison, stylishly turned out in white linen slacks and a pink angora sweater, stood on the rickety porch. I gaped at her.

If Elaine was equally surprised to see me, she didn't show it. She greeted me as if she'd expected to find me answering the door at Dwight Tanner's house. "I thought that was your car, Loren. I'm so glad to run into you like this. I've been meaning to call you to apologize for barging in that way the other night. When I saw the time, I was so embarrassed. I had no idea how late it was. Please accept my apology."

I continued to stare, racking my brain for a response. Asking if she'd had someone trash my house while she distracted me probably wouldn't predispose her to tell me what I wanted to know. I blurted out the first thing I thought of. "Dwight's asleep."

"I was hoping to talk with you sometime anyway about our mutual concern. Maybe we could grab lunch some place. I can see Dwight later."

Too astonished to process that suggestion, I reworked my murmur.

Elaine interpreted my incoherent stammering as agreement. "Fine. There's a charming little restaurant called Papa's not far from here. Let's run over there."

I didn't warm to the idea of running to Papa's or anywhere else with Elaine but, with Dwight's strong box barely out of sight, I didn't want her joining me in the kitchen. Better to talk with her someplace else.

"All right," I muttered.

Despite my nagging suspicions about her visit to my house, my interest was piqued by that phrase, "our mutual concern." I assumed she meant Connie. This was certainly a day for surprises. I didn't know how many more I could handle, but I couldn't pass up a chance to hear what she had to say on that subject.

We didn't waste time on discussion. Dwight appeared to be sound asleep, so I didn't disturb him. We were out the door in seconds.

"I'm parked behind you, so we might as well take my car," she said.

I felt a jolt of suspicion, but it seemed pointless to disagree. I climbed into her black Mercedes and we took off.

Papa's, a small, white frame building on the Hudson River, bustled with activity. A dozen people crowded around the tables on the front porch, eating sandwiches and fabulous looking ice cream concoctions. Next to the entrance, a bulletin board showcased newspaper clippings describing the restaurant's rebirth after a disastrous fire a few years before.

Elaine led the way through the main dining area to an outside deck and a table next to the railing. Below us, beyond a narrow swath of grass and a fringe of evergreens, the Hudson raced by, its fast-moving current tumbling over jagged rocks which reared up sharp and slick with spray. The beauty of the twisting, eddying water made it easy to forget the danger lurking beneath its surface. When I leaned over the railing, I saw that the river squeezed into a narrow gorge a short distance downstream before it coursed over an even steeper drop, heading for the falls which powered the mills at Corinth.

As we'd studied the menus the hostess handed us, Elaine said, "Isn't this a fabulous place? I'm so pleased you were willing to join me."

I nodded without comment, watching our waitress arrange placemats and silverware on the table. Once Elaine and I had ordered the day's special, a sampling of three kinds of salad, I couldn't take the suspense any longer. "You wanted to talk to me about something, Elaine?" I prompted her.

She didn't let me rush her. "Let's eat first, why don't we? We can talk business afterwards."

We cast around for subjects to discuss but by the time we'd finished eating, I'd had it with the small talk. "I'd like to hear what's on your mind, Elaine," I said.

She took a minute fixing her coffee before she answered. "As you've probably guessed, Loren, I'm concerned about Connie. Stephen and I are trying to figure out how to help her—both financially and in other ways. We need a plan that will work for all of us."

"All of you? I don't know what you mean," I said.

"Ted is definitely a wild card," she went on. "I'm sure you've already pegged him. Not willing to do much himself yet quick to interfere. We could use the help of an impartial third party. I'm hoping you'll consider assuming that role."

I had no idea what she was asking me to do. I wondered if she knew about Connie's inheritance, but I couldn't violate Dwight's confidence by bringing up the subject. "What kind of role are you thinking of, Elaine?"

"Stephen is talking with his attorney. He wants to establish paternity and I have no problem with that. His affair with Madeline happened a long time before I knew him and I respect that decision."

I set my coffee cup down with a clatter and stared at her. Was it possible she didn't know Stephen and Madeline had resumed their affair, or was she pretending ignorance for some reason of her own?

She didn't appear to notice my reaction. "Connie is too young to take care of herself," she went on, "and the uncle—well, you must realize he'll be a candidate for a nursing home before long."

That remark loosened my tongue. "Dwight? I can tell he's probably slowed down a little, but otherwise he seems okay."

"Loren, you can't mean that. I agree he acts sharp enough sometimes, but then he drifts away. Stephen's attorney's going to come up with a plan and I'm hoping you'll support us in our efforts."

"Elaine, I still don't understand," I said.

"You've been kind to the girl. You have stature in the area. Connie needs someone like you in her life, a woman she feels close to. You could offer some guidance…keep her from making the wrong decisions. We'd pay you for any expenses you incur you understand, along with a monthly stipend, but Connie wouldn't need to know that. She'd think of you as an understanding older friend."

Her idea of paying me set more questions buzzing in my head. Maybe she did know about the money Madeline had earmarked for her daughter after all. Was the girl's welfare really her main concern or was she trying to gain access to Connie's inheritance?

I phrased my question carefully. "Elaine, shouldn't an attorney handle matters like this?"

She pushed her coffee aside and leaned toward me. "I'm telling you this in strictest confidence, Loren. Stephen is negotiating to open a branch of his firm in South America. We'd like to take Connie with us, or at least have her join us there as soon as possible."

Now I was even more taken aback. "But what about Dwight? What would happen to him?"

"I'm sure we could find a local woman to keep house for him. He's not the best guardian for a teenage girl anyway, you know."

She might be right about that, but I couldn't imagine the two of them separated. "Elaine, this is coming as a complete surprise. I don't know what to say."

"You can start by helping us convince Connie that an extended visit to Brazil would provide wonderful opportunities for her. She seems to listen to you."

I shook my head. "I think you're overestimating my influence on her. And I can't agree without knowing a lot more about what you and Stephen have in mind."

My response had annoyed her, I could see that. She signaled for the check.

"Oh well, I'd hoped we could reach some sort of agreement today, but if we can't… I'm not going to press you for an immediate answer." She threw money on the table for the bill and tip and brushed aside my attempt to contribute. Before I realized what she was doing, she was hurrying out of the restaurant.

When I caught up with her on the porch, she was all smiles again. "It's beautiful here, isn't it?" she said. "I imagine Dwight is still sleeping. We'll have time to walk down to the water. The view of the falls is spectacular."

I glanced at my flimsy sandals. "I really don't have the shoes for it."

"No problem. The path is well worn. This is a favorite activity over here. We'll only be a few minutes." She whirled around and headed along the side of the building.

I hesitated, reminded of how she'd led the way to my dock the night my house was ransacked. Still, asking for my help with Connie had been an overture of friendship, hadn't it? I tried to shake off my doubts about her sincerity as I followed her.

The path wound through a thick stand of evergreens, then emerged close to the river's edge. The spray caught the sunlight, creating myriad rainbows. This section of the Hudson bore little resemblance to the broad, majestic waterway downstate where the wealthy Dutch settlers had established their fiefdoms. What I was seeing here was a turbulent, workhorse river which had energized the local economy as it swept harvests of Adirondack logs to the mills along its shores. A few miles downstream, near the section called the Big Bend, people had built homes, but these steep banks were as overgrown with vegetation as they'd been a hundred years ago.

As we stood marveling at the beauty of the river, a gust of wind blew a shower of water in our direction. I stepped back quickly, feeling my sandals slip on the wet grass.

Elaine motioned me forward. "Stand next to me where

you can see the falls. When the sun hits the spray down there, it's a breathtaking sight. Lean forward."

I felt her hand on my back, gentle at first, but urging me closer to the edge.

"Elaine, hold on. I'm too close." Before I got the words out, I felt her push—firm, insistent, no longer with one hand but with two, both hands shoving me toward the water. I shifted, tried to halt the momentum, tried to dig my heels into the slippery ground. My sandals, their soles slick now with moisture, slid along the wet grass.

I'd lost valuable seconds before I realized what she was doing, and those seconds were all she needed. I tottered forward almost to the water's edge, sensed her right behind me, felt her hands digging into my back. Unable to stop myself, I staggered onto a flat rock that jutted out into the river. Moss and spray had coated it with slime. I couldn't stop my feet from slipping.

"Elaine, what are you doing?"

Off balance, I slammed back with my elbow. I caught her in the hip, a glancing blow, but it must have hurt. I felt her lessen the pressure on my back. I managed a half turn and saw her face twisted into a frightening grimace.

"You bitch. You goddamn busybody. Why couldn't you be on my side? You're after that money for yourself, aren't you?"

"Elaine, stop. Think what you're doing!" I realized logic and reason were poor weapons, but they were the only ones I had. I swayed back and forth on the slimy rock, struggling to keep from falling, unable to capitalize on my momentary gain.

"I'm not letting you ruin everything for me. You fell. Madeline fell. She tried to ruin everything for me, too."

I felt her yank her hands away, then slam them hard

against my back. The blow caught me between my shoulder blades and shoved me even nearer to the edge of the rock. I fought desperately to find another foothold, but the stone was hopelessly slick. I couldn't stop myself from sliding. I pitched forward, out of control. Beneath me I saw the water churning. It was not like the lake water I was used to swimming in. It was fast moving, the current powerful and merciless. I wouldn't simply drown here; I'd be battered by the rocks as the river swept me downstream and over the falls.

I hit bottom hard. The water wasn't deep, but I couldn't get my feet under me to stand. I was pummeled and tossed as if I were weightless. I couldn't see or breathe. I struggled to get my face out of the water. My leg scraped along a submerged rock. Its sharp edges ripped a deep, painful gouge in my calf. I gasped in pain just as I was swept under again. Water filled my nose and mouth.

I fought my way to the surface, coughing, choking, flinging my hands around for something I could hold on to. Somehow I twisted my legs under me, felt for the bottom with my feet and reached out my right hand to grab the rough edge of a rock.

Elaine, her face still contorted with rage, stepped forward and brought the heel of her shoe down hard on my hand. She had apparently followed my progress as I struggled in the water. Pain shot up my arm, but I knew I couldn't let go of the rock. Before I could shift position, she lifted her foot to stomp me again.

Desperate, I grabbed for her. Somehow I got hold of the strap of her sandal. She kicked wildly; her shoe slammed into my chest, and then caught me in the mouth. I cried out with the pain and felt blood start to ooze from my bruised lips, but I knew that sandal strap was my lifeline. I had to hang on. I felt Elaine's weight tip forward. She was dangerously off balance, but she yanked her foot back and aimed another kick at my face.

"Damn you. You want that money. I know you do. But you won't get it."

Despite my grip on the strap, her shoe slammed into my nose. The pain was excruciating. I could see my blood spurt out, a fountain of blood, with everything around it shrouded in darkness. I couldn't hold on to the strap.

I slipped under the water again. The cold hurt almost as much as the kick, but it knocked some sense into me. The pieces of the puzzle fell into place. What had been unimaginable a half-hour before appeared in front of me in perfect clarity. Elaine, Don's sister-in-law, someone I d seen as a friend, was in reality a cold-blooded murderer. She'd killed Madeline Hathaway and now, more than anything, she wanted to kill me.

I couldn't let her do it. I had to find a way to save myself. I focused on what I needed to do. Somehow I managed to hold my breath and force my body upward. By the time I'd clawed my way back to the surface my vision had cleared a little. I grabbed for another rock a few feet away, hauled myself closer and braced my body against it.

Now I saw that, without my grip on her foot, Elaine was teetering back and forth, waving her arms wildly as she struggled to regain her balance. She wavered and tipped sideways. She fought to remain upright, but she couldn't do it. As if in slow motion, she tumbled onto the rock and slid off into the water. She came up sputtering, her hair plastered to her skull, water streaming from her head and shoulders.

She shoved her feet down and tried to stand. She managed one step toward me before the fast-moving current hit her and forced her back. Suddenly, she was caught in the turbulence and tossed farther out into the channel where the current was even swifter. The river seized her and in seconds she'd disappeared from sight.

I felt for handholds in the rock. Inch by inch, I dragged myself up onto a small ledge. Moving slowly, terrified of slipping off, I maneuvered my body onto a flat section. I rested a minute, wiped the blood from my eyes and face, and tried to pinpoint Elaine's location. Even from my position on top of the rock, I couldn't spot her.

I divided the river into sections and attempted to check each one methodically, but it was impossible to make sense of what I was seeing. Dozens of rocks, some needle-sharp, others smooth and slippery, thrust up out of the current. White water churned around them. Near both shores I made out deceptively quiet pools, but the Hudson rushed past them in its headlong drop toward the falls. At one point I thought I saw a head bobbing in the turbulence near the gorge, but I couldn't be sure.

Elaine had disappeared.

THIRTY-EIGHT

I TWISTED MY BODY around until I faced the shore. I spit the blood out of my mouth and called up the hill again and again, hoping someone would hear me over the sound of the rapids. There was no one to hear me, no response.

I had to make a decision. If I stayed on the rock and no one heard my shouts, how could I be sure somebody would stroll down the path and find me? At the restaurant I'd thought the day comfortably warm, but here, out of reach of the sun, the water was numbingly cold. Every few seconds a wave slammed into my face as if the river had determined to sweep me downstream to my death.

Getting myself to the bank wasn't going to be easy, but I had to do it. I couldn't hold on indefinitely and I'd seen how quickly Elaine had been gobbled up by the current.

I loosened one hand from the rock, tipped my head back and pinched my nostrils together until the bleeding slowed. I took several deep breaths through my mouth as I plotted the best route to safety. The rock I'd climbed onto seemed tantalizingly close to shore, but I realized the danger of plunging into the water and heading directly toward the bank. If I wasn't to be carried into midstream as Elaine had been, I'd need to make sure I always had something to hang on to.

Once a plan was clear in my mind, I slid off the rock

and propelled myself toward another eighteen inches away. When I had a good grip on it, I pulled myself around to the side nearest the shore to a spot a little more sheltered. I rested, then reached for the next hunk of rock poking up out of the river. I established a rhythm: fight the current for a step or two, grab another rock, rest against it, then push on. I kept up a steady pace, actually surprised when I realized I could crawl out onto grass. I intended to stand, wring out my water-logged clothes and climb back along the path to the restaurant. Instead, I collapsed on a grassy hummock and lay there, panting, unable to gather the strength to move.

After I'd accepted the fact I couldn't get up, I began shouting again, still not sure I could be heard. Finally—an answering shout, then movement at the top of the hill.

A man in a gas company uniform and hard hat pounded down the path. Two others followed close behind him. The first arrival, a red-faced, heavy-set guy, puffing from his run, leaned over me. "Did you fall in the river, ma'am? Let me check your injuries. I'm Willard Carpenter, an EMT, local rescue squad," he said.

I offered a weak smile of gratitude. "Out there…woman went in."

"Lot of blood on your face, Ma'am. What did you do? Ram into a rock somehow when you fell?"

"Didn't fall…pushed." I gasped out the words.

"Somebody pushed you? Who?"

I nodded, tried to point. "Out there."

Willard leaned closer. "You mean there's somebody still in the water? Somebody else fell in? Where? Did you see where he went?"

"She."

"A woman?"

"Elaine Morrison." Those few words and the gesture I made toward the middle of the river sapped what little strength I had left.

The other men conversed in low tones as Willard went on checking my injuries. I was dimly conscious of more people running up, most of them men. I saw their feet and lower legs as they gathered on the bank where I was lying, caught the murmur of their voices as they questioned the first arrivals about what had happened. I realized they were organizing a search, heard them talking about the falls and the danger of being washed downstream and swept over them. Everything seemed to be happening far away; it had nothing to do with me.

Willard continued his examination, his movements slow and deliberate. After he'd run his hands carefully over my skull, he wiped the blood off my face, gently inserted packing into my nose and alerted me about the scrapes and cuts he found. When he turned his attention to my body, he asked simple questions I could answer. "Does this hurt? Can you bend this arm? That one? Your legs? Can you point to where you hurt the most?"

This slow exchange lulled me until I felt as if I were drifting off to asleep. I wanted to sit up, to explain that I was all right, but I couldn't summon the energy to move.

I heard two of the men volunteer to search along the banks in case the missing woman had managed to reach the shallows. I tried to describe Elaine and tell them what she'd done, but they hurried away before I could get the words out.

I had no idea how long I'd been lying there when an angry growl shattered my relaxed state. "Good God, I don't believe this. What the hell's happened to her this time?" I recognized Jim Thompson's voice, but the string of invectives he uttered was unlike anything I'd ever heard out of him before.

"Jim." My voice sounded strange, unfamiliar.

"For God's sake, Loren, what are you doing here? How did you end up in the river? You could have been killed, you know."

I managed a disgusted look. At least I thought I managed one. Did Jim think I didn't know how close I'd come? "Elaine Morrison pushed me in and then fell in herself," I told him.

"Pushed you?" I thought I detected disbelief in his tone.

"Pushed me and then stomped on my hands when I tried to hang on to a rock. And when I grabbed her foot, she hauled back and kicked me in the nose. That's the truth, Jim."

My voice caught as I said the words, but I took a deep breath and tried again. I told him about the lunch and her suggestion that we walk along the river. Then I pulled myself together and lifted my shaking hands to show him the bruises already forming on the backs of both.

"She did this to you when you were trying to hang on?"

"And Jim, from what she said, I think she's the one who killed Madeline Hathaway, too. Shoved her off that cliff, just like she shoved me off the bank today."

"I don't believe this. We just got new charges filed on those guys who did the break-ins at your place. We thought we'd tie them up for a while. Now you got somebody else after you?" Jim shook his head in exasperation.

"So, blame the victim, Jim. Isn't that the way you like to do it?"

His expression changed. "Loren, take it easy. I'm not

blaming you. As long as the ambulance is here, we'd better get you over to Glens Falls to the hospital."

I lifted myself up on my elbows. To my relief, the feeling of weakness was subsiding. Jim's remarks had started my adrenalin pumping. "No. Let me stay here. I've got to know if you find her."

Willard gave his approval. "I don't think this woman's in any immediate danger," he told Jim. "I'll keep an eye on her if you want to get back to the search for the other victim. If she really did go over the falls, you'll be looking for her body."

"Okay. In that case, I'll leave Mayor Graham here with you. I'll check with the others, see what they need." Jim hurried off.

Fine with me. Someone had covered me with a blanket and I snuggled into my cozy little cocoon, secure in the knowledge my own EMT was hanging in close beside me while the searchers did their thing. I tried to drift back into the somnolent state I'd been enjoying when Jim arrived. I didn't want to rehash what had happened, didn't want to analyze the reasons why Elaine Morrison had tried to kill me, but I couldn't stop my thoughts. Was it because I wouldn't go along with her plan? Or had she spotted the strong box on the kitchen table? Did she realize what Dwight had showed me? She'd mentioned Connie's finances, mentioned them twice, as a matter of fact. Was Connie's inheritance what had set her off?

I heard the crackle of short wave radios as more members of the emergency squad were summoned, listened to the shouts of the men who'd been searching as they gave directions to new arrivals.

I didn't know how much time had passed before it

dawned on me that the efforts to find Elaine's body were proving fruitless. I was so sure she'd been swept downstream I hadn't considered what might happen if she had escaped the current and had gotten to shore.

I bolted upright and called to the EMT. "If she's managed to get out of the water, someone else may be in danger. I need to warn him."

"Hang on. I don't think the investigator will like this idea."

"No. Of course, he won't. I'll have to talk to him. Can you get him back here?"

I didn't understand how the EMT notified Jim so quickly, but I'd no more than struggled to my feet when he came charging up the hill. "Now what?"

"Dwight Tanner. I'm worried about him. Madeline Hathaway left money to Connie—a lot of money. Dwight was showing me papers from his strong box just before Elaine came to the door. From the way she was talking, I think she knows about them. If she's not in the river, I bet she's gone to his house after them."

"Papers? What papers? Why did he show you papers?"

I explained about the bank book and the insurance policy. "There's a lot of money earmarked for Connie. Dwight figures he won't live much longer. He asked me to look after her."

Jim made no effort to hide his astonishment. "You? Why you?"

This time I was sure I managed a dirty look. "He happens to like me. He thinks I'm reliable."

Jim barely suppressed a snort. "And Mrs. Morrison didn't cotton to that idea?"

"At lunch she suggested I should spend time with Connie, but Stephen would take care of her finances. She even suggested paying me, like that would buy my support. I suspect she's anxious to get control of that money herself. She practically admitted that to me just before she pushed me into the river."

"You'd better tell me exactly what she said."

"Can I tell you in the car on our way to Dwight's? I think we should get over there fast. I'm afraid of what she'll do."

I thanked the EMT for his care and, with him on one side of me and Jim on the other made it up the path to where Jim's car was parked.

"Shouldn't we swing by Papa's and see if Elaine's picked up her car?" I asked Jim as we set off. Maybe I was wrong about what she was going to do next; maybe the car would still be parked there…I held my breath as we swung into the lot.

Elaine's car was gone.

While we hurtled down the road toward Dwight's house, I filled in the blanks for Jim, starting with Elaine's arrival at the Tanner house that morning.

"Not much doubt she wanted to kill you," he said when I finished. "And, from what you're telling me, she came close to doing it. If you'd been caught in that current and swept downstream, you'd probably be dead now."

Leave it to Jim to make me feel even worse. "I thought that's what happened to her when I didn't see her any place."

"Well, it would appear she got out of the river somehow. And you're saying she did all this for money, money Madeline Hathaway left to Connie?"

"To Connie, but Elaine wants Stephen to get control of it. He's Connie's father, after all."

"She acknowledges that?"

"She seemed more than willing to admit it. Jim, I realized something while I was hanging on to that rock. I think Elaine's been behind everything that's happened—not just Madeline's murder, but Don's beating and the burglaries at my house, too. You should have seen her face when she ground her heel into my hand. That woman's crazy."

"Let's take this one step at a time. I agree we should start by making sure she hasn't gone back to the Tanner house."

"And that's where my car is," I said.

"Maybe, but you're not driving yourself anywhere. No arguments about that. I'll see you get home when the time comes."

"All I want is to make sure both Dwight and Connie are all right. And maybe get dried off somehow," I told him.

That was true enough. But most of all, I did want to get home. I wanted that in the worst way. A quiet evening, snug in my own house, knowing Dwight and Connie were safe and Elaine had been carted off to jail, struck me as the best possible outcome for this wretched day.

Fifteen minutes later, as Jim pulled into Dwight Tanner's driveway, I kissed that possibility goodbye. Dwight lay in a crumpled heap at the top of his porch steps, one arm outstretched as if he'd been reaching for something.

"Dwight!" I shouted as I tumbled out of Jim's car and limped across the yard toward him. "Dwight, what happened? Are you hurt?"

Jim dashed by me while I struggled up the steps. He dropped to his knees next to Dwight and felt for a pulse in his neck. "Take it easy, Loren. He's conscious, give the poor guy a chance to answer."

He was right, of course. Dwight moved at a snail's pace on his best days. Now he had to pull himself together just to find the words he wanted. Finally, he found them. "That woman," he gasped.

I bit back my questions.

"That Elaine, the one knocked on the door and asked you to go to lunch, Loren. She came back."

"I thought you were asleep then, Dwight."

"I heard her talking to you. But, like I told you, I had to rest a minute. I did fall asleep, I guess, after you two left. Then all of sudden, she was back. I heard her in the kitchen. She must've breezed right past me without so much as a by-your-leave."

Jim slipped his arm behind Dwight's head and eased him into a sitting position. "You recognized the woman as the same one who left earlier with Loren?"

"Right. Elaine Morrison. She's come here before."

"Why did she come back today? Did she tell you that?"

"I guess she wanted my strong box. She took off with it, anyway. She's married to Connie's father; says he'll be handlin' Connie's finances now and he'll want to have his attorney look over the papers in it."

Jim and I exchanged glances.

"You mean the strong box you showed me this morning, Dwight? She took it with her?" I asked.

"Yup. Scuttled right out of here with that box under her arm. I ran after her and tried to stop her. That's when I fell."

But I'd seen Elaine caught in the current and swept downstream. Had she really managed to get out of the river and back to Dwight's house so quickly? "Are you sure this was the same woman who came after me earlier?" I asked.

"Well, dressed different this time. Wearing a pair of

Connie's jeans and a blue sweater of hers. She'd got her own clothes wet some way, she said."

Jim perked up his ears. "How did she get Connie's clothes?"

"Most likely off her bedroom floor."

"Floor?" Jim and I said in unison.

"Sure. That's where Connie's clothes end up. Folks say that's typical teenage stuff. She's an angel other ways, so I don't give her a hard time about keepin' a messy room."

My brain clicked into gear. "Do you suppose I could borrow some dry clothes myself?" I asked him.

"Go right ahead, Loren. Connie won't mind you takin' something," Dwight assured me.

Jim and I lifted him to his feet and helped him into the house. After we'd made him comfortable in his recliner, I poured him a glass of orange juice and dashed to Connie's bedroom. I dug through a pile of discarded clothes and found a pair of slacks and a top that didn't quite fit to replace my own soggy garments.

When I came back to the living room a few minutes later, Jim was still struggling to extract information from Dwight. "So you think Mrs. Morrison might have gone to where Connie's babysitting?"

"Wouldn't be hard to do. Connie always leaves a telephone number for me. I heard that woman on the phone. She was probably calling it. Connie would have told her how to get there."

"Better tell me, too, Mr. Tanner. It's important we find Connie as quickly as possible," Jim said.

Dwight stumbled through the directions in his excruciatingly slow way as Jim jotted them down on the back of an envelope he pulled from his pocket. When he was satisfied he knew what roads to take, we left Dwight in his chair sipping his juice and took off for Connie's babysitting job.

Jim thrust the envelope at me. "Here…read these directions to me when we come to the turns. I want to find this kid fast."

"Elaine wouldn't try to hurt Connie, would she?" I asked, as we careened along winding country roads.

"I don't want to take any chances," Jim said. "When I left your house this morning, I stopped by Ramona's motel. Westerhall told me some things about those guys who broke into your house. Judging by what's happened today, looks like he was telling the truth."

"Take a right here. You talked with Leonard Westerhall?"

"He's a licensed P.I. Worked for Ted Hathaway for a while. Seemed tuned into what's been going on. Knew about those guys breaking in to your place, claimed they were looking for papers connected to Madeline Hathaway's estate. Said they'd already beaten one guy almost to death—meaning Don, I guess—and thought you might be next on the list." Jim gave me a quick look as if to check my reaction to that piece of news.

The shivers hit me again even more violently than they'd had in the river as I flashed back on the beating I'd seen the two men inflicting on Don. What if the sheriff's car hadn't arrived at my house when it did? Was that what had been in store for me?

But I didn't have time for morbid thoughts. I focused on Dwight's directions. "Take another right. Route 12 is what you want now."

After Jim made the turn I said, "So you think Elaine was after the money Madeline left for Connie?"

"Looks like that's what she wanted. According to the uncle, Mrs. Morrison's been dropping in over here. Probably thought once her husband established himself legally as Connie's father, they'd have access to her inheritance."

"And take her to South America, she told me. But Jim, I didn't think Stephen and Elaine needed money that bad."

"Lived pretty high, wouldn't you say? Rumor has it his business is mortgaged to the hilt. Could be the bubble is about to burst."

"That would be tough for Elaine, I agree. But what I don't understand—how could Elaine find criminals like that to do her dirty work?"

"One of them told us they hung out at a meal site where she volunteered. Passed the word they were looking for work and weren't fussy about what it was. When the uncle kept insisting he didn't know anything about the money Mrs. Hathaway left to Connie, she hired them to see what they could find out."

I smiled for the first time that day. "Dwight's good at not knowing, I've noticed."

"So there she was knocking herself out to get close to the girl and her uncle and you come along and waltz right in there. She'd gotten rid of Madeline. Now you became the threat to her plans."

"Just for taking an interest in Connie?" I said.

Jim gave me a sharp look. "You were a little more involved than that, weren't you? That motel owner in Luzerne tells us those men came to see her right after you left there that day with Mrs. Hathaway's duffel bag. Told her they were from the FBI, so she admitted she gave the bag to you."

I got the message. By the time I'd informed Jim, the bag

had been stolen. Fortunately, we came to another fork in the road. "Keep going straight. I think we're almost there."

"So the guys find out you have the duffel bag. Elaine figures it may contain those financial records of Madeline's she's looking for. She sends them to break into your house to get it."

"The McGuffin," I said.

"The what?"

"Nothing. Just thinking out loud."

"Then when they don't find what they want in the duffel bag, they try again."

"You know, Jim, I thought it was funny Elaine came to my house so late that night, then wanted to sit down at the dock. She was luring me away from the house purposely, so they could rip my living room apart, wasn't she?"

"Wouldn't surprise me if..."

Before he could say more, we spotted a farmhouse off to our left. As I pointed, Jim swung the car into the driveway leading to it.

Two children peered through the screen door, their eyes huge with fright.

Jim, his hand resting on the shoulder holster under his jacket, slid out of the car and approached the house. "Hi. You guys okay? We're looking for Connie. Thought she might be here."

The older of the children, a solemn little girl of about nine, did the talking while her brother, intent on sucking his thumb, huddled close behind her. "Connie's gone. A mean lady made her go with her. Connie told her she can't leave us alone, but she made her go anyway."

"Made her? How did she make her?" Jim asked.

For that question the little guy yanked his thumb out of

his mouth. "She had a gun, a big one! Like on TV! She was
gonna shoot Connie if she didn't go with her. And then
she'd shoot us, too."

"We were scared," his sister assured us.

And for good reason, I thought. So was I.

THIRTY-NINE

JIM DIDN'T WASTE a second. After I described Elaine's Mercedes and took a stab at the license number, he radioed instructions for all units to be on the lookout for it. I could tell he was weighing the possibility of leaving me with the children and taking off alone.

"I suppose it wouldn't be safe for you to stay here with the kids," he said, "and I certainly don't want to take them with us. Wonder where the nearest neighbor is and if it's someone we can ask for help."

Before he could make a decision, a green Ford raced down the road and swung into the driveway. The woman driving slammed on the brakes and scrambled out of the car. "What's going on? Where are my children?"

The children tumbled out the screen door and threw themselves into their mother's arms. She knelt in the driveway hugging them as she explained that she hadn't been able to reach Connie for over an hour and felt something was wrong. She had rushed home.

JIM TOLD HER what had happened to Connie.

"You and the kids stay inside with the doors locked, ma'am. I doubt she'll come back this way, but you don't want to take any chances. I'll get back to you with more details," Jim told her.

As the mother hustled the children into the house, Jim ran back to the car. I struggled after him as fast as I could.

THE RADIO KEPT UP a stream of chatter and static as we roared down the road. Sheriff's deputies had been alerted and were headed in our direction. So far no one had spotted Elaine. Jim handed out orders to the other cars. I figured the smartest move was to keep my mouth shut and, for once in my life, that was exactly what I did.

We'd covered maybe five miles on the bumpy country road when we made out a figure running toward us. Connie! Jim slammed to a stop as we reached her.

"Boy, am I glad to see you guys," she gasped, bending forward as she struggled to catch her breath.

Jim jumped out of the car. "What happened? Are you all right?"

Connie waved her hand behind her. Fifty yards down the road, the Mercedes was tipped into a drainage ditch.

"Connie, did she hurt you?" I asked, as I limped over to her.

"Hurt me? No way. She wants to adopt me. Do you believe it? Of course, she also threatened to shoot me. I guess she was willing to go either way."

"Shoot you?" Jim asked.

"When I didn't want to go with her. Told her I couldn't leave the kids alone. They were terrified. Five minutes with Elaine and Jimmy went back to sucking his thumb. She's one scary broad."

I couldn't have agreed more. I flashed on Elaine standing on that rock in the river, grinding her heel into my hand.

"How did she lose control of the car—speeding?" Jim asked.

"Nah. I couldn't do anything at the house for fear she'd hurt the kids. But as soon as we got on the road and she took her eyes off me, I yanked on the wheel. Sent us right off the road into that ditch."

Jim shook his head in disapproval. "You took quite a chance doing that. Where was the gun at that point?"

"Right on the seat next to her. It slid off onto the floor when we tipped sideways. I shoved my door open and took off. I figured once I got out of the car, I could outrun her, but I didn't have to. I think she hit the windshield and knocked herself out. I didn't wait around to find out."

I knew Jim was dying to lecture Connie about the risks she'd taken, but he couldn't afford the time. He radioed the other units with their location and updated his plan to apprehend her. "Get in the back seat, both of you. Lock the doors and stay down. There'll be a deputy here in a few minutes. I'm going to check her car."

Connie and I followed orders. As we huddled in Jim's car, I studied her face, wondering if she could use a hug. "You sure you're all right?" I asked.

"No sweat," she insisted. She gave my outfit a second look. "Wait a minute. Are those my clothes you're wearing? Not that I'd ever wear that top and slacks together."

I confessed at once. "Sorry. I'll make it up to you."

"Oh, I don't mind you borrowing something. But Elaine ripped off the new blue sweater I just bought with my babysitting money. I hadn't even worn it myself."

I murmured something sympathetic, but my attention was focused on Jim. He crouched low, skirting the edge of the ditch, as he approached Elaine's car. He'd almost reached it when the engine roared to life. The car rocked forward, spewing dirt and stones, slipped back, then cata-pulted onto the pavement. His shouts for Elaine to stop were drowned in a hailstorm of dirt as she careened off down the narrow road.

Jim pounded back toward us, his frustration obvious. I realized he wanted to take off fast after Elaine, but not with us in the car. For all he knew, she might have retrieved the gun and decided to use it rather than be caught.

Before he could decide what to do with us, another sheriff's car pulled up behind us and screeched to a stop. Jim lost no time barking out orders. "Deputy, take these women to Dwight Tanner's house. They'll direct you. And you two, get inside and stay there with the doors locked. Loren, don't even think about going home. I'll send a man to drive you when we can spare somebody."

Connie and I scrambled out of Jim's car as fast as we could. Before we'd opened the door of the deputy's vehicle, Jim had slammed his car into gear and taken off down the road.

The deputy, whose name I didn't get, delivered us to Dwight's house in record time. He deposited us next to the front porch without ceremony and took off to join the search.

Connie leapt up the steps two at a time. I hobbled along after her as best I could. Now that my adrenalin-induced energy was fading, it was a struggle to put one foot ahead of the other. By the time I dragged myself into the living room, Connie was already kneeling next to her uncle's chair.

"Dwight, are you all right? Are you feeling any ill effects from your tumble?" I asked him.

Dwight leaned forward in his recliner and rubbed his eyes. He gazed at Connie with an adoring look and reached for her hand. "I dozed off there for a few minutes, I guess, but I'm fit enough now. Especially with my girl back safe and sound."

"Take more than that to slow you down wouldn't it, Unc?" Connie patted his shoulder with her free hand and waited for him to release her. After she'd given him a half-dozen more pats and planted a kiss on his cheek, he loosened his grip on her hand and eased himself back against the cushions again.

"Let me see if I can find us some sodas," Connie said and started for the kitchen.

I wasn't sure I could handle the dozen steps required to join her, but somehow I managed to lift my aching body out of the chair and follow her.

Connie pulled cans of root beer out of the refrigerator and we sat down at the kitchen table. When I looked back into the living room, I saw Dwight was already asleep.

"You got aspirin, painkillers, anything like that in the house?" I asked as I massaged my aching body parts, one after another.

"Sorry. My uncle's not big on that stuff. Your hand bothering you?"

"Not just my hand. My face, my arm. So many places I can't even figure out which one hurts the worst. I need to get home."

She gave me a sharp look. "But that Thompson guy doesn't want you leaving, does he?"

"I hurt too much to wait around. I've got my car keys. I'll grab those wet clothes I left in your bedroom and take off. Tell Investigator Thompson I'll stay with my friend Kate until they find Elaine. He can reach me there." I jotted Kate's name and telephone number on a piece of paper and laid it on the table next to her.

"It's your call. I can't tell you what to do." Connie pillowed her head onto her arms. Her eyes drifted shut.

I limped into her bedroom. Everything appeared exactly the same as it had an hour earlier when I'd gone in to borrow the clothes. The tattered green window shades, drawn to the sills, blocked most of the light. The louvered doors on the closet yawned open; Connie's clothing spilled out onto the floor. My wet slacks and top hung where I'd left them, over a wooden chair in the far corner of the room. I glanced around, hoping to find some kind of bag to put them in.

When the door I'd come through began to swing slowly closed, I wasn't alarmed. A draft, I supposed. A breeze from somewhere. An uneven floor in an old house.

None of the above.

As I recoiled in horror, the grotesque specter of a woman—hair a wet, tangled mass, eyes wild with rage, mouth twisted into a frightening grimace—morphed from the shadows. "Stop right there. Don't make a sound," she hissed.

Elaine Morrison, wearing the bright blue sweater Connie had been fretting about, was pointing a gun directly at my heart.

FORTY

I COULDN'T BELIEVE my eyes. "My God, Elaine. Don't you know when to quit?"

I didn't wait for an answer. I'd had it with this woman. She'd hurt me too much already. My legs throbbed so I thought sure they would collapse under me. My head pounded. My hand where she'd stomped me with her damned heels burned like someone was holding an acetylene torch to it. She'd done enough damage.

I summoned every ounce of strength I had left and charged across the room at her. From some dim corner of my brain, I called up remnants of the self-defense lessons I'd taken years ago. You bank on the element of surprise, I remembered. I slammed my left arm under the hand holding the gun, hit as hard as I could and forced both hand and gun up toward the ceiling. The gun didn't fire. The phony. She must have kept the safety on.

I didn't lose my momentum. I brought my right shoulder forward, dug in my feet and smashed into her with a tackle a New York Giants lineman would have been proud of. I swung my right hand up fast and grabbed the gun as she staggered back toward the closet. She stumbled, tripping over the clothes and shoes on the floor, scrambling, struggling to stay upright. Her feet slipped out from under her as I drove her deeper into the clutter. Blouses and slacks, some of them still on their wire hangers, cascaded down, draping themselves over our heads and shoulders. I elbowed away something silky that was clinging to my face and tightened my grip on the gun. I wrenched it out of her hand and flung it across the room. It still didn't fire as it skidded under the bed.

But Elaine wasn't done yet. She braced against the closet's back wall and righted herself enough to land a hard blow on my left cheek bone. Her big diamond ring—the one I'd admired on happier occasions—gouged out a chunk of flesh from my cheek. That was the last straw. That cheek was one of the few spots on my body which didn't already hurt. I couldn't handle any more pain. I brought my knee up fast and slammed it into her midsection. I heard her gasp as the wind went out of her. I shoved her sideways with all my strength. She slid down into a heap to the closet floor. At least she would have made it to the floor if not for the pyramid of clothes crumpled under her.

I disentangled myself—first, from her, and then from the blouse still sticking to me. I backed out into the bedroom and pulled the louvered doors together. They were lightweight, too flimsy to hold Elaine for long. No lock of course—that would have made it too easy—just handles with open spaces in the center.

I could hear her harsh, ragged intakes of breath and the rustlings of the clothes as she tried to claw her way up from the floor. I grabbed one of Connie's leather belts which had tumbled out and looped it through the spaces. Then, fearing it wouldn't hold, I found a cloth belt, wound it round and round through the apertures, and tied it tight.

I staggered out into the kitchen. Connie, already half asleep, lifted her head from the table. "What's the matter?"

"Quick. Come and help me. Elaine Morrison's locked in your closet, but I don't think those doors are strong enough to hold her."

Connie didn't waste time on questions. She sprang up out of the chair and ran after me into the bedroom. The closet doors were shaking from the force of Elaine's blows as she kicked and pounded against them.

"The chest of drawers. Let's move it over there," I said.

We each grabbed hold of one side of the heavy chest and wiggled it back and forth, working it across the floor until we could position it in front of the closet.

"That should hold the doors shut," I said.

"You better sit," Connie ordered. "You look like you're gonna pass out. I'll get the phone. We have to call 911."

I sat down on the side of the bed. "You call. I'll talk when you reach somebody."

Connie didn't hesitate. She ran for the phone and hit the numbers with a steady hand as she rushed back into the bedroom. She stood quietly next to me while I gasped out my story to the sheriff's department dispatcher and gave directions to the house. "Contact Investigator Thompson, too. Tell him to come over here as fast as he can."

My brain felt as if it had embarked on a roller coaster ride as Connie and I perched side by side on the bed, keeping watch over our makeshift prison. I didn't think Elaine could force her way out as long as the chest held the doors shut, but the intermittent banging from inside the closet signaled she hadn't given up. I couldn't afford to take a chance.

When we heard the doorbell a few minutes later, Connie bolted up like a jack-in-the-box. "That was quick. A car must have been right nearby."

A minute later I heard her light step and turned to see her escorting a deputy into the room. I pointed to the closet doors. "She's in there. Elaine Morrison. She tried to drown me earlier and she just attacked me again now."

Before any of us could make a move, Jim Thompson and two more sheriff's deputies burst into the room.

I took a breath and dug deep for the energy to explain. "I came in to get my clothes. She was here. She pointed her gun at me but I got it away from her and locked her in the closet. The gun's under the bed."

I could tell Jim was making a valiant effort to keep his face impassive as he marched over to the windows and put up the shades, but I saw his jaw twitch. One of the deputies dropped to his knees and fished Elaine's gun out from under the bed. The other, a burly guy who must have done a lot of weights, slid the chest of drawers away from the closet as if it were made of cardboard. He pulled a Swiss Army knife out of his pocket and cut through the belts. Jim, his own gun drawn, yanked the doors open.

Elaine lurched forward, blinking in the sudden brightness. She stood with her head bowed, not glancing at either Connie or me while Jim cuffed her hands behind her back and told her she was under arrest.

As soon as he'd informed her of her rights and told her the charges she'd face for her attack on me, he and the deputy escorted her outside. "There'll also be charges connected with Madeline Hathaway's death, Mrs. Morrison," he said.

Elaine didn't reply.

Connie and I watched from the front porch as Jim and the deputy bundled Elaine into the back seat of a sheriff's car. Before the car could pull away, a black BMW roared down Dwight's driveway and slammed to a stop within a few feet of the house.

Stephen Morrison threw open the door and sprinted toward the car holding Elaine.

Jim blocked his path. "Stop right there. Better tell me who you are."

Stephen complied, but with his usual take-charge manner. "I'm Stephen Morrison. I believe I have the right to speak with my wife."

"Not right now you don't, Mr. Morrison." Jim said, as he signaled to the deputy to pull away. "You can come to the Municipal Center in an hour or two and bring your attorney. Your wife's being charged with assault. Other charges are pending—we're investigating her role in a recent murder."

Stephen staggered back as if Jim had struck him. "Murder? What are you talking about? Elaine didn't kill anyone."

"Mr. Morrison, your wife attacked Ms. Graham this afternoon," Jim informed him in a matter-of-fact tone. "We also have evidence that she killed Madeline Hathaway."

The color drained from Stephen's face. "No. You're wrong," he shouted.

"I think you'll find you're the one who's mistaken, Mr. Morrison."

"Elaine didn't kill Maddy. Her husband did."

Jim's expression didn't change, but I sensed Stephen's words had surprised him. "What makes you say that?"

"Ted Hathaway did it. He found out Maddy and I were seeing each other. That's why he killed her. I thought you realized that, figured you were waiting until you had evidence enough to make the charges stick."

"You may be right about the reason behind the murder, Mr. Morrison," Jim told him. "But Ted Hathaway didn't do it. Our evidence indicates that your wife killed Madeline Hathaway. And today she assaulted Ms. Graham. She'll be charged in both crimes."

Stephen swayed back and forth. He glanced wildly around until he focused on me a few yards away on the porch. "Loren, that can't be true, can it? Elaine wouldn't hurt you."

The feeling of white water pounding against me rushed back. I couldn't speak, but Stephen read the answer in my face, saw my bloody cheek and blackening eyes.

"No." His cry was full of anguish.

Jim reached for his arm and supported enough of his weight to keep him from falling. "You need to sit down, Mr. Morrison. Why don't you come in the house? I'll be asking these folks some questions about what happened here this afternoon. Maybe you should hear what they have to say."

Jim guided Stephen up the steps and into kitchen. He eased him into a chair at the table and motioned to Connie and me to sit down as well.

Stephen sank back, then quickly grabbed the edge of the table and pushed himself away. "No, I don't have time for this. I have to see about Elaine."

"Sit right there a minute, Mr. Morrison." Jim's voice was loaded with authority. "I'll make this quick. I guess everyone in the room knows you're Connie's father. You've known that for a while now yourself, haven't you, young lady?"

Connie glared across the table at Jim. "He's my biological father, I guess. My real father died last year."

Stephen didn't flinch, but he couldn't meet her eyes.

Jim turned back to him. "Maybe you'll fill us in on a few things, Mr. Morrison. When did Madeline Hathaway get in touch with you about your daughter? I believe that must have happened sometime last fall. Is that right?" He waited for the answer.

Stephen repeated the story he'd told me in his office. "Maddy ran into Don somewhere. Last September, I guess it was. Came to my office and told me about Connie, said her adoptive parents had died. That was all."

His voice held such a note of sadness that I reached over and touched his hand. "But that wasn't all, was it, Stephen?"

"At first it was." He swung around to face me. "Then all the old feelings came back. It was like I was seventeen again. She felt it, too. I know she did. She wanted me to see our daughter, find out what a beautiful girl she was." He sneaked a glance in Connie's direction, but she refused to meet his eyes.

I had a question I needed answered, so I jumped in and asked it. "That night at the center, Stephen, when I saw the body in the display case. Did you and Madeline have something to do with that?"

His words tumbled out slowly, as if he were dredging up something painful. "I still can't believe what happened that night. Maddy left a message with my secretary to tell me about a meeting there. We never saw each other in Emerald Point, so I realized something was wrong. She'd found out Ted had hired a private detective. She wanted to warn me, but she was afraid to do it on the phone."

Jim took over. "You're referring to Leonard Westerhall, I believe. I spoke to him earlier today. So go on—Mrs. Hathaway asked you to meet her at the center?"

"Maddy had a key to the building. She thought she could lose the detective."

"But he followed her there?"

"He must have. We'd no more than got there when we saw this guy nosing around outside. He came in the front door. I snuck up behind him, grabbed a hunk of board lying there and hit him with it. Next thing I knew he was knocked out on the floor."

I interrupted again. I couldn't stop myself. "Stephen, you did what?"

"I know. I know. I couldn't believe it myself. But Maddy was scared to death. She didn't want Ted to find out about us that way. She planned to tell him herself when the time was right."

Did she? I wondered. Ted had been so sure that would never happen.

Stephen took a deep, ragged breath and glanced over at Jim.

"You're not going to arrest me for that, are you? He had no business being in there anyway. And I knew he was just knocked out."

Jim ignored his question. "Please go on, Mr. Morrison."

"I was going to leave him there. I figured he'd come to in few minutes. But before we could get out of there, we heard a car drive up."

"Was that when I came in?" I asked him.

"I didn't know it was you, Loren. I swear it. I thought if I pulled the guy into that display case, he might not be noticed. When I heard someone at the front door, I shoved in the lock on the case and took off out the back. I never knew who came in until Don called the next day and told us what had happened to you."

"But how did the paint and ladder get tipped over?"

"Maddy did that. After you left, she ran back inside and did it. She thought it would confuse things."

"She figured that right." I wanted to tell him how Leonard Westerhall had managed to get out of the display case and rent a cabin at Ramona's motel, but I could see it didn't matter to him. All he cared about was getting to the Municipal Center. The minute Jim gave his okay, he charged out the door.

Once Stephen was gone, Dwight shuffled in and joined us at the table. His hands shook as he handed Jim a packet of papers. "Think this might be what everybody's so het up about. I had it hid good but I got it out and showed it to Loren here earlier today, then she got sidetracked by our visitor."

I recognized the packet from his strong box. "I thought Elaine took all that with her, Dwight," I said.

He allowed himself a small cackle. "So did she. But, after you gals left here, Loren, I saw how you tried to cover the strong box up when she came in. I figured you didn't trust her any more than I did. I didn't cotton to her much myself the way she's been poppin' in here lately and snooping around."

"Really? Elaine's been coming here?" I said.

"Told Jim here. She's turned up a lot lately. Knew she was after something. Wanted to take Maddy's place, I guess. So this morning, after you two went off, I took the important stuff out of the strong box and hid it. Then I left the dang thing right under that newspaper where you'd slipped it. When she came back, she grabbed it without checking inside at all." He gave me a broad wink.

Jim glanced down at the packet. "What do you plan to do with this now, Mr. Tanner?"

"This here's going to pay for Connie's college education, so I want it kept safe. Maybe Loren here will help me decide the best way to do that. I say we look through it right now. Then there won't be any question about what we've got."

I turned away so no one would see my smile. No matter how Dwight came across sometimes, he was a sharp old guy and he wasn't about to take any chances with Connie's inheritance.

FORTY-ONE

THE NEXT AFTERNOON I was curled up in the only comfortable chair in Don's hospital room, giving him a play-by-play of the events of the day before, when Jim stuck his head in the door. He'd made good on his promise to have a deputy drive me home from Lake Luzerne, so I'd escaped the lecture I knew he was itching to deliver.

"Okay to come in?" he said, then choked off a horrified gasp. "Yikes. It's hard to tell which of you looks worse. Has somebody checked those bruises on your face today, Mayor? Isn't your nose broken?"

"The doctors say not. They claim the swelling will go down in a couple of days."

Jim shook his head in disbelief. "You look even worse now than you did yesterday."

No sense taking offense. I knew he spoke the truth. "I'm supposed to get checked again in a day or so."

"Make sure you do," he muttered.

His disappointment was palpable. He'd psyched himself up to read me the riot act for playing detective and now after one look at me, he felt obliged to put his lecture on hold. He shifted the conversation to Don.

"Have you talked with your brother yet?" he asked him.

"Late last night. He's devastated. Never suspected Elaine...killed Madeline. Thought Ted...after private detective's report…" Don's voice was still raspy, but the long pauses between his words were fewer and farther apart.

Jim pulled his chair closer. "Do you have any idea what he'd planned with Mrs. Hathaway? Would he have left his wife for her, do you think?"

Don mulled over the question, then shook his head. "Couldn't know what Madeline would do. Might choose Ted…like before."

I remembered Ted's vehemence the morning before in my kitchen when he'd insisted Madeline wouldn't have left him. Stephen must have suspected that, too.

"Let me bring you both up to speed," Jim said. "Last night we got sworn statements from Don's assailants. They're not the sharpest guys around, but they'll make credible witnesses against Mrs. Morrison."

"That should help with a conviction," I said.

"And you're right about your brother, Don," Jim continued. "When he got to the Municipal Center yesterday, he still wasn't convinced his wife killed Mrs. Hathaway. Then, besides that, we had to tell him she was responsible for your beating, and that it was meant for him."

"He told me…last night. Couldn't believe Elaine would do that to him…" Don said, "…wants to go off someplace…for a while anyway. Think things through."

I remembered Stephen's reaction the first night he came to the hospital to see Don. "You know, I think he suspected right away the beating was meant for him, but he assumed Ted was behind it."

Jim agreed. "He wasn't the only one, Mayor. A lot of folks saw Ted Hathaway as the bad guy in this, but he's in the clear. Your burglars will testify that Mrs. Morrison killed Madeline Hathaway herself, and then hired them for the rest of her dirty work."

"I find all this hard to believe myself," I said. "How could Elaine arrange to have them beat up her own husband like that? Why would she do that to him, especially after Madeline was already dead?"

"Payback. Wanted him punished for the affair, I suppose," Jim said. "Maybe didn't intend those characters she hired to go as far as they did—and certainly didn't expect them to beat up the wrong guy."

"Then, as long as she was on a roll, she decided to kill me?"

Even after everything that had happened I still had trouble getting out those words.

Jim managed a sympathetic look. "Remember, she'd already killed the woman she thought was taking her husband. All she needed to do was get friendly with Connie and help Stephen get access to the money Mrs. Hathaway left the girl. Then, you arrive on the scene, all chummy with Connie and her uncle, posing another threat to what she was after. And she wanted that money, wanted it bad."

"But I wasn't after the money. I just thought Connie could use a friend."

"How was she to know that?" Jim said.

I realized he was right. Elaine had offered to put me on her payroll. If I hadn't balked at her suggestion that day at Papa's, maybe she wouldn't have tried to kill me.

At least, not until I crossed her the next time.

THE NEXT MORNING, I layered on extra makeup and went back to work. It was summer, after all, our busiest season. Diane was keeping the center humming and she always needed another pair of hands to help out.

Don spent several more days in the hospital and a week in rehab before I talked him into driving up to the house one night for dinner.

"Just dinner?" he asked. "You're not going to try to have your way with me in my weakened condition, are you?"

"Furthest thought from my mind," I assured him.

But of course, it wasn't. And after I'd served him spaghetti with herbs and hot sausage made according to his own special recipe and a glass of his favorite Chianti, the thought wasn't far from his mind either.

THE DAY AFTER Labor Day, while most of Emerald Point was celebrating the end of another tourist season, Connie pulled into my driveway in a snappy white Toyota.

"You're driving? You got your license?" I cried, as I ran out to greet her.

"Permit. I need a licensed driver with me still, but I'm doin' great. Aren't I, Unc?" She bounced the question to Dwight who sat beaming in the front seat next to her.

"She sure is. A little fast sometimes, but otherwise…"

"And the car? That can't be yours, can it?"

"First thing we got with the insurance money. Not brand new, of course. Unc says college has to be the top priority. Ted's probably gonna get back most of the bank account, but he can't touch the house or the insurance."

"Terrific. Come in and I'll get us a cold drink to celebrate."

As they got out of the car, Connie, quick as always, stepped around to help Dwight disentangle himself from his seat belt and struggle to his feet. I saw clearly then what had changed since the day of Ted's reception at the beginning of the summer.

Connie looked taller and slimmer now, her brown hair

curling around her shoulders, her sports outfit crisp and well pressed, not at all like something scooped up from a bedroom floor. She moved differently, too, with a grace that reminded me of someone. It took me a minute to realize how much like Madeline she'd become.

After we'd eaten a makeshift lunch and Dwight and I were lingering over our coffee, Connie walked down to the dock to check out the lake.

"You know, Dwight," I said, "you were right about something you told me a while ago. That girl's grown up every bit as lovely as her mother, just as you predicted."

I watched the smile start at the corners of his mouth and spread across his face.

"But fortunately, you were wrong about something, too."

"And what would that be, Loren?" he asked.

"You said you wouldn't live to see it, but you have."

"Yes," he said. "I have, haven't I?"